FRESHWATER BOYS

FRESHWATER BOYS

ADAM SCHUITEMA

DELPHINIUM BOOKS

HARRISON, NEW YORK · ENCINO, CALIFORNIA

Designed by Jonathan D. Lippincott

Library of Congress Cataloguing-in-Publication Data available on request.

ISBN 978-1-883285-36-4

10 11 12 RRD 10 9 8 7 6 5 4 3 2 1

These stories appeared, in somewhat different form, in the following literary maga-
zines: "New Era, Michigan" in *Orchid*; "Sand Thieves" in *Glimmer Train*; "Restraint:
A Confession" in *Black Warrior Review*; "Debts and Debtors" in *TriQuarterly*;
"Camouflage Fall" in *The Florida Review*; "Deer Run" in *The Carolina Quarterly*; "The
Lake Effect" in *Crazyhorse*; "Curbside" in *Passages North*; "The Feel of Meridians" in
The Cream City Review.

My thanks to the editors of these magazines for their early support and the showcase they provide for new short fiction.

FOR JENNIFER

For in their interflowing aggregate, those grand fresh-water seas of ours,—Erie, and Ontario, and Huron, and Superior, and Michigan,—possess an ocean-like expansiveness, with many of the ocean's noblest traits; with many of its rimmed varieties of races and of climes. —Herman Melville, *Moby Dick*

CONTENTS

ACKNOWLEDGMENTS

My thanks to the many friends, colleagues, and mentors in the English Department at Western Michigan University who assisted me in countless ways during the writing of this book. I especially want to thank Stuart Dybek, Jaimy Gordon, and Dan Mancilla for their insights, suggestions, and support.

I would like to thank my agent, Donna Bagdasarian, for her dedication, encouragement, and belief in these stories. Thanks also to my editor, Christopher Lehmann-Haupt, for his keen judgment.

And finally, loving thanks to my parents, in-laws, and especially my wife, Jennifer. To list all the ways in which they've supported me and my fiction career would require another book.

FRESHWATER BOYS

NEW ERA, MICHIGAN

You start with a name, and the rest follows: youth and age and the scattering of ashes. The town was named in the 1870s. Darryl read the brief history on the menu's back cover at the Trailside Restaurant. He'd read it before. A local doctor/sawmill owner had been fascinated by the dawning of that wondrous technological time: telephones, typewriters, elevators. Darryl was twelve years old and, sitting in the restaurant, was a little young yet to notice that some people in town—some sipping coffee in the vinyl booths around him—still waited wearily for that dawning to end and the full daylight of a new era to begin. He was a little young to notice that only a handful were content with the time—with the dawn—and felt it was the moment when the light was near-perfect.

Darryl Pickle thought a lot about names because of his own. He'd checked the phone book, which covered everyone along Lake Michigan from Ludington down to New Era and as far east as Walkerville and Walhalla, but his family was the only Pickle. He'd heard there were a few in Muskegon and a few more in Grand Rapids, but he'd never checked the phone books in those cities. And he thought a lot about the word "hermit," which he'd always found funny, and the name Joseph Doornbos, which was the name of the hermit down the road.

He'd once asked his dad what a hermit was, and found out, "A hermit's a man without a woman or anyone else," which made

Darryl think of a lot of people he knew, mostly divorced uncles on his mom's side. But they weren't hermits. They weren't like Joseph Doornbos, severed from the earth and sky as much as from family and friends.

Darryl stayed close to the earth. For his birthday—in addition to a video game, a bright silver compass, a pair of flannel slippers, and some other assorted clothes—his parents had bought him a new dirt bike. His birthday was in June, and he washed the bike every day, even now at the end of August. Part of what makes summer so perfect up here in the country—especially for kids whose parents both work full-time—is the freedom to get on a bike and vanish for hours. Darryl took it everywhere, through town and out of it, and especially to the woods by his house.

He searched for uncommon trees and animals. Sometimes he'd park the bike at the edge of the woods and wear his new flannel slippers into the moist rot of moss and dead leaves and fallen branches. The bottoms of the slippers were leather, and he pretended they were moccasins that helped him walk without sound. The woods made him feel invisible to the outside, but the moccasins made him feel invisible on the inside. He held the shiny compass in one hand, though he knew the woods by heart, and they were too small to ever get lost in. In the other hand he held a field book that helped him identify different trees. The beeches were his favorite, their smooth silver skin and almost muscular trunks like the legs of elephants. A few of them were along what people called Refrigerator Trail, because an old refrigerator had been dumped among the brown leaves. These beeches were larger than any others he'd seen in the area, their huge limbs diverging from the squat trunks close to the ground and curving upward on all sides so that they looked like monstrous hands, or a jail cell.

Darryl often brought a spiral notebook into the woods with him. He hunted without guns. He crept along the trails, which were overgrown from under-use, and tried to catch a glimpse of something rare. When he spotted an animal, he marked it down in the notebook, each sighting a vertical pencil mark next to its name. He didn't count squirrels or common birds like robins or even cardinals; there were too many. But he'd seen seventy-five white-tailed deer in his life, fifteen at once, gathered at twilight in his neighbor's cherry orchard. He'd counted a few falcons and owls, wild turkeys, and several raccoons. Once he came across a white llama, being led down the trail by a girl who lived with horses down the road. He didn't count the llama; it seemed like cheating since it wasn't native. He always hoped to find a bear, but knew there weren't any for at least a hundred miles this far south.

His rarest find was two bald eagles that he'd seen at Claybanks Park on the lake, one circling above the trees and one later perched high in the branches farther down shore. That night, he wondered if he'd just seen the same eagle twice, but he didn't erase the two markings in his notebook. It was easier to tell his family that he'd actually seen two, instead of clouding a good story with doubt.

Darryl liked to be alone. He enjoyed hanging out with his older brother, Jesse, sometimes, but outside of his family he didn't have any real friends. Jesse always had to be with people, always had to have background voices and someone to ricochet his jokes and observations and even his moments of silence off. Darryl slipped away when Jesse's friends came over. He went inside when the guys were out, outside when they were in. Jesse played football and basketball. Darryl's favorite sports were distance running and swimming—no teammates really necessary. He played board games by himself, jumping with the black checkers as well as the red, trying his hardest to win both ways. Last school year at lunch, when he finished eating and other kids started to wander in cliques through the cafeteria or sit across from each other to play paper football, Darryl would go to work with sharpened gray pencils on a pad of plain white paper, sketching the trees and animals from the woods. His favorites combined both, birds in maple branches or deer peeking out from behind birches.

The fall and the school year were coming—both too quickly. It already felt like mid-September. Scattered maples through the county were turning already, flaring out in an orange that seemed gaudy with the asparagus fields and most everything else still green. The cherries throughout the local orchards had fallen more quickly than usual, and the apples were already getting big and red, the slim branches bending down as though strung along with heavy ornaments. The weather was unusually cool. Acorns cracked with metallic sounds, bouncing off the hood of his dad's Buick. Darryl's stomach felt light and nervous. He didn't want to return to school.

He spent most of the last weeks of vacation on his dirt bike. Each morning, his dad walked the three blocks to his job at the canning company, and his mom walked the two blocks to the Reformed church, where she was the secretary. They left Jesse and him lists of chores. Darryl often had to pick up something at the hardware store, and even though there was one in New Era, he usually used the excuse to ride three miles to the True Value in Rothbury.

He rode the straight stretch down Oceana Drive. New Era is in Oceana County. It's another sly name meant to convince outsiders, and even locals, of a great importance in the area, as if the lake a few miles from here was really the fifth and unnamed ocean, that if you charted a course west for the horizon, you'd not only hit the shores of Wisconsin but also continue onward to Japan and Russia. On warmer summer days, the country road wavered in the sun as if seen through gas fumes, mirages both north and south. On cooler days, a sharp wind swooped through the open fields. Halfway to Rothbury, Darryl would skid onto the shoulder of the road to ensure that a dust cloud rose from his back tire. He went to the hardware store out of town so he could stop and look up at the bus.

The yellow school bus rested on top of a sand dune back from the road—an inland dune forgotten perhaps by ancient waters. It looked as though the bus itself had been washed onto the top and marooned after a great flood. Its wheels had sunk into the soft sand, and its windows looked covered on the inside with black plastic. The side read MUSKEGON PUBLIC SCHOOLS. The black paint of the letters was flaking off, revealing an inner, silver skin. This was where the hermit, Joseph Doornbos, had lived for fifteen years, since before Darryl was born.

The hermit was rarely seen, and even then it was from afar, from the road below, as he wandered around his property at the top of the dune. Darryl had spotted him once. It was like the eagle sighting, both startling and, later, something he began to doubt. He'd expected the hermit to have long hair and a ratty, unkempt beard that nearly dragged in the sand as he walked. But from a distance he looked clean-shaven and either bald or with a head of very short white hair. A loose T-shirt hung from his gaunt frame, tucked into brown work pants. He must have been well over eighty years old. And he must have seen Darryl that day, watching him from the road, because he froze for a moment before quickly shuffling to the far side of the bus, disappearing like a deer.

Everyone toyed with the rumors. Darryl even heard them tossed about at home, around the dinner table. He and his family tried to guess what the hermit lived on, if he had any family, and why he chose isolation. Darryl thought hard about the last question. Before this, he'd never thought about adults being completely alone, and he'd never considered they could die that way.

"What's he eat?"

"I don't know."

"Someone must bring him food."

"Who?"

"Who knows?" said Darryl's dad. "I hear he's rich, so he can buy all the help he needs. Like an eccentric millionaire. I think his granddad was a lumber baron. Maybe he just eats all that money and jewels of his. Feeds on dollar bills like white bread." He took a fierce bite out of his roll. They all laughed.

More than the hermit himself, the rumors of what he kept inside the bus were the most fascinating, and speculative. The treasure theory was popular, among kids and adults. But Darryl's mom thought the bus was probably stripped empty to its essentials inside and that the hermit had forsaken the material and devoted himself entirely to God. Kids Darryl's age liked to think more grimly, that the hermit was a murdering kidnapper, that there were children's dead bodies sitting upright in all the rows of the bus, seat belts clicked shut across their cold laps. Kyle TenBrink and Randy Dodge claimed they'd snuck up there when the hermit was away and that the inside was lit with a kerosene lamp. They said they'd seen a decapitated chicken in a rusty cage, a puddle of blood collected in a pan underneath it. Stepping through the dim bus, they could read in sloppy redness the names of victims, past and future, written like finger paint on the inside walls.

"One said Pickle," said Kyle TenBrink, retelling this in the cafeteria last school year.

"Of course," said Randy Dodge, "'cause Pickles are tasty."

Darryl eventually left for a table in a distant corner of the room to work on his sketches. He didn't believe the story. He didn't believe the hermit would ever leave in the first place, and if he did, he wouldn't leave the bus unlocked. And he didn't believe Kyle and Randy had the guts to check anyway. Sitting at a corner table, Darryl softly shaded the bark of a beech tree with his pencil and got frustrated because he could never get it to look three-dimensional. He made sure to stare at his work and not look up until lunch was over. He didn't worry about murdering kidnappers, just about kids like Kyle TenBrink and Randy Dodge.

·

The secrets soon eroded like sand. Darryl, Jesse, and their parents went to the Trailside Restaurant on the second-to-last Saturday morning before school started. They did this every week. The boys tried to steer their thoughts away from school, but a cold front still draped the lakeshore. They ate pancakes with more syrup than their mom thought was necessary, and she and their dad commented over and over about how good the coffee was today.

The place was filled with farmers, friends from the canning company, and members of their church congregation. Deputy Martinez entered through the glass doors wearing his glimmering badge and his brown uniform. He took off his brown hat to reveal thick black hair, combed straight back. He shook hands with people and waved to others as he made his way among the cluttered wooden tables and chairs to the counter for some coffee. Darryl's dad stood and followed him to the counter to pay the bill. The two of them shook hands and smiled. They talked. Darryl wiped syrup from his chin with his fist and tried to read lips. He couldn't. His dad and Deputy Martinez had gone to school together, and sometimes they still hung out on Sunday afternoons to watch football. His dad looked surprised and shook his head. Deputy Martinez nodded, spoke some more, and waved his hand at something beyond the walls of the restaurant.

A few minutes later, Darryl's dad returned with a toothpick in his mouth and a handful of peppermints for the boys. His eyes said he had news.

"Our old friend Mr. Doornbos passed away yesterday."

"You're kidding," said Mrs. Pickle.

"Who's that?" asked Jesse.

"Your hermit."

"He's not *my* hermit," said Jesse.

"He's not my old friend, either," said Darryl. Unlike Jesse, he hadn't forgotten the hermit's real name.

"You know what I'm gettin' at," said their dad. "Jorge just told me. They got a call from his daughter and found the body yesterday morning. Sent it to a funeral home."

"He has a daughter?" their mom asked.

"Guess so. She's an old bird herself, but I guess she lives just up in Pentwater. Jorge said she used to bring Mr. Doornbos food and such."

The family stood up from the table and walked outside into the bright, cool light. It reflected off cars and shop windows. Across the street, one of the early turning maples was lit in autumn red. The Pickles walked the few blocks home.

"What are they doin' with the bus?" asked Darryl.

"I don't know," said his dad. He was sucking on his toothpick, flipping it over with his tongue, nearly scraping the roof of his mouth with the sharp points. "Gettin' rid of it somehow. I guess the daughter owns all of it now, and she wants to sell the property. Nobody's gonna want that thing straddlin' the hill."

As they approached home, Darryl and Jesse began to walk a little faster, ahead of their parents.

"Slow down, boys," called their mom. "You're not goin' anywhere for a while. Play inside or play ball out in the yard."

"Why?"

"'Cause," said their dad, "we know where you'd head to if we let you take off on your bikes. I don't want you up there by that bus." He slid the toothpick from his teeth and threw it into the grass. The boys turned back toward the house, looked at each other, and spoke without words.

•

On Monday their dad was back to work, their mom was behind her desk in the church office, and Darryl and Jesse were like other kids in town, gone on their bikes. Jesse was the only kid Darryl ever rode with. He rode his dirt bike, and Jesse rode their mom's old Schwinn with the metal basket on the front. His own bike had a busted chain. Jesse wanted a promise that Darryl would trade on the way back, but Darryl wouldn't do it.

"It's my bike. You'll just have to look like an old lady."

"I could still beat your ass in a race."

They raced in the cool August morning, and the wind chilled their arms and legs. They refused to wear jeans or long sleeves just yet. They raced, but they would have ridden fast anyway because their mom came home early for lunch, and although she was never suspicious of their being gone, she always got suspicious when she saw them leaving. Jesse's bike couldn't compete with Darryl's, so Darryl held back and taunted him in one of those rare moments when the younger brother had the power. He cupped his hand over his mouth to amplify his voice. "If you raced a pregnant lady you'd come in third."

"I'll turn around," said Jesse, struggling and standing up as he pedaled to get more power. "And if I do, you won't dare check out the bus alone, so you'll never find out what's inside."

"I'm just kiddin'," said Darryl. It was true. This was one thing he didn't want to do by himself.

Oceana Drive was busy with cars and semis, and a county sheriff's car even passed, maybe Deputy Martinez. Darryl was nervous. They rode to the inland dune where the bus rested on top like a tarnished, crooked crown.

"It's wide open," said Jesse. They'd expected yellow police tape to be wrapped around the trees and strung all the way up the hill, blocking off the land. But it looked the same as always. Darryl's anxiety faded a little. It started to feel less like a crime.

"We should go up the back side," said Jesse. "Someone will see us goin' right up the front."

"Is there a trail through the woods on the other side?"

"I don't know. I think there's Christmas tree farms back there anyway. We'd get caught cuttin' through there, too."

They decided to charge the hill. The opposite side of the road was an asparagus field that had gone to fern. The fuzzy leaves rose up to Darryl's waist and made the field look as though it was blanketed in a soft green fog that stretched in three directions. They laid their bikes down in the field so they were invisible from the road. Oceana Drive was flat, and the boys could see for miles south toward Rothbury and a mile north toward New Era. When there were no cars in sight, they rushed across the road and into the sand. Darryl had imagined scaling the dune with long strides, bounding up to the top and the cover of the high trees with only a little trouble. The closer they got to the dune, the less they could see of the bus at the top. The hill was high and steep. They climbed the lowest sands, looking for any shallow footprints that they could use for traction, but the sand was smooth and untouched. No one had been there. The sands slipped away under their feet, making it impossible to run. They dug in with their hands, and the earth fell away like handfuls of air. So the boys steered to the right, where a cluster of dead, leaning maples clung to the eroding duneside, their exposed roots like cobwebs in sunlight. They climbed and used the roots to pull themselves up.

"God, hurry. A car's comin'."

A pickup rumbled near and passed, and the sound slipped away.

"They saw us," said Darryl.

"Keep goin'."

Their legs burned and shuddered, and their lungs felt dry and crumpled in their chests. Once at the top, they ducked around the bus to hide themselves from the road. Darryl leaned forward, gasping, with his hands resting on his knees. Jesse put his hands on the top of his head the way he'd learned in football practice.

"No wonder he never left the bus," said Jesse, still breathing hard. "He'd never frickin' get back up."

The bus looked even worse up close, as if it had once been in an accident. The side hidden from the road was smashed in. Headlights were shattered. Most of the tires were flat. Maybe the hermit *had* been a kidnapper, thought Darryl. Maybe he'd wanted this bus because a lot of little kids had died in a crash and he liked living and sleeping in a tomb, among the souls of second- and third-graders.

"How'd he get this up here?" asked Darryl.

"How are they gettin' it back down?" asked Jesse.

On the opposite side of the dune were woods, and beyond, a Christmas tree farm and some other fading fields. A path slithered down the back of the hill into the trees. Years ago it might have been a set of two-tracks that a bus could have climbed up, but no cars would make it through now with all the low branches, brush, and saplings in the way.

Darryl peeked around the front of the bus and looked down at Oceana Drive. They still seemed to be sneaking. Jesse stared at the narrow door to the bus.

"Push it open," said Darryl.

Jesse didn't say anything.

Darryl knew he had to be the one. He pushed the door at the middle hinge, and for a second it got stuck, rust scraping against rust. Then he leaned his weight into it until the door folded in on itself like a dying houseplant, leaving a black patch of air that smelled sour and dark.

"I don't wanna go in," said Jesse.

"Neither do I." Darryl didn't care that he'd said it out loud. He tried to identify the smell that leaked out of the door into the sunny outside air. Then he remembered that the hermit's body could have been rotting in the bus for days or weeks. Maybe his daughter only visited him once a month, and found him three weeks into his decay. Darryl stared into the dark rectangle of the open door and thought some more about ghosts—of children, or of the hermit himself. It was quickly pushed aside by a new fear. There could be someone inside right now—the daughter, or some other blood-lusting hermit squatter who'd taken up residence.

"It's pitch black," whispered Jesse.

"I told you we shoulda brought flashlights."

"You never said we should bring flashlights."

"Bull. In the garage before we left."

"Shut up," said Jesse. "We'll just have to rip the plastic off the windows."

He stepped past Darryl and climbed the first high step. Darryl hesitantly followed, and the shaft of light from the door revealed a steering wheel and speedometer and wide mirror above the windshield that let the bus driver spy on the kids—all the traits of normal buses he'd taken on field trips. The rubber floors at the front were the same, and so were the vinyl seats. But that sour smell still coated everything. Jesse reached to the inside of the front windshield and pulled away the plastic. They were black trash bags, duct taped at the edges. The tape held tight, so he had to stretch and tear the plastic itself. Yellow light burst through. The front section of the bus emerged from shadows.

There were two rows of green vinyl seats, but most of the bus's seats were gone. Darryl stepped to one of the small side windows and began ripping away trash bags. Now they could see the floor, and at first they thought the inside was covered in sand. It coated the front seats and made things toward the back glow, reflecting the little light that made its way into the dark. Darryl ripped another trash bag off a window. And then there was enough light that they could see it wasn't sand, and they realized what it was they were smelling.

"Look at all the sawdust," said Jesse.

Darryl ripped away more plastic.

"That's enough," said Jesse, sounding scared. "If the cops come back they'll know someone's been up here."

Darryl looked back at all the stretched, tattered plastic. Bits of it still hung from the duct tape on the edges of the windows. "They'll already know."

There was plenty of light now, and they could see the source of all the sawdust. Halfway down the aisle of the bus, shoved against the wall, was a wooden workbench. The boys approached. A small stool stood in front of it, and tools were strewn across the top: hammers, rulers, wrenches, dull pencils, coffee tins filled with nails, tubes of wood glue. But most of the tools were small hand saws and files. A little metal kit sat open on the bench, and inside were five small files, all with different-colored handles and of different metal widths and degrees of roughness. And there was a large file that Darryl picked up and found was as heavy as a lead pipe as he turned it over in his hands. He brushed his fingers against each side. One had little spikes like the teeth of a cat, and the other was as fine as the dune sand outside.

Most of the rest of the bus was what they'd expected. No chickens in cages. No bloody finger paintings on the walls. In the very back, still veiled in darkness, was a sleeping bag on an air mattress, a pillow, a pile of blankets, a kerosene heater, and two Coleman coolers. There was also a set of crude, handmade shelves, squeezed in next to the coolers. Darryl walked carefully, leaving footprints in the sawdust and stretching his hands out in front of him. Jesse stopped him cold.

"Holy shit, look up."

Darryl turned and looked. His eyes were adjusting to the dimness, and now he could make out images on the arched ceiling of the bus. There were small posters and glossy photographs ripped from magazines and taped up in a rough collage. It was like a planetarium, but instead of stars there were animals, pictures of bears and deer and coyotes, trout and geese, wolves and moose. There were pictures of Indians too, and of canoes and totem poles.

One of the pictures was so large that its top began on the ceiling, but the rest of it curled down the rounded corner of the wall and ended right above the workbench. It was a huge calendar—1975—advertising Hills Bros. Coffee. The top half was a picture of an arctic landscape. Two men in parkas stood next to a fully packed dogsled. Six huskies in harnesses stood in front, staring out at something off the page, their mouths open and tongues draped over their fangs.

"Let's go," said Jesse. Darryl could tell he was uneasy, but wasn't sure why. Maybe it was all the gold-rimmed eyes peering at him from the pictures above his head.

"Just a sec," said Darryl. He turned and walked to the back of the bus. His eyes could make out everything now. He stared for a moment at the sleeping bag to make sure it was actually flattened out—that no body was still tucked inside—and then examined the shelves.

They were lined with carvings, smooth sculptures made from single pieces of wood. There was the bear in the poster above him, reaching for salmon, its coat stained to a shiny bronze. There were deer and moose and wolves, their eyes carved to lifelike stares, their claws and hooves filed down to points and curves without a trace of roughness. Darryl looked up at the ceiling again, and in the posters and magazine photographs he saw the same deer, the same moose, the same wolves. There were more carvings: Indians and canoes and other birds and mammals.

He walked back to the workbench to see if he could find any others. He brushed the film of sawdust off some newspapers and then pushed the papers aside. Underneath was a half-finished carving. The original piece of wood had never been perfect, nothing bought from a lumberyard. Half was only a scrap of tree limb Darryl might see when walking through the woods in his moccasins. The bark was stripped off, there were knots, and even tunnels maybe left from termites. But the other half of the log was reborn: six huskies, harnesses draped over their chests, tongues and teeth and eyes that mirrored the picture in the calendar above. A million individual hairs looked carved into their fur, tossed about by an invisible wind. The dogs stood in a wooden line one after another, and their harnesses stretched back into the unfinished log, where the sled would be, still unseen and uncarved, buried under the rings of wooden age. The dogs looked as though they were unsheathing themselves, pulling themselves free from the marrow of the log.

"You ready?" asked Jesse. He stood next to the door, washed in sunlight.

"Yeah."

They walked down the steps into a blue sky, squinting as Darryl pulled the door at the hinge to close it behind him.

"What a waste," said Jesse.

Darryl said nothing. He was still thinking of the dogsled, the way it seemed to be molting in anticipation of a new life. Glancing back at the bus, with the sky as a clean, pure backdrop, he imagined its yellow skin being peeled back so that people on the road could see all of the carvings, and the hermit's life could also be seen by everyone, pulling free from all the rumors and horror stories. But he knew there must have been some reason the hermit kept himself and his work hidden, ugly and knotted like the uncarved pieces of wood.

As he and Jesse left, Darryl noticed a small woodpile stacked by the rear tires. Some of the wood looked bleached, like bones. Driftwood. Maybe the hermit's daughter had brought it for him from the beaches in Pentwater.

The boys scanned the road from their high spot on the hill, and when there was no one in sight let themselves yield to gravity, cascading down in huge strides only sand dunes would allow.

•

Jesse held the syrup jar over his pancakes, raising and lowering it as the syrup dribbled onto his plate. Darryl reached for the butter and looked at Jesse. "Hurry up with the syrup."

A man with a black mustache and wearing a gray suit walked past their table. Nobody ever wore a tie in the Trailside, not even

on Sundays after church; on Sunday the restaurant was closed. The
man tapped Darryl's mom on her shoulder. "Morning, Sue."

"Oh, good morning, Leon." The man nodded at the rest of the
family and sat at a table by himself, adjusting his tie. Darryl's mom
turned around to face them. "Leon Mears. Director of the funeral
home in Shelby. I'm on the phone with him all the time when
there's a funeral at the church."

"Is that where the hermit was sent?" asked Jesse.

"Mr. Doornbos," said his dad. "Now that he's deceased, let's
have a little respect."

"Mr. Doornbos. Is it?"

Darryl wanted Jesse to shut up. Jesse was the type who would
get too excited during a conversation and let secrets slip, like their
search of the bus last Monday.

"It sure is," said their mom. "Although I wasn't involved in
coordinating that one. None of the churches were. There wasn't
even a funeral."

"Why not?" asked Darryl.

"No one to go," said his dad.

"Be good," said Darryl's mom. "Actually, Leon and I were talking a little bit about the hermit's daughter—I think her name's
Margaret—and from what I hear she had him cremated and scattered his ashes in Lake Michigan up in Pentwater."

"Mom called him hermit," said Jesse, laughing.

"Mr. Doornbos. You know who I mean." She tore open a packet
of sugar and poured it into her coffee. "Lately I've heard of lots of
people who live on the lake who feel they need to be cremated and
buried at sea." She shook her head.

Darryl had never thought much about cremation, or about
dying and having no funeral service because you'd cut yourself off
from everyone.

"What's gonna happen to the bus?" he asked. "Is the daughter
gonna take all his jewels and stuff?" He threw this lie into the

conversation so that, just in case Jesse later slipped, there'd be less of a trail and he could cover the scent of sawdust.

His dad took off his hat and rubbed his forehead. "What Jorge says is she was up there the other day and took out anything she wanted. The rest is goin' the way of the landfill." He put his hat back on and smiled as he raised his cup of coffee to his lips. "From what he says, there wasn't any treasure, unless it was buried in the sand where X marks the spot. Just some tools and blankets and junk. She didn't take much."

Darryl and Jesse looked at each other across the table. "How'd an old lady get up that hill?" asked Jesse. But they both knew—there must have been an easier climb through the wooded backside.

Darryl chewed his forkful of pancakes slowly. He tried to remember all of the details of the dogsled carving. It was the perfect fusion of tree and animal, his two favorite things. He wondered if the hermit's daughter had taken it.

•

Darryl made two markings in his spiral notebook next to the word "Deer." That made seventy-seven. He saw them right through his bedroom window, running through his backyard to the orchards across the street. They were does, like the wooden deer in the bus, captured the same way in Darryl's memory and overlapping there for a second. It had been almost a week—school started this coming Tuesday—but he could still envision many of the carvings. They were so much more real than his little pencil sketches—three-dimensional and warmed by the rich textures of the wood. And they were done alone, in silence. When Darryl worked on his drawings in the quiet of his nighttime bedroom, the pencil lead scratched loudly against the clean paper. It probably resembled the sound of the hermit's files as he sat in his metal home and gently shaved away wood in the middle of the night, the sawdust of all his creations drifting to his feet like snow.

Darryl wanted to go back. He figured the hermit's daughter probably took all of the carvings on the shelf—they were like trophies, why wouldn't she?—but maybe she'd missed the half-finished dogsled under the newspapers, or had just felt it wasn't worth taking because it looked, in a way, so crude. Maybe she was like Jesse. But that crudeness was what Darryl wanted to see again, the beauty that could come from something once neglected and raw. He tried to remember if he'd covered it back up with the papers. He didn't think so.

It was Sunday afternoon and his parents were home, but his dad was in the basement watching TV and his mom was taking a nap. Darryl walked outside to the garage. In the rafters, above the bikes and riding lawnmower, his dad stored a lot of miscellaneous junk like planks of wood and storm windows and some old burlap sacks. Darryl jumped up and grabbed one of the sacks. He bunched it up so that he could hold it in one hand while riding his dirt bike. But then he remembered that he might have to carry things back home, and he wouldn't be able to hold it then. He'd have to ride the Schwinn.

He set the empty sack in the front metal basket and left, riding down Oceana Drive, fiddling with the three gears and never getting into any sort of rhythm. He couldn't feel sleek and fast on the Schwinn. He felt like his mom. He rode until he got to Tonawanda Drive and turned into the little community of cottages and trailers around Lake Tahoe. Then he quickly cut through some open fields in the area that led to the Christmas tree farms and the back half of the hermit's dune.

The old Schwinn bounced through the fields, and his legs burned even in first gear as he ripped his way through the overgrown trail. The high grasses made his legs itch. He refused to wear long pants even though the cool weather still lingered over the area, circling over the lake instead of moving east as usual.

Darryl found the trail that ran up the dune. He couldn't see the bus from the field, but he recognized the patch of elegant beech trees and white birches that graced the woods near the hermit's property. He grabbed the burlap sack and ditched the Schwinn, letting it fall and clatter amid the trees. Then he hiked up the hill. The sand was packed harder, and the tree roots gave it a foundation. He climbed easily.

The door to the bus was open this time, probably left like that by the hermit's daughter or the police. Real animals might have made their way inside by now, birds nesting in the corners, or squirrels burying acorns in the sawdust. As he walked up the rubber steps, a flash of panic flooded his head and heart. He started to sing "Twinkle, Twinkle Little Star," something he used to do when he was real young and had to walk through his basement in the dark. The plastic bags over the windows still hung in tatters as they had a week ago. The same light filtered in.

The sleeping bag was gone. So were the coolers and air mattress and most of the tools. But the posters and magazine pictures were still plastered on the curved ceiling, and the carvings that had stood on the shelves were piled in the back corner. The daughter had removed them before taking the shelves. Darryl's fear grew, and it stemmed in part from being alone.

"Like a diamond in the sky . . ."

He usually loved his solitary world, in shadows and forest shade, knowing no one could see him. But the echo of his footsteps in the bus and the darkness of those areas still concealed by black trash bags were claustrophobic. As he glanced around to see what else had changed since his last visit, he noticed all of the footprints in the sawdust. Most were smaller, either his or Jesse's or the daughter's, but along the edges, and between the rows of seats where no one else would step, were large prints made by work boots—traces of the hermit's final days. Darryl approached one of the footprints and slowly placed his own foot on top of it. To his amazement, his bulky white high-tops almost filled the entire print—only edges of the heel and toes showed through. He quickly pulled his foot away, turned to the workbench, and flung the newspapers to the side. In his rush of worry, he accidentally knocked the dogsled onto the floor. He picked it up and tried to inspect it in the dimness. It looked fine, the half-living tree limb, the dogs that tried to pull loose.

"Twinkle, twinkle little star . . ."

Darryl went to work. He put the huskies in the sack first and then began scooping up the other carvings in the corner: the deer, the bear, and others he hadn't noticed before. There was a carving of a topless Indian woman. Darryl looked behind him in the bus, and then rubbed his thumb slowly over the smooth wooden breasts before slipping it in the sack with all the rest.

He rode down Oceana Drive with the heavy sack leaning against his handlebars in the front basket. He swam in waves of relief, feeling as if he'd rescued something beautiful and fragile, like kittens. The carvings shifted sometimes as he rode over bumps, and once almost spilled out onto the road and the bordering asparagus fields. But he made it home with all of them. His dad was still in the basement, and his mom was just waking from her nap and thought he'd been playing in the backyard the whole time.

He hid the carvings in his room, in the back of his closet, under a pile of old clothes that didn't fit him anymore. He wasn't sure exactly why they had to be hidden, but in the cloudy gloom of a Sunday afternoon, with all his blinds closed and school starting in two days, he began to feel guilty, like a thief who steals art from museums. He tried to convince himself that all the carvings were going to be trashed, that the daughter had taken what she wanted and wasn't coming back. But maybe she was. Maybe, before gathering up the hermit's most precious belongings, she was going to return by herself one last time to say a prayer and say goodbye just as she must have done when she left his ashes floating offshore.

Darryl tried not to think about that. No, he was sure. She'd taken what she wanted and that was it. She probably thought the carvings were junk made by a lonely old man with nothing in his pockets but time. But he still knew he had to hide them so that his dad wouldn't find out he'd trespassed when told not to, and so his mom wouldn't find the carving of the naked Indian woman.

•

Darryl woke up in the middle of the night to go to the bathroom because he'd had too much Gatorade before going to bed. In the smog of thought that comes at that hour, he imagined the animals in the carvings, how he could almost put another mark in his spiral notebook next to the word "Deer" because the deer carving looked so real. He could finally mark the empty space next to "Bear." He flushed the toilet and walked through the dark hallway back to his room. The old floorboards creaked under his steps and reminded him of the hermit's footprints.

Darryl got into bed and thought about ghosts. Earlier that summer he'd spent some lazy time on the patio reading books like *The Ghostly Gazetteer* about real-life haunted landmarks. Sometimes the hauntings began when dead people's possessions were removed from their old homes. He remembered a story of two old portraits— a man and a woman—that were separated, and the portrait of the woman began to weep real tears.

He rolled onto his side. His sketch pad and pencils were on his nightstand beside his alarm clock. He never showed the sketches to anybody, even his family. But he often hoped that his mom or someone else would see the pad of paper and casually flip through the pages to see all that he'd created. Darryl questioned how the hermit's daughter could just leave her father's artwork to be trashed with the rest of his junk. What had he done? Severed himself almost completely from her? His separation from the world might have started with his job and his church and his friends, and eventually spread to his family.

Darryl loved the solitude of his room, but he still liked knowing that his parents were on the other side of his wall, and that Jesse was right across the hallway. But maybe this would change. After all, he'd once liked the kids at school too.

He turned onto his other side so as not to think any more about his family, or about the hermit's ghost shifting through the sack of carvings like smoke, or especially about the topless Indian woman weeping real tears.

•

Whatever he'd brought home with him from the bus was too troubling to keep. Darryl woke up at five fifteen and stared at the numbers on his alarm clock until they came into focus. His sketch pad also came into focus, and his earlier thoughts about the hidden sack of carvings sharpened in his mind. He closed his eyes to sleep again but kept thinking about the hermit's ashes, floating alone among the waves. When the weather cooled and the waves went gray, there was nothing lonelier than the lake. The hermit wanted to be separated from people, but not from everything. Even after death, just as during his life, he would have wanted to be with his animals. And if there were spirits inside the animals, they probably wanted to be with him too.

Darryl got out of bed. He knew he had to get rid of the carvings. School started the next day, so he had to do it this morning. His parents would leave for work thinking he was still sleeping in bed; as long as they didn't hear him leaving, he was fine.

Darryl wore the same T-shirt and sweat shorts he'd slept in, and then slipped on his flannel slippers that let him walk without sound. He crept to the side door of the house with the heavy sack of carvings slung over his shoulder. Even though he wore the slippers, the floors creaked in places, but it was still so dark outside he knew no one would wake. He left the house and opened the garage door only halfway because it was so loud, and then walked the Schwinn underneath it before lowering the door back down to the gravel driveway. He lifted the sack into the basket and started pedaling, the gravel crunching under his tires until he made it to the paved road. He was going to return the carvings to the hermit.

There was no way he could ride all the way to Pentwater, so he had to settle for another lakeside park close to New Era. He headed for Claybanks, where he'd once spotted a bald eagle, or maybe two. He pedaled down Oceana Drive with the stars still out and watching him like eyes, the sky curving over him like the ceiling of the bus.

It took him nearly an hour to get there on the slow Schwinn, made slower by the final leg on the hills of Scenic Drive. He needed to yawn but was breathing too hard. His legs burned from the early-morning exercise. First light sprayed out over the sky to his right, but to his left, there were still stars, over the lake that he still couldn't see because of the tall oaks that separated the road from the beach.

The campground at Claybanks was fairly empty from the cool weather and the unofficial end of summer as kids got ready to start school the next day. There were a few RVs and tents, a few smoking fire pits, but the place was still, everyone asleep. Darryl parked his bike at the far end of the grounds where the woods began. His legs felt shaky as he switched to walking, and the sack over his shoulder added to his weight. He headed down the sandy trail that led to the water. The dawn's light cast a soft, calm pink overhead, but it disappeared as he walked down the trail under the dark, sprawling branches of oak and beech and white pine. As he hit the dunes, the trees gave way and the sky's fresh light returned, like the hue of an infant's skin. The beauty reassured Darryl. It was right to bury the carvings at sea.

He couldn't hear the whitecaps breaking on the shore and guessed that the water was simply as calm as the sky. But as he climbed a small hill covered in tall grass and walked over the hill's crest to where he could finally see the lake, he realized the dune had

been blocking the sound. Now the roar of the water crashed everywhere in front of him as waves at the edge of the lake turned sharp
and white like teeth. The burlap dug into his shoulder, but he was
almost there. His flannel slippers squeaked against the hard-packed
sand, no longer soundless. There was no one on the beach in either
direction. But there were ladybugs, thousands of them, lining the
wet boundary of sand where the waves reached. They covered the
blades of dune grass that rose in tufts from the sand. He saw them
covering seagull feathers, scraps of garbage, and even a dead mon-
arch butterfly at the brink of the water. He'd never seen so many
ladybugs, and didn't know if they had flown there or been washed
ashore with the sand.

Darryl almost said a prayer while staring out at the lake, something to honor the hermit and replace the old ghosts with the Holy
Ghost. But he felt stupid, and then felt guilty for feeling stupid
with nobody watching him but God. He dragged the sack toward
the water.

He failed, twice. His first attempt to scatter the carvings at sea
mimicked an Olympic hammer throw. Clutching the sack by its
scrunched-up opening, he spun around, gaining momentum with
each spin, until he released and hurled it into the water. It didn't
go far, and immediately began floating among the waves and tumbling back to the shore. He looked around to see if anyone had
witnessed his failure. He felt like an enormous idiot, and even if
God was the only one who'd seen, that was humiliation enough. Of
course a sack filled with wood—especially driftwood—was going
to float. A few of the carvings, the coyote and the bear, came out of
the sack and were bobbing among the waves by themselves. Darryl
took his slippers off and waded into the cold water up to his thighs,
trying to hold onto the sack while chasing down the ones that had
escaped, even more conscious of the scene's awkwardness because
of the sluggish way he moved through the somersaulting water.

He wondered what had happened to the hermit's ashes, if any had drifted from Pentwater and were floating now around his legs.

His second attempt involved kneeling on the beach and trying to fill the sack with enough sand so that it would sink. He dragged it behind him, leaving a long groove that ran to the water, and began wading through the waves again. The cold burned his skin as it moved from his legs up to his groin. The water was low, so he was able to walk a long ways with the water only rising up to his waist. As he walked, he noticed the bag floating beside him.

"Shit, shit, shit." He scanned the beach. There was no one to hear him. "Shit."

With his clothes clinging to him, his teeth chattering, and the sack heavier than ever, Darryl walked back across the sand and up the trail leading to the campground, unsure of what to do.

There was a smoldering campfire off by itself. It looked as though the people who'd used it late last night were gone. He stood in the smoke, coughing, his eyes stinging, but feeling a little warmer and dryer. After a few minutes he wandered around near the edge of the trees, gathering kindling. Orange embers still winked at the bottom of the pit, and when Darryl threw some of the smaller sticks on, they caught fire quickly. He spent about a half hour stirring up the embers and throwing on larger and larger sticks until the fire was fully rekindled and giving off real heat.

Darryl sat on a rock with the sack next to him in the grass. There was some activity now around the campground, people wandering to the outhouses and kids climbing the colorful play equipment. The sun was fully out, and Darryl felt bad that he'd missed that moment at dawn when the burial at sea would have been near-perfect.

He turned the sack over and spilled out the carvings. Most had stayed fairly dry, and even the coyote and bear were only wet on one side. He stared into the flames and let himself be hypnotized for a short time, feeling exhausted. When he blinked away his stare, he noticed how much white ash had accumulated in the fire pit. Whoever had lit the fire before him must have let it burn for hours and hours. Darryl wondered if a person's ashes looked like that after cremation. He wondered if things—artifacts—could be cremated.

With a motion that felt reflexive, he tossed the wooden deer sculpture into the fire. Its stained bronze skin went black, its fragile legs, still stretched into a gallop, succumbed to the flames first. He threw the bear into the flames, the wolf, the naked Indian woman—all of them. They burned for nearly an hour. Nobody ever wandered close to Darryl. Like most things, he did this alone. He hesitated when he got to the last carving in the sack, running his hand along the polished wood and feeling all of the tiny grooves of the fur with his fingertips. But then the half-finished dogsled followed the others, the huskies eventually blackening and caving in on themselves, becoming a mound of ash at the bottom of the pit.

The sun had cleared all the trees and risen high into the blue sky. Even though the light of dawn had passed, he felt glad about what he was doing. There was a water pump that he used to fill some empty pop cans. He made several trips between the pump and the fire, but eventually the flames hissed and steamed and died away. When they were cool, Darryl gathered the sticky, wet ashes in his bare hands and scooped them into the sack. They stained his hands black and gray.

He returned to the beach and waded into the lake one last time. The sack felt weightless. He pulled the wet handfuls of ash out and let them fall in clumps into the water. They diffused and floated in all directions.

As he walked back to his bike, he remembered the hermit's name again: Joseph Doornbos. He'd try to refer to him by his proper name now, although he really didn't want to talk about him anymore. What could words say that ashes couldn't?

There was no fire now to warm him, so Darryl threw the burlap

sack in a garbage bin and got on the Schwinn. He didn't want to
ride back at all. He was too tired and cold, and he didn't want
to explain to Jesse where he'd been. He couldn't imagine speaking
to a single person at school tomorrow, not even his teachers. In the
cafeteria after lunch, he'd find a quiet table to work on a new sketch.
It would be a drawing of a dogsled, emerging from old wood like an
infant animal emerging from the womb. It would not be fully free
of the wood, but it would be finished, and he would leave it on the
table for someone else to find.

SAND THIEVES

Uncle Lucien spent the summer surrounded by horseflies. They left the rest of us alone, except my mom, who blamed the scent of Aqua Net for luring them into her hair. During Memorial Day weekend my two cousins and I knelt in the sand at the top of the beach. Terry and Caleb had dug a wide hole and filled it with water to hold the turtle they'd just caught. I'd dug a narrow but deeper hole that swallowed my arm up to the shoulder. The underground sand was cold and moist. It was older than the soft stuff on the surface, and had probably been brought to the cottage years earlier.

Uncle Lucien walked slowly in our direction, swinging his old double-edged weed cutter with the long wooden handle, slicing dandelions and tall grasses along the top strip of beach. We were in his way.

A swarm of horseflies circled his shoulders and head, and a few other flies buzzed around his ankles, scattering and returning with each low swing of the blade.

Caleb looked in his direction. "You got a fly on your foot," he said.

Uncle Lucien stopped and picked up his can of beer from where he'd set it in the sand, then lazily waved his hand over his ankle, the way a cow in a pasture swings its tail. "They're lookin' for protein for their eggs," he mumbled. He stood still and took a long sip. The fly landed on his foot again. Uncle Lucien didn't move, but watched it out of the corner of his eye. A tear of blood slowly swelled and somersaulted off the side of his big toe, darkening a small circle of sand like an old penny.

"They got some teeth if you let 'em use 'em," he said. He took another long sip of beer, swished it around in his teeth, and then spat it onto his foot, scattering the fly again. "Get," he said. He set the beer back down and returned to swinging the blade, making it hum against the air and the grasses. My cousins and I reluctantly stood and let him pass.

He was my mom's uncle, and I tried not to think about him unless he was in my field of vision, within earshot, or unless Terry was making fun of him and I was chipping in. Uncle Lucien was as bald as a dolphin and always wore a beat-up Tigers cap to protect his head from the sun, but the flies still stuck close to him. He never seemed bothered. As long as we kids didn't disturb him while he worked on the beach, he moved steadily through the day, with horseflies bouncing off his head.

"Like dog shit," said Terry. "He's like a big, steaming pile."

Terry was fourteen, two years older than me and ready to enter high school the next fall. His parents had been the first to divorce, and although his dad lived just three blocks down from his house in Fruitport, Terry rarely saw him. Terry showed up that summer of 1985 with a thin, black mustache and black tufts of armpit hair, which I noticed the first time he took his shirt off to swim. He and I and our ten-year-old cousin Caleb spent most summer weekends up at our family's cottage in New Era. The three of us were close. None of us had any siblings. We all lived alone with our moms after our parents divorced. We could have been brothers, except Caleb had bright orange hair—his dad's orange hair—and he didn't look dark like the rest of the family.

Uncle Lucien once noted this. "He's the only red-head fruit in our Polack family tree."

Weekends at the cottage were a time for us to breathe a little easier, to be relieved of the strange dynamic that results from single moms living all year with only their sons. That summer was the first without Grandpa, and although none of us talked about it, we seemed to keep busier and closer. The three of us boys joined up and disappeared for entire mornings or afternoons, and our moms gave us that freedom, happy, it seemed, to be back in their own clique for a time. They acted girlish when they were together, laughing, whispering, pointing at the young, shirtless men who put shingles on the Drysdale cottage across the street. They smoked cigarettes and drank wine coolers, cassettes of Dionne Warwick and Neil Diamond providing the soundtrack. Sometimes the three of them would recline on the beach, passing around a can of cashews—one of their weekend luxuries. Aunt Dee Dee, Terry's mom, wore a leopard-print bikini that I tried not to look at but sometimes did. She, my mom, and my Aunt Tess sunned themselves in the early heat of Memorial Day, lying next to one another on their stomachs with their eyes closed, speaking dreamily about vacations they'd never take. They fell silent when we boys came near. Sometimes I think they were talking about men. Maybe the shirtless men across the street. Maybe our dads.

The cottage rested on a hill above Lake Tahoe, with a small lot of land—beech trees, moss, and a root-choked trail—bridging the cottage and the water. Lake Tahoe was a small lake. A big pond. All comparisons with the more famous lake out West end at the name. Instead of casinos there were trailers. Instead of mountains there were asparagus fields. Dogs without leashes chased kids through ferns and old leaves, around charcoal grills and propane tanks. Motorboats weren't allowed by ordinance, only quiet fishermen in rowboats and loud families churning away in paddle boats that—for all their rocking and jostling—couldn't manufacture any waves. In the morning, the lake looked still. At dusk, it looked stagnant. And if we stood close by the dirt road when cars or pickups drove by, dust filled our eyes and grit scraped our teeth. The cottage doesn't sound like much, but we loved the place, in large part because of Uncle Lucien's beach.

I call it *his* beach because it wasn't a natural geographic formation. He was a sand farmer. He farmed sand in the sense that he tended it each morning of every summer weekend, nurturing it so that it could thrive in the warm months and be consumed by the family—although he wasn't thinking of the family when he set out to work. To farm sand, however, he had to first become a sand thief.

Terry, Caleb, and I all lived within thirty minutes of one another, but I only met up with them on summer vacations and some holidays. It was the same with Uncle Lucien, only I didn't miss him the way I did the rest of the family. None of us did. And that summer of '85, Aunt Dee Dee's indifference ran deeper, into layers of resentment. A few years earlier, my grandma had died at the veterans nursing home in Grand Rapids after years of living in the haze of Alzheimer's. Grandpa went to the same home after he suffered a stroke in 1984. He died later that year.

But even though Uncle Lucien lived only about five miles from the home, he never went to visit Grandpa, and never explained why. Our moms tried not to talk about it in front of us boys, but they avoided him during that whole three-day weekend, looking down at him from their perches on the deck while he raked the sugary beach.

•

I stumbled out of the road, and the firecracker exploded behind me. Caleb's fingers were in his ears. Terry was off looking for dry leaves to ignite. It was early June, still a month before Independence Day, but the three of us were already lighting Black Cats with a magnifying glass. I focused the white beam of light on the tips of the wicks, but staring at it was like staring at the sun. I had to rely on the hissing sound to know it was lit, and then blinked away the black, floating spots in my eyes as I got out of the way.

"God, my eyes," I said, rubbing them. "We need a lighter."

"Our moms said no," said Caleb.

"Do you know how many lighters they got inside? The junk drawer's filled with 'em. They're not gonna miss one more little plastic lighter if you just stick it in your pocket while they're out on the deck."

"*You* do it, Lance. You want it."

"Fine," I said. I began walking through the trees to the cottage.

Terry ran toward us with an armful of brown leaves. "Guys," he said excitedly, "you should hear the old man down there."

"What?"

"He found some more four-wheeler tracks on our property. Messed up his ferns. He was down there all yellin' to himself, 'Four-wheeler cock beaters!' It was great."

Uncle Lucien did this often. He raked the sand on his small beach with his shirt off, his thick shoulders and arms flexing with each motion. He hunched over slightly with age, still carrying the burden of his own, lasting strength. Early in the summer his skin burnt red under the curls of white chest and back hair. By mid-June he would be tan. While he worked, he would find things that angered him: four-wheeler tracks, dog shit on the beach, loud or lazy children. He shouted and swore to the sky, spooking robins out of trees. Voices of swimmers on the other side of the lake would carry across to our side, so I can only imagine what nearby property owners thought when they heard the words of this crazed old man—parents on other shores clasping their hands over the ears of young children, carrying them indoors, where the windows were closed and the radio turned on, the volume high.

I tossed the magnifying glass at Terry's feet. "That thing sucks. I'm frickin' blind. We're gonna get a lighter from inside."

"*You're* gonna get a lighter," said Caleb.

"Shut up," I said.

When I returned with it, Terry pried it from my fingers and picked up a new Black Cat off the ground. "Check this," he said.

He jogged to the crest of the hill and looked down at the beach. Then he crouched against the smooth, gray skin of a beech tree. "Wanna scare him?"

"Terry, don't," said Caleb.

"You chicken?"

"Don't do it," I said. I turned to my left to look at the deck. Our moms relaxed in lounge chairs reading paperbacks. "They'll see you."

"So what? They don't care."

"He'll kill you."

"No he won't. He'll forget about it five minutes after it's over. He's nuts."

Terry peeked around the tree trunk. Uncle Lucien was resting and looking out at the lake. His left hand held the rake, and the right tipped back his can of beer. Terry flicked his thumb over the lighter several times, but it only sparked.

"Shit, how old is this thing?"

After a few more tries, a short flame rose up from it. Terry touched the wick to the flame until it started to hiss. Caleb turned to run, and I followed him as Terry stepped around the tree and tossed the Black Cat in Uncle Lucien's direction. I didn't watch where it sailed, but I heard the blast as I sprinted toward the back of the cottage.

"Goddamn it!"

Caleb and I ran all the way to the shanty at the back of our property. Terry was a few strides behind with a smile on his face, mimicking Uncle Lucien. "Goddamn it! Goddamn it!"

We stopped running. "Did you hit him?" I asked.

"God, no," said Terry. "It blew up way above his head. But he probably pissed his beer right out of himself."

Our moms never said anything to us. And later, when Uncle Lucien confronted us and called us all no-dick sissies and a waste of our daddies' sperm, they didn't say anything to him, either. When they were our age, they'd heard similar words, what Aunt Dee Dee called his "oral flatulence."

Terry wasn't deterred. The following weekend he found an old UAW baseball cap in the kitchen junk drawer, along with a pair of enormous plastic gag glasses that resembled Uncle Lucien's. With Uncle Lucien out of sight, Terry grabbed a rake from the shanty, pulled his shirt off, and scooped up handfuls of wet dirt from under the leaky garden hose. He smeared it over his chest and shoulders. I noticed that he looked stronger that summer, but his muscles were still lean compared to Uncle Lucien's.

"Check this out," he said. "Little bit of chest hair. I'm like the great gorilla himself."

"It needs to be white to look like his hair," I said.

"Nah, brown's cool." With the dirt stuck to his body, Terry stooped over and shuffled around, raking lines in the sand and sometimes looking up through the gag glasses, speaking to the sky.

"Come here, girl!" he yelled. "I got some protein for your eggs."

I laughed, my face instantly red and my eyes wet. Caleb was reluctant and embarrassed, but he laughed the loudest.

"Dude," I said, "you got problems."

"Come here, goddamn it! I said I got protein for your eggs!"

Terry had started swearing more often that summer. He squinted and bunched up his face to make it look old, and Caleb and I laughed so hard that our voices evaporated into a pure, silent laugh that shook our bodies.

"Let me give it to you, baby!"

The wet sand dried and fell in clumps from Terry's chest. As I wiped my eyes with my hands, he turned the hose on and began to wash himself off, still wearing the huge pair of plastic glasses.

•

My grandparents bought the New Era cottage during their retirement, and as my grandpa's only living sibling, Uncle Lucien had been invited over every summer weekend. When I think of the two men together, I remember them storing warm cases of Pabst in the rotting wooden shanty, never facing each other during conversations but moving through words carefully, settling into them. Grandpa sometimes smoked a pipe, and once I saw the two of them leaning against a parked car in the driveway and passing the pipe back and forth—their eyes never meeting—and puffing up clouds that floated between them. Their conversations were like that too: Grandpa could speak to Uncle Lucien with the ease of smoke, the words slipping back and forth amid their breath, inhaled and exhaled. It was a skill or trick the rest of us never figured out.

Most Saturday afternoons, Uncle Lucien would turn the key in his car, roll the window down, and from the front steps of the shanty the two of them would listen to Tigers games on AM radio. They could patiently sit together through a fourteen-inning pitchers' duel, standing only for more beer or to piss in the ferns by the horseshoe pit. The only other time either of them sat so still was around the fire after dark. Otherwise, they were in motion, my grandpa playing flag football with us boys, taking us on errands to Jack's Market, or letting us sit in the back of his pickup and driving down the two-tracks, tree branches whipping us as we laughed in the wind. Uncle Lucien was tireless in a different way, tending the beach, pruning the trees, pulling the weeds.

He married and divorced before I was born. He didn't have any kids. When I was about five or six, Uncle Lucien had a string of relationships with young, obese women. He occasionally brought them to the cottage on the weekends. I remember playing tetherball with one of them. And I remember Aunt Dee Dee speaking to my mom through unmoving lips in the kitchen while stirring a new pitcher of cherry Kool-Aid.

"I don't even want to *know* my uncle has a fat fetish, let alone witness it every week. If he's here to plump her up on my potato salad, tell him to just leave now. I'll give her a doggy bag for the trip back to Fat Rapids."

He worked for years at the GM Metal Fabricating Division in Grand Rapids, living in an apartment without a yard or a garden. He drove a Plymouth, feeling no loyalty to his company or union or anyone else. In the winter, he hibernated. In the summer, he returned to the sand. He woke early every Saturday morning when it was still dark, driving his baby-blue Duster to Duck Lake State Park before the rangers arrived. The park was on Lake Michigan, and he brought four plastic buckets with him that were so large I'd once stuffed myself into one of them during a game of hide-and-seek. When empty, they bounced against Uncle Lucien's knees as he clumsily trudged along. He kept an old army hand shovel in his trunk, and I can imagine him kneeling in the sand, digging during the hour when shadows and stars share the morning. I imagine him lugging the heavy buckets over to the car and dropping them in the trunk so that it sank a few inches. The big lake was probably starting to glint like an unsheathed blade as he left for the cottage. By the time the rest of the family arrived around nine o'clock, Uncle Lucien had already poured white Lake Michigan sand over the small square of beach at the east end of our property, pouring it like sugar over our coarse, inland dirt. He raked and tenderized it, making crisscrosses in the ground so that it seemed new and perfect. We kids never dared to step on the beach first. We waited for our moms to ruin it with their dirty yellow flip-flops.

When Grandpa died in December of '84, my mom spoke to Aunt Dee Dee on the phone, arranging the funeral but also arranging the aftermath, trying to resolve the Uncle Lucien situation. In other words, was he still welcome now that the sisters owned the cottage? Aunt Dee Dee said they should cut him off for abandoning Grandpa at the veterans home.

There was a blizzard the day of the funeral. I'd never seen Uncle

Lucien in the snow. I'd never seen him wearing a stocking cap and gloves. During the service, he kept his eyes closed and his head bowed, like a prayer, but also like when he'd bury his face in his hands as Willie Hernandez took the mound for the Tigers with two on and two out in late innings.

I sat apart from the adults at the luncheon that followed the funeral. But afterward, as we walked to our cars, my mom called, "We'll see you Memorial Day, Uncle Lucien."

His future was secured. He returned that summer.

It didn't surprise me. Even if they did mock him behind his back and ruin his sand with their flip-flops, I think our moms felt he needed to keep coming. Terry thought it was because they wanted the sand. It was as if Aunt Dee Dee had sat across from Uncle Lucien at the luncheon, piercing kielbasa with a plastic fork and scribbling a barely legible but completely binding agreement onto a prayer card or dessert napkin, outlining each party's terms, asking him to sign the deal that would keep him in business at the beach.

But no such words, if any, were exchanged. They wanted to fulfill Grandpa's wishes and keep inviting his brother up every weekend. And they wanted Uncle Lucien there for our sakes. He wasn't Grandpa, but at least he was a man. As for all the bizarre displays and "oral flatulence"? They were things to ignore, like horseflies circling our heads.

•

A cardinal landed on a tree stump a few feet from where Uncle Lucien sat. It was the Fourth of July, and I was by myself on the other side of the beach, reading a baseball card price guide. I looked up occasionally at Uncle Lucien and the bird.

"Hey, sweet thing." He stretched his arm out at the cardinal. "How are you?"

The cardinal cocked its head and took two quick hops in his direction.

"Pretty bird," he whispered. "Pretty bird. Pretty bird."

The cardinal flew away. I'd seen this before. Uncle Lucien spoke to animals more than he spoke to the rest of us. He said he read the minds of birds and fish. When Terry and I were real young, we used to think he was a wizard. Then I saw a falconer at a Renaissance festival near Detroit and thought they shared the same gift. As if Uncle Lucien could extend his right arm and horseflies, big ones, would land on his wrist. As if he could send them on command to hunt cats and black squirrels.

Once, Uncle Lucien emerged from the lake, where he had been pulling weeds offshore, and leeches were stuck to his thighs. He took his time removing them, walking up the sandy trail to the deck, where the rest of us were at the picnic table eating hamburgers. He wanted us to see the leeches, to be both sickened and enlightened by the truths of the natural world. He picked up a plastic knife from the table and plucked the leeches from his skin.

A year or two later, when my parents split, he took me aside.

"Come here, Lance."

My name sounded raw coming from his old mouth. Uncle Lucien held a humming coffee can in his right hand with air holes poked in the plastic lid. He lowered his voice.

"Bees."

He led me by the shoulder into the cottage and closed the screen door behind me, while he remained outside. Down on the beach, Terry and Caleb were digging trenches in the sand. Our moms were reading magazines beside them. I was seven years old. And Uncle Lucien was the only person with me, bending down to look at me through the other side of the screen, his eyes at the same level as mine.

"Get closer."

I leaned slowly forward until my nose brushed the filthy metal mesh of the door. Uncle Lucien removed the lid and pressed the open mouth of the can against the screen. I couldn't see the bees, but

I swear to God I heard each wing slice the dark coffee can air. They seemed to kiss my lips. But the fear of stings was less than the fear of moving from where I was told to stand. I kept my nose to the screen.

"Some people run like hell from bees," he said, "and others tell you to stay still because they only sting in defense. Just stay real still and they'll leave you alone. And I say fuck the little prick of a bee sting. Don't worry about an itty-bitty boo-boo here and there. Some things are dangerous. Some just hurt for a second."

He removed the can from the screen, and the bees diffused into the sky. Uncle Lucien's eyes never left mine. "Divorce is like a bee sting," he said.

•

He took down Grandpa's American flag without asking our moms. It was the first weekend after the Fourth of July, and he replaced it with a blue state of Michigan flag. Grandpa was a proud patriot who'd fought in Europe during the war. Uncle Lucien never talked about his own time in the service. He'd been a mess cook stationed in Goose Bay, Labrador.

"A cook," said Terry.

I took the old globe from the cottage coffee table and searched all over Europe for about fifteen minutes before Terry, sitting across from me, pointed at his side of the globe.

"It's here," he said. "Christ, it's all the way over here."

I turned the globe on its axis and saw the word stretched over northeastern Canada, an ocean from the closest German tank. Labrador.

The blue Michigan flag slapped against the front door of the cottage, pressing its nylon skin against the kitchen window when the wind blew hard. An elk and a moose stood tall on their hind legs in the center of the flag. A river ran to a pretend horizon.

Uncle Lucien was a Michigan jingoist. Later that weekend, while the family lounged on the beach and he took a break from his work, he explained that we—meaning the entire state—could secede from the Union and survive on our own.

"We got everything we need." He extended a hard, knotted finger with each word. "Lumber. Fruit. Iron ore. Fish. Christ, we could send tankers filled with fresh water down the St. Lawrence. Swap it with the Arabs for oil."

That, of course, was horse shit. He wouldn't give the water to any outsider.

He then quizzed us on Michigan history, geography, and wildlife.

"What's the state fish?"

"I don't know."

"Brown trout, you dope. How about this tree, right here?"

"Pine."

"*White* pine. State tree. Ever look away from the TV to see one in real life?"

He hated how the suburbs had ruined us. He hated our surprise when we overturned rocks in the woods and found insects in the cold dirt. He hated our grimaces when we swam in the lake and brushed against the submerged weeds. Even when we were younger and still followed him around, he wouldn't let us travel to Lake Michigan when he loaded his sand-thieving tools into the trunk of his Duster. The big lake was his shrine, and he protected it from the ignorant—from us.

Later in July, he sat in his green lawn chair and read an article in the *Chronicle* about how the state of Arizona wanted to run a pipeline and pump the lake's water to the desert. Uncle Lucien didn't shout, as I expected, but shook his head and exhaled deeply as if suddenly exhausted.

"If we ran low on sandstone would we take a jackhammer to the goddamned Grand Canyon?"

•

In early August, on the northbound highway headed for New Era, my mom told me that Aunt Dee Dee had been dating a guy named Pete.

"I wanted to let you know," she said, "in case you overheard anything this weekend. But you got to promise not to say anything around Terry. She's waitin' till it's right to tell him, and it's not right yet."

I nodded and knew what she meant. Terry was still angry about things. I didn't say anything to him all summer, and I wished I hadn't known at all. It got me thinking about my own mom. She wasn't the youngest sister, but she looked like it, since she never permed her hair, choosing to leave it long and straight. I started thinking about her with other men on those nights when I went to a friend's house to sleep over. Maybe Terry was keeping something from me, too.

August was a sad month. The weather was hottest and time passed the quickest, seeming to accelerate as the school year approached. Weekend tumbled over weekend. The three of us played a lot of horseshoes, Frisbee golf, and tetherball. We drank Pepsi with sand in it. Since Terry was the teenager in the family, our moms asked him to man the grill. He let Caleb pour the charcoal, and I could spray the lighter fluid, but he always lit the match. The warm, blue rush of flame made Caleb and me step back, while Terry stood as still as a soldier guarding his post. He flipped chicken breasts and poked at bratwursts with the two of us looking over his shoulder or playing close by in the sweet smoke. Our moms joked and talked loudly inside while arranging condiments, slicing tomatoes, and boiling corn. Uncle Lucien was waist-deep in the lake, pulling weeds from the water that he heaped into a compost pile. He was clearing the lake, but back then I only noticed the stench of the rotting weeds.

On a Saturday night in mid-August, when the sun set and the lake darkened, Uncle Lucien gathered logs and placed them just so in the fire pit. Terry had drawn a large circle in the sand for us to hold wrestling matches in, and he and I were trying to pin each other before all light left the sky. At one point he rolled on top of me and sunk his knee in my chest. He was definitely heavier than he'd been the previous summer.

Uncle Lucien walked over and rolled Terry off of me with one hand. "You, get some dry leaves." He pointed at me. "You, little sheep shit. Twigs."

He turned back toward the fire pit, while I scrambled in the dusk for kindling. Terry sat in the middle of the circle, his legs bent and his arms resting on his knees. His hair was messed up. His T-shirt was stretched out. In the failing light, he looked confused and frustrated.

Aunt Dee Dee, Aunt Tess, and my mom came down the sandy trail after dark with marshmallows and the sticks to roast them on. We picked our places around the fire, Uncle Lucien already settled in his chair, wordless and still, staring at the flames with huge eyes behind huge glasses. Our moms talked until they tired, and we all eventually fell silent like Uncle Lucien, entering his world for a few brief moments when the shared space of family felt comfortable, when it seemed like Grandpa was sitting with us again, the quiet moderator between generations. The lake was black glass and broken only by the occasional splashing lunge of a fish. I sometimes jumped from the splash in surprise, but Uncle Lucien remained unmoving. I remember wondering once if he had died, he was so still. Maybe he had died with his eyes open, like people sometimes do, and the cottage would feel more like ours with him gone. Terry and I would become the family sand thieves.

And then he moved, making me jump again.

Our moms were the first to yawn repeatedly and then stand up from the fire to say goodnight. My cousins and I could have fought fatigue longer, but we didn't want to sit alone with Uncle Lucien.

We hiked up the trail, stubbing our bare toes on roots and piercing our heels on acorns. We left him there in his green chair, which, as the hours passed, seemed to slowly sink into the week's fresh batch of white sand. An orange light glowed over the cottage door, and moths and earwigs clung to the screen. We opened the door quickly and ran our fingers through our hair to make sure no bugs had landed on us.

And when we woke Sunday morning, Uncle Lucien was shirtless and barefoot on the beach as always, raking the damp sand. I wondered if he'd slept the night before. He and my grandpa used to share one of the bedrooms, while all the women shared the other and we boys slept on the living room floor. But I hadn't seen him go to bed that entire summer since Grandpa had died.

I imagined that Uncle Lucien did hibernate—saving his rest for the winter, returning full strength in the summer like the flies. Maybe, in those times I thought he had died open-eyed by the fire, he was sleeping. Or maybe, long after the rest of us had gone to bed, he slipped inside the house like the spiders we'd always find, and then slept on the couch without making a sound. Our suburban eyes probably couldn't adjust to see him in the darkness of country nights.

I had started thinking like a young kid again, about wizardry.

The next day, when I spoke to Terry about this, he just shook his head. "It's nothin' magical." He turned and looked at the Duster parked in the gravel driveway. "He wouldn't share a roof with just us. He sleeps in his car. And our moms are cool with it."

"No way," I said. "They wouldn't let him sleep out here."

"Sure they would. They hate him."

"Yeah, but not that much. They let him keep coming."

Terry raised his eyebrows and stifled a smile. " 'Cause it's good sand, man. You can't deny that."

•

On a humid Saturday in late August—just days before school started—our faltering two-against-one badminton match ended because, even by himself, Terry whipped Caleb and me. I threw my racket in the dirt and found my yellow Wiffle bat resting in the rafters of the old shanty. I left for the public boat landing one lot over, an area hardly used by anyone any more, although it was a graveyard for overturned rowboats and canoes. Many had been smashed by downed tree limbs or by bored children who stomped on their underbellies.

I'd been watching black-and-white reruns of *Home Run Derby* and started smacking stones out into the lake, choosing a line of ripples in the water as my fence. The round stones felt solid on the bat, blooping far out from shore into a home run epicenter. I practiced so I could challenge and beat Terry.

He followed me down to the concrete strip of the boat landing, carrying a red plastic fishing pole—a kid's fishing pole. Caleb trailed him, still with his badminton racket. Terry's fishing line was tangled, and the gears popped and ground from sand the way our teeth did when we wrestled in the circle.

"Go look for worms," he told Caleb.

"I'm not touchin' any worms. They're sick."

Terry dropped his voice so it was low and quiet. "I said go get me some worms, Caleb."

"And I said *no way*. Like you'd even do it yourself. You're all scared to even rip 'em in half, so they're too big for the hook and come off on the first nibble."

"Butt licker."

"Shut up."

"Scrotum sac."

Caleb yelled out at the lake. "Free food for fish! The worms will come right off!"

Terry struggled to attach the sinker to the line, gritting his teeth. "Midget," he mumbled.

Caleb stuck his tongue out at him. He had to keep it playful, because if he did something serious, like give Terry the finger, Terry would rush him and tackle him right there on the concrete.

"You're probably small enough, midget," Terry said. "I could stick a hook in your belly and you'd probably stay on."

I kept my back to them, glancing occasionally out of the corner of my eye at Uncle Lucien. He carried rock after heavy rock across the beach to make a little dam that would redirect rainwater as it ran out of the woods, away from his perfect patch of earth. I picked up a crumbling sandstone, tossed it a foot or two in the air, and swung. It exploded, the dust stinging my eyes and sprinkling into the lake.

My mom called down to us from the deck of the cottage. "Boys, are you gonna be hungry if we eat sandwiches in about an hour?"

"We're starvin' right now!" yelled Terry, still weaving the hook through the jungle of tangled line.

I swung for about twenty minutes, until my shoulders turned sore and the bat started to fray and grow sharp barbs where stones had nicked away the plastic. Caleb sat on a tree stump, sifting pebbles through his racket. Terry sat on a smashed red canoe.

"Finally," he said and stood up. The long fishing line swung freely. He looked at Caleb. "Let's go fish."

I wasn't interested. I dropped my bat and walked up to the cottage for a Pepsi. My mom and aunts were on the deck drinking wine coolers and laughing. They didn't see me approaching through the trees.

"He probably has a mirror above the bed."

"Oh, stop it, Tess!"

"She said they took Polaroids."

"Damn you. I don't tell her all your sordid Friday night tales."

"Not as sordid as I'd like."

I emerged from the leafy trail, and they immediately stopped talking. I walked through the hushed voices, returned their smiles, and crossed the deck to the back door. I grabbed a can of pop from the refrigerator and drank slowly at the sink, out of their sight, trying to make out the resurfacing whispers from the deck. I wondered if there would ever be other men at the cottage besides Uncle Lucien.

I kept listening, but didn't hear anything. After a few minutes, I left out the side door and walked to the tire swing that hung from a maple by the shanty. I slipped my legs through the center, twisted the rope, and tried to drink my pop as I spun. I was still young enough that I never got dizzy.

An echoing chatter emerged from the lake. Down the path, Terry held the cheap kiddy fishing pole, which bowed toward the ground as he reeled in a fish.

"Holy cow, check it out!" he yelled, although Caleb was right beside him. Terry's voice squeaked in excitement—something he'd worked hard all summer to restrain. I slipped out of the swing, dropped my pop in the dirt, and ran down to the lake. He held on to the line with a blue gill at the end, its dorsal fins like needles.

"Take it off," he ordered Caleb.

"*You* take it off."

Terry saw me. "Lance."

"No way. You caught it."

He let go of the line so that the fish dropped into the dirt, its gills flapping, the hook still in its mouth.

"God, it won't stay still," said Terry. "And it's sharp as anything."

He reeled the line in slowly, the fish ascending to the end of the pole. Then Terry reached back, threw his arms forward, and cast. The blue gill—still on the line—arced over the water, smacking the surface just as Terry jerked the line back again. I ducked and covered my eyes as the hook shot toward our heads.

"Jesus, Terry!"

When I looked again, he held the line with the hook—a piece

of green flesh the only thing dangling from the end. "Sick," he said quietly. And then louder, "That was sick."

"That was awesome," said Caleb.

It happened all over again about a half hour later, this time with a sunfish. Caleb held the red pole, and it looked just right in his small hands. He struggled to bring the fish ashore. Its fins were fanned in shock, and Caleb high-stepped away from it as it lay in the sand, choking on air.

"You pussy." Terry picked up the pole and started to reel in the fish, but it fell off the hook, onto the concrete boat landing. "Shit."

It flailed, turning muddy in the gravel bits that covered the concrete. I picked up the yellow Wiffle bat and started to prod the fish, flipping it toward the sand and water. The fish writhed its way down the slope of the landing. Terry shoved me aside, stepped forward holding Caleb's badminton racket, scooped the fish up, and flipped it in the air. It hit the ground like a wet shoe.

"Oh sick, man," said Caleb, covering his mouth. But I could tell by his bright eyes that he was smiling. I probably was too.

Terry scooped the fish up again and flipped it high enough that he had time to swing the racket and strike it on the way down. He hit it the way I hit the stones. The fish landed on the shore about a foot away. It didn't move.

"Oh, man. Put it back in the water," said Caleb, laughing through the words. It must have been the laughs that snared Uncle Lucien's attention, because when Terry tried to scoop up the fish one more time, Uncle Lucien was rumbling toward him. He snatched the racket from Terry's grip, and their shoulders struck. Terry slipped on the loose gravel, landed hard on one knee, and clumsily rolled onto his side amid the boats. The back of his head slammed against the sharp prow of an overturned canoe.

Caleb yelled, and I held the Wiffle bat with both hands, down near my waist like a sword. Uncle Lucien stooped to pick up the sunfish. He smoothed the dorsal fins down with his hard hands and submerged the fish in the shallows by the lily pads. It began to twist in his grip, its scales slick again with the mud washed off. It swam away beneath the lily pads, but it circled back, circled back, confused and beaten.

Uncle Lucien looked past me. He looked at Terry.

"Aw, shit," said Terry, moaning quietly in pain. His hand was pressed between his head and the canoe, and when he removed it, dark hair and blood leaked through his fingers. He stared up at Uncle Lucien. "Crazy senile fuck," he said.

But he didn't move, and neither did Uncle Lucien. The old man was alert, but not yet threatening. He was ancient and massive.

Caleb turned to run toward the cottage, but our three moms were already descending the trail. Aunt Dee Dee led them as always. Her flip-flops slapped happily, but her furious eyes were locked on Uncle Lucien.

"Goddamn you, I saw that!" she screamed, striding toward us. Her voice was sharp. She, too, had heard all the commotion and seen everything from high up on the deck.

She kneeled and touched her son's head. "Jesus, Terry." Then, smoothing down his hair, staining her hand with his blood, she mumbled, "I told myself, if he touches him, he's gone. If he touches him, he's gone." She turned and looked up at Uncle Lucien. "I swear to God I don't know what we were thinkin'. You abandon Dad and then you show up to keep screwin' with the rest of us. God, find another family to hate."

Uncle Lucien stayed quiet, moving only slightly to stare at her and then down at Terry. Terry started to cry, snarling through quivering lips. "Crazy fuck uncle."

Uncle Lucien turned his head and slowly scanned the family. "Uncle," he said with a strange smile, shaking his head, sickened. "Uncle." He turned his hairy back to us and began to walk up the boat landing, over the loose gravel. Then he ascended the trail toward his car, dipping into the shadows of the trees.

I heard him start the Duster and pull out onto the dirt road. When it happened, I figured he was heartbroken for having to leave. But now I think he wrote us off—wrote the cottage off—the second he started his car. Fuck the white pines. Fuck the horseshoe pit. Terry's blood? Fuck Terry's blood—it was less than the blood of a smashed horsefly.

Terry was fine, anyway. He stood, the blood already drying in rusty smears on his hand and head. The rest of the family began to wander back to the cottage for lunch, while Aunt Dee Dee and Terry kneeled on the shore, cupping water in their hands and washing off the blood. Terry protested and pushed her hand back, but then let her clean it.

A few hours later we left in our three separate cars and drove home. Even though school began that week, we agreed to return the next Saturday for the long Labor Day weekend. We'd spend two nights with the water and the beach. We'd close up the cottage for the season. We knew we'd have to rake our own sand.

And we were right about Uncle Lucien not showing up that next weekend, but he came to the cottage earlier that week—maybe several times by the scope of the work. My mom and I arrived late on Saturday, and we walked down to the shore, where Terry, Aunt Dee Dee, Caleb, and Aunt Tess were sitting in the lawn chairs around the fire pit.

Who knows how many trips Uncle Lucien had made back and forth between Lake Tahoe and Lake Michigan that week? He probably came at dawn, filling the plastic buckets with the sugary sand and driving to Duck Lake State Park before the rangers arrived, pouring the sand back onto the Lake Michigan shore, returning it to its birthplace, depositing it for people who deserved it.

My mom and I walked down the trail, and everyone turned to look at us, to read our reactions. Then they turned back to look at the hollow where the beach had been. All the soft sand was gone, leaving a scar of roots, dark dirt, and a gaping mouth in the earth that the lake began to fill. He left us a lagoon.

We closed the cottage that day, locking doors and windows, returning the grill to the shanty, and tearing down the badminton net. We didn't sleep over. Terry, Caleb, and I stood on the edge of the fire pit. Horseflies were everywhere, searching for blood. They landed on our necks and in our hair.

"It's like they're lookin' for him," I said.

"Fuck him," said Terry.

Caleb got down on all fours beside the lagoon, his nose almost touching it. He was quietly looking for minnows and tadpoles to see if any new life had cropped up in the new water. Terry stood behind him, and under the bright sky I could see their reflections, slightly distorted in the shallow pool. Terry's mirrored body loomed over Caleb's, out of proportion, bigger than it really was.

Aunt Dee Dee honked her car horn. We headed for the trail, where my mom stood with our suitcases and uneaten groceries. I traced the missing beach with my footsteps, walking around the perimeter and counting years on my fingers. Thirteen, fourteen, fifteen, sixteen. In four years, I'd have my driver's license. I pictured having my own car, the back end sagging from a trunkload of sand as I roared through the state park at dawn, the rangers just arriving to an already smaller beach.

RESTRAINT

A CONFESSION

When their knees hit the floor I felt the collision in my heels. It was like when someone in my bowling league dropped a ball two lanes over. Brondyke pressed his weight onto Trevor. He bled on him.

I'd been looking out the window when the fight started. A darkening gray sky outside looked like it meant to turn purple and storm. It was the end of the day on Friday, toward the end of the school year, and the clouds made things dimmer and dreamier, like everyone was on the other side of mosquito netting. The window was closed, but the outside air leaked in. It smelled like spring, blooming and wet.

Curtis started it. Our middle school had a building-wide rule requiring alphabetical seating charts, so Curtis McRae sat behind Trevor Lewis in all three classes they shared. I was in the back corner of Brondyke's geography class: Zack Vanderlaan.

The two of them sat in the middle of the room, and I could hear the taunts from my desk. Kids used their fists to cover discreet grins as they stared at Trevor and watched his face for pain. Brondyke snapped his fingers. "Hey, eyes up here, folks. Let's get all the eyes up here." He was a rookie teacher straight out of Western, tall and tan, whom girls would talk about in the hall between classes. Sometimes he stayed for an hour after school playing basketball in the gym with a group of guys. Sometimes I watched.

He'd take his tie off and roll his sleeves up. He could dunk, so we respected him immediately.

But some in geography began to think Brondyke could hear Curtis taunting Trevor yet didn't do anything because he was afraid. "Curtis is big," said Chip Elkins. "He's not messin' with him." When the taunts came I watched Brondyke for a sign that he was hearing but ignoring them. I didn't spot one.

"How's your mom, Trev?" Curtis whispered. "Heard she dances at the Vu. Totally naked."

Trevor looked down at his notes, trying to concentrate, squinting a little to give the illusion of focus. He was skinny like most of us, with a blond crew cut and pale skin. Blue veins showed through his temples. Nobody believed the stuff about his mom, but nobody said so. And the taunts, which had started out random and scattered, had become more urgent as the school year's momentum pushed us toward exam week.

"Shit Stains, they let your dad out of the rubber room yet?"

Some kids said Trevor's dad was in the Kalamazoo State Hospital down the road. The Asylum. He'd been arrested for drugs once, so it was easy for some to believe. Shit Stains was a separate rumor. Someone said they'd seen Trevor use a locker room toilet two days in a row without wiping his ass. This report was suspect. There were doors on all the stalls. And who watches something like that anyway? Why hadn't we mocked *that* kid? But it became part of our middle school vernacular. "We had to work in pairs today and I got paired with Shit Stains." I'd said this once to Roy. He always called him just Trevor.

There were other taunts. Curtis claimed he'd stolen some pills from an uncle's medicine cabinet, and at lunch some day when Trevor wasn't looking he was going to drop them into Trevor's chocolate milk or applesauce. "Some will make you crap. Some will make you puke. Some might give you a heart attack. Never can tell, Trev." But I don't think Curtis ever did anything beyond words,

until that day when he used his sharpened pencil and the whole
blister of harassment split open.

Brondyke passed out a worksheet, and we had to figure out the
latitude and longitude of cities like Paris and Moscow. Trevor went
frantically to work, resting his head on his left arm as he wrote. The
room fell surprisingly quiet for a Friday. Pencils scratched against
white paper. I didn't look up until the loud grinding of the pencil
sharpener broke in. It was Curtis, standing at the front of the room
in his bright red shirt, slowly cranking the sharpener and grinning
at the class. He blew the tip of the pencil, brushed the point with
his thumb, shook his head as if disappointed, and then sharpened it
a little more before walking back to his desk behind Trevor.

Silence settled over the room again. I could hear Brondyke at
his front desk chewing a piece of hard candy. He stood and walked
out into the hallway. It stayed quiet for another couple of minutes
before I heard a loud bang against a desktop. I looked up and saw
Trevor rubbing his back, trying not to turn around. His sad, hurt
eyes reminded me of Roy's. Curtis's face was red from holding back
a loud laugh. He checked the door before poking Trevor in the back
again with his sharpened pencil. Trevor jumped as if the lead was
electric, his hands slapping the top of his desk and his knees knocking the underside. Curtis did it a third time.

Brondyke returned, striding swiftly back to his desk with a
handful of papers. He sat down and began stapling them. Nobody
was working anymore. We all stared at Trevor, whose face was buried in his arms. His pencil moved like he was working, but he
wasn't. There were three little dimples on the back of his shirt that
made a triangle. Each dimple had a gray dot in the center. When
nothing happened right away, people's eyes began gradually wandering back to their worksheets. I leaned back and pressed my head
against the wall. The bumpy cinder blocks felt nice and massaged
my skull when I rolled it back and forth. Something crashed.

I turned around and saw Trevor's desk tipped over on its side.

Trevor stood in front of Curtis with a handful of his red shirt blooming from his fist like flowers. Then Trevor started hammering him. The rush of release was audible as his anger cracked free. Most of the punches landed on the top of Curtis's head, but a few caught his cheek and jaw. They didn't snap like the punches on TV, but they connected.

I never saw Brondyke coming up behind Trevor. He wrapped his arms around Trevor in a huge bear hug. Some of us stood up from our desks in shock. A couple of kids yelled in surprise. One kid said, "Sweet," but said it quietly.

Trevor twisted and flailed, still trying to get at Curtis. Then he started kicking at Brondyke's shins, stomping on his feet. He lifted his legs off the floor and kicked at the air. Brondyke's arms flexed so that the veins showed through. He had dark, serious shadows around his eyes, and next to Trevor's pale skin, I could see the difference between a boy and a man. While Curtis sat at his desk holding his jaw, snot blew from Trevor's nose. He went limp like a noodle, trying to slip right through Brondyke's arms to the floor. He gazed out at the rest of us, looking suddenly saddened that we weren't helping him. It seemed like he'd just give up and let Brondyke take him to the office.

Then he threw his head back. It smashed Brondyke's nose, kicking his own head backward and shooting a white flash into my eyes. But Brondyke still held Trevor tight. Later someone found a fine spray of blood over the papers on Brondyke's desk, but most of it poured straight down, over his chin and onto his clean white shirt. He started to bend at the knees, and I thought it was over— Trevor had floored him. But he was bending them so that they pressed against the backs of Trevor's knees. Trevor crumpled, their knees hit the floor, and Brondyke fell on top of him, his arms still wrapped tight in a violent hug.

Erin Bylsma ran out of the room, and everyone else stood now

in a little semicircle around the action. That was all we did. Trevor
started screaming for Brondyke to get the fuck off him. It was the
first time I'd ever heard fuck said to a teacher. Brondyke just whispered into his ear, the blood falling in rhythmic drips onto the kid's
pale cheek. "Shh. Shh. Trevor, relax. Shh. It's okay."

Trevor's body deflated. Brondyke waited a few moments, then
slowly loosened his grip, but Trevor tensed up and immediately
began to kick. Brondyke put all his weight on him again until he
collapsed a second time, deep into the carpet, exhausted. He cried.
Spit bubbled over his mouth. Erin Bylsma rushed back into the
room with Ms. Blue, a math teacher. Brondyke gently lifted Trevor
to his feet and whispered something to him. Trevor nodded, rubbing his chest and keeping his eyes away from us. Brondyke had a
smattering of blood over his mouth that made it look like a gro-
tesque smile, a clown's smile. He guided Trevor slowly out to the
hall with his open hand barely touching his back. Even from the
back corner of the room I could see circles of blood on the floor that
had turned the blue carpet black. I hoped that the janitors wouldn't
be able to get the stains out. I wanted them there on Monday, like
Purple Hearts, so all the kids who said Brondyke wasn't tough
would be reminded of what he did and shut their mouths.

•

Charcoal clouds huddled on the near horizon. Lightning pierced
them, but was too far away for the thunder to be heard. I walked
down Howard Street, slowly enough to ensure that I'd get caught
in the rain, fast enough that I knew Roy wouldn't catch me until I
was a little ways from school. It was embarrassing to be with him
in front of other friends. I heard him coming up behind me, slapping his feet and breathing hard. His bulky black trombone case
smacked his knee as he ran.

"Zack, wait up."

I kept walking without looking back.

"Miracle Ear," he said. "What, you couldn't hear me or you're just too cool?"

"Both," I said. Roy was my best friend, but I liked to tease him. Sometimes he felt like a little brother, even though he was two months older than me. I didn't have any siblings. Roy had four. Lately, we were only best friends outside of school. I'd been manager of the basketball team over the winter, and I was trying to be friends with those guys and the cheerleaders. But Roy and I still hung out at each other's homes a lot and bowled on the same team every Saturday morning. I never told any of the basketball players that I was in a bowling league. We didn't have any classes together, and his locker was in a separate hallway with the rest of the band and orchestra people whom everybody else mocked.

Roy's cheeks were red, and he was breathing hard. Sweat formed on his dark brow. He wasn't athletic. "You need to switch to flute, man," I said. "That slush pump's gonna kill you." Slush pump was my dad's name for it. He'd played trombone when he was a kid.

We crossed Oakland and headed down the hill toward Western Michigan University's campus. I lived in the married housing at the bottom of the hill, and Roy lived in the married housing on the north side of the school. I wanted to talk about what had happened with Brondyke and Trevor, but I didn't know how to bring it up. Roy had been picked on that year too, by a kid named Brian Baxter and his friends. Roy said it was because he was Muslim and it had started during Ramadan. Since he couldn't eat until sunset, his stomach had growled loudly every day in English right before lunch, and Brian Baxter had given him a hard time. But there were lots of other Muslim kids who went to our school, and they weren't picked on. It was just something about Roy that made him a target—the timid, anxious way he carried himself. Or because he hadn't unlocked the secrets of invisibility and herd mentality like the rest of us, the arts of being faceless in a hallway full of faces. Either way, he was labeled a pussy.

To our right, through the gray skies, rose the asylum water tower. It was brick with ramparts and a green copper roof. It looked like it had once belonged to an old castle but was now stranded in the middle of Kalamazoo. You could see it from almost anywhere in the city, shooting up from the asylum's courtyard. Roy and I tried to see it up close once, but guards kicked us off the property. Roy had been terrified by the guards. When I thought of the tower, I thought of Trevor's dad locked within its brick walls.

The first few raindrops fell. "It's gonna pour," I said.

"Too bad there wasn't a tornado watch today. They would've let us out early."

"If there was a tornado you'd crap yourself."

"Kiss mine," said Roy.

"Not after you crap yourself."

Roy's real name was Muhammad. His parents called him Roy; I never found out why. They were from Malaysia, but he was born in Battle Creek. His dad went to graduate school at Western, like my mom.

Roy dragged his trombone case along the sidewalk. "This sidewalk sucks," he said. There was a thin brown trail that snaked down the hill, perfect for riding bikes home, screaming alongside traffic just a foot off the curb.

"Yeah," I said, "it sucks for bikes."

"We'll have to go ride in the woods."

We'd started riding our bikes in the nature preserve behind the YMCA. A few weeks earlier we'd found a stack of dirty magazines someone had hidden beneath a small pine tree. Lots of kids hid their magazines in the woods. The flesh tones and brightly colored words on the covers had caught our eyes. We stared at them for a while and got mad at ourselves later for not taking them with us.

We both wanted to go back there to stare at them again, but we acted like we were just going for the good bike trails and jumps.

I looked over at Roy. His left hand held the trombone case, and his right held a long apartment key. He gripped it in a fist so that the silver sharp-toothed edge stuck out through his index and middle fingers. His dad had taught him how to do that. It would make a dangerous punch. He'd started holding it like that after his first fight with Brian Baxter. There were a lot of things Roy was afraid of, and his dad and I often jokingly called him a worrywart. But I didn't tease him about the way he held his key.

When we reached the bottom of the hill, the raindrops became large enough to splash off the sidewalk and hit us on the way back up. We were at my apartment complex.

"Later," I said.

"You wanna hang out tonight?" he asked.

"Yeah."

"I'll come over."

"No, I'll go to your place," I said.

"No way. It's too packed and hot."

"We won't stay in. And then you don't have to walk all the way back."

"Fine," he said. "Call me."

The light at the Stadium Drive intersection was green. Roy turned and started running, the trombone case beating against his knee. The pedestrian sign started to flash DON'T WALK, and he stopped immediately. There was plenty of time to cross once the DON'T WALK sign first appeared, but he stopped and stood in the rain. He never took chances, not even with intersections.

·

The white stucco of married housing was streaked brown and black down the outside walls, where rainwater falling off second-story ledges stained it with whatever it had absorbed. Sandboxes surrounded the cracked asphalt courtyard. The sand was littered with sharp stones, but kids dug holes or made castles or just sat in it playing their Game Boys. Most of the kids were Malaysian. All were younger than I was. The basketball hoops didn't have nets; they were never used. The soccer field was worn to mud in the center and in front of the goals. It was used all the time, by people from countries where soccer was popular. There was an exotic smell that drifted out of many open apartment windows, some tangy food or spice I could never identify. It lingered in the air and felt warm on my skin as I walked past the windows, like walking past an open oven door. The smell filled Roy's home, although I never asked him what it was. My mom hated it, but it always filled our apartment. Married housing was hot all the time, so the windows stayed open with a fan pressed against the screen, even in the winter. Heat leaked through the vents in the summer. My mom believed that the smell was coming through our heat register, so she lined the vents with dryer sheets. Our apartment smelled like flowers and chemicals. I couldn't smell the food or spice after that, but she still could. She turned our fan backwards in the window so that it sucked the inside air out. My mom knew the apartment was seedy, but it was cheap and right across the street from school, and we didn't have a car unless we borrowed Roy's family's station wagon.

You didn't have to be married to live in married housing. You could be an international student, a veteran, or a single parent.

•

Brondyke showed up with a pointed white bandage on his nose that made him look like a bird. Students and even a couple of teachers inadvertently smiled when talking to him. I'd played the whole fight over in my head during the weekend, especially in bed during the dim half-dreams just before sleep. I'd looked forward to school on Monday.

But nobody said much when Monday came. Even with his

injury, the focus was off Brondyke and on Trevor and Curtis. Brondyke abandoned the alphabetical seating chart and moved Curtis to the front corner, by the door and next to Erin Bylsma. Trevor sat against the back wall, two rows over from me. I was glad he hadn't been suspended. It would have meant missing exams, which wasn't worth the hassle. I'd never noticed how small and dark his eyes were. Against his milky face, they made him look like a blind baby animal. I felt like talking to him after class to be nice, but figured he'd sense the pity.

A couple of times on Monday I saw him pressing his back all the way against the cinder-block wall behind his chair and gently rolling his skull against it the way I did, probably reminding himself that it was still there, the cool, hard feel of safety.

•

My mom was getting her degree in holistic health and nutrition, but left me lots of frozen pizzas and pizza rolls for dinner on nights she wasn't home. She had class three nights a week. During the day she worked at the university bookstore. "I won't always let you eat this stuff," she said, preheating the oven for a pizza, "but I don't have time to cook yet. It doesn't count until I'm certified." She winked. The only thing she really didn't want me to have was Coke. When she was little, her mom—my grandma—told her that if you dropped a human tooth into a glass of Coke it would disintegrate by morning.

My grandparents had moved to Arizona. We saw them twice a year. They almost decided not to move because my dad died at the same time they were selling their house, and they thought they should stay by my mom. My dad had had a heart attack when he was thirty-eight. I was ten. He was a lot quieter than my mom. He would read a whole book in a single night, lying in bed and eating Cheez-Its as he flipped page after page. He was thin and athletic. He had a bad heart.

My mom taught me the rules of football. I didn't participate in any sports, except for bowling, but I followed them all. She took me to Waldo Stadium to watch Western's games and predicted the plays before they happened. She quizzed me. What's an I formation? Why'd they go for two there instead of one? It was better than when I went to Lions games with Roy and would have to explain everything to his dad. My mom was the expert. I was always afraid at these games of running into someone I knew from school, but I never did.

My mom used to play Nerf basketball with me too. We hung the plastic rim from the bookshelves and played throughout the cramped apartment, crashing into furniture and appliances. She wasn't afraid to foul. By the middle of seventh grade I didn't want to play with her anymore. Even when we were alone in our apartment, I started feeling embarrassed and wanted her to be quieter and more distant, like other moms I knew. We didn't have room for distance. She slept in the only bedroom in the apartment, and I had the hide-a-bed in the living room. I didn't mind it usually—I could watch TV in bed—although there was nowhere to hide things if I needed things hidden.

My mom once read the entire Bible. She was a notoriously slow reader, and usually only read things assigned for class. She read three chapters of the Bible a day and finished in a year. We never went to church. The Bible was mine, given to me by my Catholic grandma after my dad died. My mom was standing at the kitchen counter when she finished the last lines of Revelation. I was watching TV. I heard her close the book, and I looked up. She was crying, her face wet from eye to chin and her mouth open in one of those huge, sad wails that don't make any sound.

•

I began hating not having a place to hide things. I didn't have my own closet. My shirts and pants were folded on the top shelf of the

large hallway closet that also served as the pantry and the place
we kept the vacuum, even though we didn't have carpet. My socks
and underwear were stored in large Tupperware containers on the
floor.

I started thinking more about the woods behind the YMCA
and biking there by myself. I wanted those magazines. I searched
for hiding places throughout the apartment, so if I ever did find
them I'd have a place to keep them. By getting on my knees and
reaching my hand underneath the hide-a-bed, I found a tear in
the fabric, a slot between two pieces of cloth where a magazine
could fit. But I still didn't dare. My mom let me watch plenty of
gory movies and read all of Roy's violent comic books, but sex was
another matter. It was worse than Coke. If I was walking down the
sidewalk, she'd rather I see a man gunned down in the street than
a woman's skirt blow up in the wind. We used to rent a lot of movies together, but without saying anything, we both stopped. There
were too many love scenes, and it was unbearable watching them
with each other in the room.

But she kept a lot of women's magazines around the house, like
Cosmo and *Mademoiselle,* with glossy covers and beautiful women
and pages that smelled like perfume. From a distance they looked
like the ones in the woods. On nights when she had class I'd go in
the bathroom with one of the magazines and masturbate.

Once she came home early from her class because she'd had a
test. I was in the bathroom with one of her magazines. I flushed
the toilet and sprayed Lysol to make it seem like I was just in there
going to the bathroom. Then I tucked the magazine into the front
of my jeans so that it curved around my waist and walked out of the
room with my shirt hiding it.

"Hi, honey." She approached me for a hug.

"Not right now," I said. "I don't feel good." My hands were in
my pockets to hide my erection.

"Okay." She sniffed the air, picking up the scent of the perfume samples but not recognizing it. She opened the freezer and reached for a frozen dinner. I turned the corner and walked quickly to her room, putting the magazine back on her nightstand and getting out before she saw me. The need for my own room was never more apparent. I didn't need it so that I could privately look at magazines but so I wouldn't have to look at or talk to my mom if I didn't want to. I was afraid she knew what I was doing, that she could see the lust on me, smell the semen on me. A feeling of uncleanness came over me when I was around her. I felt bad for not being a boy and for not being a man.

·

Being labeled a pussy like Roy was one thing, but it was worse being known as a masturbator. Late that year, an eighth-grader named Kyle Jackson was supposedly caught jerking off in the bathroom between classes by a seventh-grader with a hall pass. It was an enormous joke all year. Kyle Jack-off. We wrote it on chalkboards and in folded classroom notes, often with illustrations. When I saw him in the hall it was all I thought about. People actually said, "He's always gonna be known as Kyle Jack-off." And he was. Years later, while he crossed the stage to receive his high school diploma, someone yelled, "Way to go, Jack-off!"

The rest of us should have been cheered. Our luck in escaping all those years without great public embarrassment deserved some honorary certificate at graduation.

·

Roy always wanted to hang out at my place because it was quiet and felt bigger than his, even though it wasn't. But I liked his apartment because of all the activity and noise.

When we first met and were better friends, I'd spend most afternoons there playing video games. The air was heavy with that warm, spicy smell that my mom hated but that I'd started to like. His family had two bedrooms. Roy slept in one with his two younger brothers. His sister and the baby slept in his parents' room.

Everything they owned seemed to line the walls, always within reach. Pillows and bed sheets were draped over living room furniture. Clean laundry was stacked on the kitchen counter. Dirty laundry overflowed from a hamper in the bathroom. Books were stacked in corners, sometimes leaning and ready to fall. A pair of skis poked out from underneath the sofa, even in July. And children's watercolors and construction-paper collages were the only artwork they hung, covering the entire apartment like wallpaper.

Roy acted differently at home. He was like a third parent, yelling at a brother for misbehaving, hugging his sister for being sweet.

His mom would serve us hot tea with two spoonfuls of sugar. The first sip I took was the hottest thing my tongue had ever touched. Roy gulped his tea while I blew on mine, too embarrassed to ask for an ice cube to drop in the cup. His mom wore a shawl that framed her huge brown eyes and gentle smile. She called me Zachary. She was like a young and pretty grandma. It wasn't her fault, but I always felt guilty and imperfect beside her.

Roy's dad was easier to be near. He had long black hair and a black goatee that hung in a point like a dark icicle. "Call me Faiz," he said. "First name, okay?"

"Okay."

And as a joke, he always addressed me formally: Mr. Vanderlaan. He joked all the time, and sometimes we'd gang up on Roy and tease him. I never felt bad if I did it with his dad. I felt like family, a blond, light-skinned cousin or something.

There was a map of the world above their dinner table. Malaysia and Michigan were circled in red. England was circled in green. Faiz was getting his Ph.D. in psychology, and he and his wife talked for months about him continuing his studies in Birmingham, England. He'd talk in an English accent sometimes. "The tea's bloody hot.

We have to clean the flat." It's sad that a year later their plans all fell through, and they moved across state to Ypsilanti.

On Tuesdays he and Roy went to Chronic Comics when the new issues came out. I wasn't big on collecting, but I always wanted to go with them, to be part of their routine. I'd drop hints, how I didn't have any homework that night, how my mom wasn't going to be home until ten.

"Would you care to join us on a trip to the comic store, Mr. Vanderlaan?" Faiz asked. "Magic powers, eh? Evil monsters versus men with no fear?"

I played Nintendo and played dumb. "Whatever. Sure. But it's not a big deal if you two just wanna go alone."

"I insist," he said, smiling and winking. He picked a bath towel off the floor and wrapped it around his neck like a cape. He flexed his muscles. Superhero.

Roy usually liked it when I went. We'd sit in the back of their beat-up station wagon and quiz each other on baseball statistics. Occasionally we'd argue about something.

Other days we didn't talk, and Roy would sit in the front seat and leave me alone in the back. I'd look out my window and he'd look out his, and I wondered if it was sometimes like that even with brothers.

.

Aidan Delaney was my CHUM. It stood for College Housing Undergraduate Mentor and was such a bad name long or short that I tried never to say it either way. Earlier in the school year my mom had signed me up for the program without asking. It paired kids who lived in married housing, whose parents were really busy, with college students studying elementary or secondary education. The girl who led the program said we were supposed to "learn and grow together through the fruitful rewards of mentorship." All the other married housing kids in the program were under ten. I demanded that I be paired with a guy.

My mom had already made that request, so I got Aidan, the only guy in the program. I didn't tell anyone at school about him, and I lied all year to keep it a secret from Roy. I figured he'd want a CHUM too, and he'd demand a guy, and since Aidan was the only one, we'd have to share.

Aidan reminded me of Brondyke. He was tall and tan and only three years younger. He was athletic and could probably dunk. Since they'd both gone to Western, I asked him if he knew anyone named Brondyke.

"What's his first name?" asked Aidan.

"I don't know."

He shook his head. "No. It's a big school. I hardly know anybody." I felt good when he said this because my middle school felt big, and I hardly knew anybody either.

Aidan showed me a college life that my mom never had. We went to the student rec center, where I'd ride an exercise bike and watch him lift weights. But my eyes always drifted to the girls who worked out there. They were sleek and beautiful, like girls in music videos. Aidan talked with most of them. He knew more people than he'd said. I once met his girlfriend, Therese. She also looked like a video girl.

Aidan took me to his apartment a lot. We'd hang out with his roommates, Bill and Cushy, and play Nintendo all day. They were just like Roy and me, except their refrigerator was filled with beer. Cushy always wanted me to drink a can. It was all a lot of jokes until one day he tried to pry my mouth open and pour it down my throat.

"Goddamn it, Cushy," yelled Aidan, "you fucking little whore! Leave the kid alone."

Cushy looked hurt. "I'm sorry, man. Just funnin'." He looked at me. "Sorry, man."

He called everybody "man."

Aidan played sports with me and taught me all the on-field strategy that I never learned from watching from the stands or on TV. We went to the movies. He helped me with my homework. My mom kept saying all spring that she wanted to invite Therese and him over for dinner one night. After not hearing from him for a few weeks, I called him in May. The line was disconnected. I think he went home to Detroit once the school year ended. I tried the same number again in the fall, but it was still disconnected. He probably moved to a new apartment, but I didn't know where.

•

By the last week of school Brondyke's bandage was off, Trevor seemed less nervous, and everyone wore shorts because of the new season's heat. Brondyke would only be my teacher for a few more days, which I wasn't happy about. My mom made a request to the school, asking that I have him the next year for eighth-grade American history.

We only had half-days because of exams. I'd felt bad those last couple of weeks about ditching Roy after school all the time, and I wanted to do something right and honest: be proud of a friendship, stick around. I didn't want to be like Aidan Delaney. So I stood outside the baseball dugouts and met Roy there. On the last day of school I even walked to the band and orchestra hallway to meet him at his locker. Kids were emptying out their folders of loose papers and just throwing them all over, covering the hall. It shocked me to see Roy caught up in that same excitement. He let his old quizzes and assignments float and flutter to the ground, not worrying about getting caught by the janitors. He smiled at me. "School's out. Teacher let the fools out. Whoo!"

I smiled back but felt terrible. Even when he would conquer his fear and worry, it was easy to tease him for his joy.

•

The comics were bloody and teeming with large-breasted women. My mom said they were what the male illustrators saw in their warped little dreams. If so, they must have also dreamed of the perfect man. Heroes all had lantern jaws, V-shaped torsos, rippled abdomens, and hair that stayed perfectly parted and in place, even while they flew or got in fights. I never had a good haircut.

The comic store felt wet on my skin and smelled like cat pee. Two cats actually walked around the store, slipping in and out of customers' legs. The owner, Captain Carl, lived upstairs. We went there a lot that summer before eighth grade. Roy knew comics; Faiz had taught him everything. They read *Cerebus* and *Sandman* and other comics that Captain Carl reserved for them in a little cubby behind the cash register. I couldn't keep up with their conversations, so I usually wandered down the aisles by myself. I wondered if it was against Roy's religion to read them, with all their sex and violence. I was pretty sure it was against mine.

I wandered alone through the store. Toward the back was a glass case containing rare and exceptional trading cards. The cards sat on shelves connected by what looked like a bicycle chain. A button on the top of the glass made the shelves climb up in the case and circle back through. I idly pressed the button, not really caring about what I saw. Most were comic characters. Captain America. Iron Man. Until I came to the cards with the naked women. There were tons of them, and they weren't covered up or anything. I glanced to my right to see if anyone was watching me. The only other people in the store were Roy, Faiz, and Captain Carl, and they were deep in discussion. I held the button down and watched the cards rotate through the case again.

Behind the counter, barely covered by a ragged little curtain, were shelves of magazines, vintage *Playboys* with pictures of women who looked old and young at the same time. I turned and walked back to a shelf of comics, away from Roy, Faiz, and Captain Carl.

I crouched down and flipped through some comics without really looking at them, trying to hide the shame on my face and elsewhere.

•

By the next day it was easy to put that shame aside. I rode my bike to the woods and looked for the dirty magazines by myself. The heat index was over 100 degrees, and sweat soaked through my shirt. After an hour of searching, I found them, moved from their original location but still under a pine tree. I took just one magazine, *Gallery*, and rode home with it hidden under my shirt, tucked into my waistband.

•

I tried to read the entire Bible, like my mom, but I never got past the Pentateuch. There were several false starts, from the beginning, but I couldn't bulldoze my way through all the laws and customs of Leviticus. I became very familiar, though, with Genesis and Exodus.

I enjoyed just holding the book in my hands. It was a St. Joseph Edition of the New American Bible with a red leather cover, gold lettering, and pages that were thin and brittle, like birch bark. One of the pages had a smashed bug inside, a gnat or mosquito. I remembered how my mom sometimes read it outside at night in the open-air stairwell. The bug was right next to the story of Dinah, which I always read closely.

Dinah was raped. I understood that word better in eighth grade, and my mom told me never to use it when joking around. Dinah was raped by Shechem, who then asked the girl's father, Jacob, for her hand in marriage. Dinah's brothers, concealing their wrath, claimed to approve of the union, as long as all of the able-bodied Shechemites were circumcised. These men agreed, and on the third day, while the Shechemites were still healing and in pain, Dinah's brothers entered the city and put all of the men "to the sword." Any other type of wound, and maybe the Shechemites could have put up a fight. But they fought as something less than men, so their city was sacked and raped.

The story made me scared of sex. I'd already begun to worry that my mom would find the magazine under the hide-a-bed, in the tear between the two pieces of fabric. I imagined her cleaning one day when I was at Roy's, moving the couch out of the way to dust and the magazine falling out onto the floor. I imagined her horror. When this fear and shame arose, I waited to see if they would pass again, overwhelmed by the fluorescent lust on the page.

At night, lying in bed, I sometimes heard loud, strange voices echoing up through the stairwell and the metallic sound of footsteps. And sometimes I wished, as my mom slept in the next room, that I owned a sword, and that someone would try to kick in the door.

•

Faiz adopted Lake Michigan. He knew it better than his native South China Sea. In August, he took Roy and me to Van Buren State Park in South Haven and made us walk a long way down the shoreline to get away from all the loud families clustered near the parking lot walkway.

"This is my spot," he said, waving his hand in disgust toward the distant crowd. "Leave that part of the beach to them. This is what I was made for." He unfurled a bed sheet and let it float to the sand. His yellow shorts couldn't really be called shorts; they covered his knees. And when he took his shirt off he revealed a large, round belly that I'd never noticed before.

It was like our own private beach. Roy explored the dunes and the woods that covered their peaks. I stuck close to Faiz, digging in the sand, trying to get tan. I looked so white next to him. He fell asleep on his back, his golden belly perfectly round. It was hilarious, like a soccer ball. I wanted to kick it.

Roy came stumbling down a thistle-filled dune trail with his hand pressed against his thigh. "Ow, ow, ow, ow, ow!" He limped to us. A small trickle of blood ran down his leg. Faiz sat up to inspect it.

"There's a barbed wire fence up there," said Roy. "I was walkin' through the trees and ran up against some stupid rusty barbed wire."

"You'll need a tetanus shot," I said, "in the butt."

"In the arm," said Faiz, smirking and shaking his head. "And you won't need one. Go jump in the lake to wash it up."

"Why's there barbed wire in the park anyway?" asked Roy. "They're gonna kill some little kid."

Faiz turned and looked south down the shoreline. "To block off the power plant's property." He nodded toward a huge gray-blue building that stood in the sand right on the water's edge. It was the same color as the lake. "It's a nuclear plant."

"What?" said Roy. "We're gonna get cancer or something."

"Your hair will fall out," I joked. But I didn't like the plant either.

"If you come here at night," said Faiz, "the water glows green."

"Bull," said Roy.

"I've seen it," I said, trying not to smile.

"No you haven't. When do you ever come to the lake without us?" Roy looked out at the water. "It doesn't glow. But I'm not washin' my leg off in there now."

"It's fine," I said. I stood up and jogged to the waves. The lake was calm, the waves almost silent. My first few footsteps crashed loudly in the water before I spread out my arms and did a belly flop. I pulled my face out of the water, looked back at Roy, and yelled. "No! It burns!"

I took a deep breath and did the dead man's float, rising and gently falling with the small waves. My ears were above water, and I heard someone else splashing into the lake. I thought at first it was

Roy, but it was Faiz. He scooped me right up out of the water and started walking toward shore. "No!" he yelled. He jogged across the sand so that my teeth rattled. I kept my eyes closed in fake death. "Give him room!" He set me on the bed sheet.

"Dad, shut up."

"It's eating away at his skin. We have to act fast."

I peeked through my eyelids to see Roy walking away, back toward the dunes. "Stupid," he said.

"Yes, good," said Faiz. "Go for help. Mr. Vanderlaan's probably got a half-life of three million now. They'll have to bury him deep in the sand in a titanium coffin."

"Kiss mine," called Roy.

I laughed through my death. Faiz and I high-fived.

⋅

When throwing away pornography, it's important to choose the right locale. I decided to do it at the end of August as a sort of New School Year's resolution. The guilt began to emerge not just from wondering what my mom would think, but from what people like Faiz and Brondyke would think if they knew. I didn't dare throw it out in the dumpsters at married housing because I believed that, no matter how late at night, someone in one of the apartments would see me out there with the skunks and raccoons and know what I was up to. After removing the magazine from its hiding spot, I rolled it up tight and sheathed it in three paper bags so that none of its bright colors could be seen. Then I stuffed it in my backpack and rode my bike around the area, looking for just the right place. I also brought a couple of empty pop cans so that anyone who saw me would think I was just throwing away a sack lunch.

I almost settled on the dumpster at Second Reformed Church on the corner because there was no one around, but in the end I felt too guilty about defiling a place of God. I rode around Western's campus. It was crowded with returning students. I glanced around for Aidan Delaney, but it was a big school. I knew I'd never see him.

My shoelace came untied, so I stopped in an area where all of the campus maintenance vehicles were parked. Looking down, I saw a sewer grate tucked behind a tree-lined area. And that was it. The trees would hide me from view, and if anyone did see me, they couldn't go and check what I'd thrown out.

I pulled the magazine—still wrapped in three paper bags—out of my backpack. I crouched down and tried to casually slip it through the grate, but when rolled up, it was too thick and got stuck halfway. I panicked. No doubt there was some returning college student who saw the silhouette of a boy stomping on a paper bag. But it eventually fell through, splashing slightly as it hit bottom. I hopped on my bike and rode home, my feet slipping repeatedly off the pedals because I tried to go too fast. In bed that night, I was certain that sewer workers would find the magazine and trace it back to me or that, at the very least, I'd clogged someone's toilet.

·

I was an eighth-grader and enrolled in Brondyke's sixth-hour American history class. He looked tanner than usual and seemed relaxed. I was glad. He went back to using an alphabetical seating chart, so I was at my same desk in the back corner: Zack Vanderlaan. I tried hard not to look out the window when he lectured. I wanted him to see my respect.

Roy and I didn't run into each other much, but I knew Brian Baxter was giving him trouble again. Faiz took two days off work in a row to drive him home from school after getting a couple of frantic, sobbing phone calls. Roy refused to walk.

Brondyke broke a ballpoint pen on Tuesday of the second week of school. He was sitting at his desk taking roll and he cracked it. He grabbed a tissue and wiped his hands, thinking he'd cleaned all of it, but the black ink smeared. When he scratched his head or rubbed his chin while lecturing, he left black fingerprints on his face. None of us said anything; we didn't want to embarrass him. I wondered when he finally noticed. In his rearview mirror driving home? Or did his wife say something at the dinner table? I worried that it would still be there the next day, faded gray, over pink skin that was rubbed raw from the grit of a rough washcloth. Kids laughed as we filed out of the room. They had good reason. He looked ridiculous.

The cafeteria served spaghetti on Thursday. I walked past the teachers' lounge just as someone was leaving it, and for a moment I could see inside. There were round tables, a beat-up burgundy couch, and Brondyke. He sat alone at one of the tables twirling spaghetti around his fork. As the door swung closed, I worried that I'd see him sixth hour with spaghetti sauce splashed against his white shirt, or over his lips and chin.

·

If you bought a large Coke at the concession stand it came in a plastic collectible cup with the Lions logo on it. They were down by twenty-four in the fourth quarter, and the Silverdome was already emptying out. At the two-minute warning, the aisles filled up even more, and people left all their garbage scattered underneath their seats. Hardly anyone took their collectible cups home with them.

Roy and I climbed through the empty rows and gathered them up. We stacked them in huge towers that bowed toward the ground. We had no idea what we'd do with them, but we were definitely taking them home.

"Hey!"

We looked down a few rows where a group of men was staring at us. One guy with red hair and a red sweatshirt yelled. "Hey!"

"Yeah?"

"Those your cups?"

"People just left them. They're not comin' back."

The red-haired man looked at Roy. "Hey, Indian." Roy didn't respond. He bent down to pick up another cup. "Indian, that ain't your cup." The other men laughed, and one started throwing peanuts at us. He said he was trying to toss it in our cups, but he kept drilling me in the chest and back.

Faiz saw what was happening and clumsily but quickly climbed over the seats to get between the men and us. He didn't say anything to the men, just stared.

"Hey, it's another Indian. The big chief!"

A peanut hit Faiz on the top of the head. "Damn, I was aimin' for the beard." They laughed. There was nobody else in our entire upper-deck section of the stadium. Faiz kept staring. I was still behind him. I wish I could have seen his eyes.

"Hey, I'm not spendin' all night tryin' to get out of the goddamned parking lot," said one of the men. He stood up and the rest followed, waving at us as they went.

"Were they drunk?" asked Roy.

"And cowardly," said Faiz.

•

Roy and I never walked home together that fall. I started playing basketball in the gym with the guys from last year's team and thought about trying out instead of just being the manager. Brondyke stopped by a couple of times, but when he did it was only to take a few perimeter shots before leaving. No dunks.

We didn't play on Fridays, so I walked home one afternoon right after school. As I crossed the baseball diamond, I casually looked around for Roy, not really expecting to see him. But I did.

He was on his knees, surrounded by Brian Baxter and two other kids. They were on the far side of some trees, out of view from the school, but I could see them from where I stood next to the dugout. Roy's backpack was in the dirt, and his trombone hung awkwardly out of its half-open case. The boys punched him in the stomach, and when he fell to his side they kicked at his ribs. I was close enough that I could hear him sobbing and see the wetness of his eyes. They slapped his face and the top of his head. They beat him like grown men, ugly and unembarrassed.

The school buses started turning onto Howard Street beyond them, filling the air with exhaust and their low, melodic drone. They drowned out Roy's voice. For a moment, it was easy to hide in that noise and feel more distant than I was. I tucked myself behind the corner of the dugout, and Roy never saw me. He moved to Ypsilanti a year later, never knowing. Faiz never knew, Brondyke never knew, that even if I'd had a sword, I would have failed to use it.

DEBTS AND DEBTORS

Zeke Mockerman's new white truck rumbled down our road, bright as a comet with a tail of country dust behind it. He pulled into our dirt driveway and extended a thin arm out the window, waving at my dad and me with a spidery hand. My dad had just heard about Zeke's good fortune at the casino. He didn't return Zeke's wave.

We'd heard the truck coming a half mile away. The roads around our Zeeland house were straight and quiet, crossing in mile intervals, dividing the land into the perfect squares of the farmer's geometry. Through the soft buzz of insects and clatter of treetop crows, we'd heard the dings of stones being spit up by tires into the steel belly of the truck. When it came to a stop by our granary, my dad slung the wooden bat onto his shoulder like a lumberman resting with his ax.

Zeke dropped out of the high driver's seat, stumbling and hopping on his good leg before gaining balance. "Sergeant Major!" he yelled, waving his arm over his head. He was about a hundred yards off, and I had to shield my eyes with my glove when looking at him, the hot sun glistening off the truck with the silky shine of an egg white. Zeke headed toward the field, limping our way.

My dad said nothing. He'd been quiet all morning, working alone in the gray cinder coolness of his basement wood shop before surprising me at noon by offering to hit me some fly balls. We stood in a field that once grew alfalfa, like the rest of our property, but which had been cleared that spring and used only for baseball that summer. It was the week of my birthday, the first time my dad had ever been home for it. I was thirteen, had grown six inches that year, and even back then I realized the field was still being used to grow and harvest something: a ball player.

I looked away from Zeke and looked at my dad. "Come on," I called. "One more." I punched the leather palm of my glove, making it snap beneath my knuckles. "Deep this time. No lazy pop crap."

"One more," he said, still watching Zeke. He clenched the handle of the bat, tensing the ribbons of muscle that ran up his forearms. He turned to me. "One more, and then scoot on inside for a bit. Or take a bike ride."

In high school they called him Cannonball because of his all-state pitching arm, and to that day, when he was fifty, his closest friends called him by that same name, referring now to his body type: short, stocky, but powerful. His build, along with his short-cropped hair, were his only stereotypical features, the only ways a person would know he'd been a Marine.

The heat was unmoving on that breezeless afternoon, typical of summer in the middle of some field, where the wind had all the room in the world to swish back and forth against our skin, but never did. Zeke was halfway to us, moving slowly. I looked over my shoulder and trotted through the tire ruts and weedy waves of the uneven field, scratching my legs on thistles and rough grasses because I wore shorts. My dad wore blue jeans and a short-sleeve plaid shirt—same as always—and his chest had a U-shaped sweat stain dipping down to his round stomach. His blue Vanderwood Plumbing hat was dark and wet just above the bill. He usually refused to play ball in the middle of the day because of the heat, waiting instead for the sun to approach the horizon and duck behind the steel column of power lines that cut east through our fields. The heat seemed to bother him more each summer, along with his pain. He had problems with his sciatic nerve, and pain ran like a current down his right hip and leg. He always stood in the shade of an apple tree while he swung the bat, and over the summer his feet wore that patch of field down to bald dirt. If I made an errant throw back to him, he'd mumble something, step out of the shade, and limp to the ball.

He tossed the ball to eye level, and the bat slid from his shoulder with the ease and grace of ice on ice. The swing made the familiar cracking sound of nearly all his swings, fully connecting with the ball. I used the glove to block out the sun, the way he'd taught me, before hauling the ball in easily, one-handed.

"No showboatin', Jackie," my dad said. "Use your right hand to snap the webbing shut."

"Barry Bonds does it all the time."

He approached me. "And some might accuse him of bein' a showboater." He winked. "Ten hot-shot catches ain't worth that one God almighty dropped ball that'll come when there's a runner on third and everybody's watchin'."

I stared at the ground, nodded, and dripped a long string of spit from my lips, aiming for an egg-shaped stone half-buried in the dirt.

"Look at me," he said. I looked. "It's comin'." He smiled, held the bat out like a fencer's foil, and playfully poked me in the ribs. "It's been a happy summer knowin' I don't have to hold back any more when I pitch to you."

"*Hold back anymore*," I said, smiling back. "You never held back."

"Yeah, you keep thinkin' that. Last summer if I'd a rifled one up and in, you'd a bailed sure as shoot. But now you stand in there. Takes more than a little discipline."

I looked down at the earth again, embarrassed but happy. He never withheld his praise but always dressed it up in enough humor that it never wedged too much awkwardness between us.

"I wanna work on my pitching," I said. We'd started to draw strike zones on the back side of our granary with a piece of chalk, and he'd stand behind me, coaching me on my curve ball.

"After dinner." My dad looked up. "Go head on in now. I gotta talk with Zeke."

Zeke stepped toward us, happily—some in town would say stupidly—grinning at me. "Playin' ball?"

"Were," said my dad. He slung the bat back onto his shoulder, gripping the handle like he was wringing out a towel. This was what he'd wanted, the reason why he'd invited me to play and sweat under the midday sun. For Zeke. For effect. There was no mistaking now the bat's use as a dangerous prop for the coming interrogation.

He removed one hand from the bat and stroked the underside of his chin. I would see him do this when balancing the checkbook late at night, when trapped in heavy traffic, or when I wouldn't do what he asked. Then he removed his hat to wipe his forehead, exposing his short gray hair. Normally, these days in June were when he'd spend two weeks in Twentynine Palms, in the Mohave Desert, for mountain warfare training ATD. This was the time of year when he'd go to the barber and get his hair cut even shorter than usual, "high and tight." And although he'd retired from the Reserves a few months earlier, that June he still asked the barber for the same cut.

Zeke squinted in the shadeless field. He was twenty-one, tall and lanky, with cut-off jeans hanging off narrow boy hips and wearing a black T-shirt that said "Bullet Proof." His thick, black hair had grown long, curling down his neck and over his ears, making his head look too big and round for the slim trunk of his body. He reminded me of a palm tree. He'd grown up a couple of miles down the road, and after high school he'd joined my dad's Reserve unit in Grand Rapids. He'd been one of my dad's men. But a couple of years after that, he was in a car accident that destroyed one of his knees. He was medically discharged, but he had no medical insurance.

Zeke approached my dad and stumbled for a moment as he stepped into a tractor tire rut. He extended his hand and nodded. "Sergeant Major."

We could have used some wind then, to drown out and whisk away the awkwardness of his gesture.

"You can call me Jay nowadays," said my dad. They shook hands.

The Marines were like a secret society that my dad used to attend at short but regular intervals and rarely spoke of when he returned. One weekend a month and then the two weeks in the desert. The rest of the time he was a plumber, driving his truck to houses in Zeeland and Holland, growing a little alfalfa that he sold to farmers in the area. He'd started buying cows after his final month as a Marine.

"Zeke," my dad said, "I wanna show off my new Angus. Jackie, why don't you get me and Zeke a couple a beers."

"That'd be great, Sergeant Major," said Zeke. He looked at me. "Thanks, Private. Het-hut!" He clicked the heels of his running shoes together, drew a sharp right hand to his forehead, and stood tall and straight. A palm tree in alfalfa fields. I returned the salute.

As I walked toward the house, grasshoppers brushed against my bare legs, their wings humming over the dry grass. Cicadas filled the fields with their shrill, rising sounds and then faded away. I walked slowly, listening through the sounds to make out what my dad would say to Zeke with me gone. And I did.

"Thanks for comin'," he said.

"It's okay, Sergeant Major," said Zeke. "I can still follow orders, I guess."

•

The title of Sergeant Major was important to my dad, even if he played it down to Zeke. He'd been one of only sixty-five at that rank out of the forty thousand enlisted soldiers in the Marine Reserves. After his promotion from first sergeant, he had to leave his Grand

Rapids unit to take the only opening for his rank in the country: Fort Worth, Texas. He'd buy a plane ticket and fly down there once a month. It cost him more money than he made. He was proud of the promotion, but he knew he'd reached the ceiling, the highest rank an enlisted soldier could obtain. After two years of service, they forced him into retirement. He didn't go to Twentynine Palms again. He was home for my thirteenth birthday.

Zeke wasn't the only one to refer to my dad by rank. Other soldiers—active or retired from duty—addressed him formally. One Friday a month, my dad would drive to the Creston VFW in Grand Rapids, just down the road from his old unit. Sometimes he'd let me tag along. Eight or nine men—usually the same eight or nine men—sat clustered around the bar or at one end of the hall. The rest of the place was empty except during fish fries and cribbage night; the lights kept off in the back of the hall to hide the vacant tables and chairs and the unused stage with its piano and drum kit. Framed black-and-white photographs of somber, uniformed soldiers lined the walls amid mirrored Miller Lite signs and dart boards. My dad and I usually sat with three other men: Bill Peterson, Charlie Atkins, and Theodore Prusinowski. All were Vietnam veterans, like my dad. They'd left the service as corporals and staff sergeants, and so insisted on formality.

"Let me buy a drink for the sergeant major."

They sipped one-dollar Buds around a small table, looking up occasionally at NASCAR time trials on TV. I drank Coke and ate salty popcorn. Sometimes my dad would get a little drunk and turn quiet and tell short bursts of stories about the war, like how he'd been playing AA ball in Birmingham, Alabama, having been drafted by the Oakland A's, only to be drafted a few months later by Uncle Sam. He'd usually tell light-hearted stories, winking at me from across the table because he knew I'd heard them before. The nighttime fire fight in which they shot round after round into the darkness because someone had spotted movement in the trees, only to find a few murdered water buffaloes when the sun finally rose. The time they went against orders and launched red, green, and white flares into the sky on the Fourth of July. The two-inch flying cockroaches with the "antenna like a moose's antlers" that weren't fazed by Raid unless the soldiers lit the spray with a match and used the aerosol cans as flame-throwers.

We'd respectfully watch my dad take another sip of beer and turn quiet, rubbing his neck and the underside of his chin with the back of his hand. It would always seem like he was about to tell one more story, but instead he'd smile gently, content to end on a lighter note. And the other three vets would keep nodding, saying nothing but probably understanding the silent story, the one I'd learned that Christmas Eve from my cousin Bobby.

We were at my grandparents'. My dad and uncles were playing poker in the basement, the women drank rum and Cokes in the living room, and Bobby and I stood in the back alley, knee deep in snow, not wearing jackets, using the lids of aluminum garbage cans as shields and trying to thwart each other's snowballs. During a truce, as he scooped up new snow in his red hands, Bobby said, "My dad told me something about your dad. About the war."

"What?" I dropped my arms to my side, the garbage can lid resting against my thigh.

"Don't you know?"

"Know what?"

"He told me not to say anything, but I thought you already knew. Forget it."

"What'd he say?"

"No."

He threw a snowball at me, which I deflected with a bare hand. Bobby was only a year younger than me, but we were at the age where each year made a major difference in terms of height and weight. I rushed him, tackled him, and pressed his face into snow.

"You hole licker. Tell me." And that's when I learned how my dad had killed someone, not from the distance afforded by a bullet, but with the butt of his rifle, caving in a man's skull.

Bill Peterson, Charlie Atkins, and Theodore Prusinowski probably told their own secret stories to themselves, or told them telepathically to one another at the table. In the dim light of the windowless club, they nodded in agreement at something unspoken, leaving me thirsty, eating salty popcorn, the only one not knowing.

So my dad stuck to the funny tales, and his best was about an eighteen-year-old private with horrific teeth who'd been poor and never went to a dentist while growing up. During their two weeks in Twentynine Palms, my dad had persuaded the commanding officer to let the private have leave. The base dentist in Twentynine Palms never had much to do and excitedly treated this private as an experiment, a showcase of all his dental talents. The private never spent any time during those two weeks firing mortar rounds or sleeping on the desert sands. He stayed with the dentist, and every few days, when my dad and his troops would return from the field, they'd find the private lying in bed, his cheeks and jaw swollen, his lips full of Novocain, as he recovered for the next day's round of treatment.

"Five thousand dollars in dental work, all for free," said my dad, smiling. "One night, in one of them nitrous oxide hazes, the boy is lyin' on his back, and he grabs my sleeve, and he's cryin'. He's so thankful, and he tries to mouth the words, but his face is swelled up like a balloon about to burst."

The other three men at the table laughed loudly. My dad winked at me and whispered, "Zeke Mockerman."

·

I began running to the house. I wanted to get the beer and get back before my dad stopped talking about cows and started talking about the real reason he'd invited Zeke over: the debt. This one had nothing to do with teeth.

I bounded up the rickety steps of our back porch. Hank, our old black Lab, stirred underneath, in the shade beside one of his many outdoor water bowls scattered around our property. He gave a hoarse grunt as I passed over. Inside, my mom sat at the dining room table folding laundry. Our house was meant for winters: dark wood paneling, a massive stone fireplace, trophies from deer hunting trips lining the walls of the den. There was no air conditioning, and my mom patted her forehead with a dish towel while she worked.

"Slow down," she said as I ran into the kitchen. She was folding whites, mainly underwear, and had made two piles of briefs. My dad's: huge, with blue and yellow stripes on the waistband. Mine: narrow leg holes, red stripes on the waistband, some stains. The stacks rose about eight-high on the table where we ate our meals.

"Zeke's here," I said.

She looked up, eyes wide. "He is? I must've been downstairs when he pulled in." She stood and walked to the kitchen's back window, then delicately lifted the mini-blind with her middle finger. "Where?"

"By the cows. Behind the granary."

"I can't see them." She lowered the blind and took a deep breath. "Stay in here awhile."

"Dad said to get beers." I opened the refrigerator and rummaged in the vegetable crisper where he kept the cans extra cold under celery and cucumbers.

My mom wiped her forehead again. "He's an odd bird."

I held a beer in each hand and closed the refrigerator with my rear end. "That's not nice," I said. "He's your husband."

She snapped her dish towel at me like a locker-room prankster. "Shush. You know I mean Zeke."

I did, but the entire situation was an odd one. My dad went to great lengths to keep his home life separate from his military life. Once, when I was being a smart-ass at Thanksgiving dinner, my grandma told my dad, "You should make him scrub the bathroom floor with a toothbrush," and he said, "I don't believe in treatin' family like grunts," and sent me to my room.

Now he was at home with one of those grunts. When Zeke had arrived, my dad's voice had straddled some invisible fence as he tried to speak kindly in front of me but tersely in front of a former soldier. I was fascinated by the strange fusion of worlds. I noticed that his cannonball body, which had always seemed to me made for fastballs, was really built for long, lumbering hikes through deserts and jungles with equipment and weapons slung over his broad shoulders.

"How much money did you guys loan Zeke?" I asked my mom. She glanced out the window again. "None of your business."

"Was it 'cause of his knee?"

"That and other matters."

"Like what?"

"Jackie—"

"What costs money?"

"Jackie, you have no idea what doctors cost if you don't have insurance. Nor can you conceive of the pressures it puts on others in the family." She looked right at me. "Thank the world that you don't have such worries."

"You guys paid the doctors?"

She walked back into the dining room, sat down, and began folding another enormous pair of my dad's briefs. "Don't call your father and me *guys*."

I looked out the window. Zeke and my dad were out of sight. I walked with quick strides past my mom, then ran through the living room when I was around the corner, pushing open the thin screen door and leaping from the back porch in the direction of the granary. In a moment I saw them, walking with their backs to me, approaching the barbed wire of the cow pasture. Zeke limped from side to side, putting most of his pressure on his left knee. And my dad limped alongside him, putting pressure on his left hip.

•

I'd learned about the debt the night before. My parents and I had been settled around the dinner table, and my dad cut at his steak so hard that the knife squeaked against the plate.

"What?" my mom had asked.

He shook his head and continued to put food in his mouth as he talked. "He bought a truck."

"Who?"

"Zeke." He cut into his potato. "I ran into Andy Dykema when buyin' a coffee this morning, and he said he'd seen Zeke drivin' around all week in a brand-damn-new truck."

My mom stopped eating, sighed, and performed the sign of the cross. We weren't Catholic. "Do you know it's his?"

"Sure do." He looked up with a phony smile. "Because Andy also told me he heard Zeke had been up to the casino in Mount Pleasant and won a bundle on the dollar slots." He chewed angrily, shaking his head. "Said they took his picture holding a big novelty check."

"There's nothing you can do," said my mom.

"Heck I can't."

"You told him it wasn't a loan."

"It ain't just that." My dad went quiet for a few moments, staring at his plate while he ate. Then he said, "Dumb kid. It was one thing when he was scrapin' to get by. Strikin' oil is another matter. But I don't want his money. I wanna teach him manners."

•

I slowed to a walk as I approached them, falling into a casual stroll I hoped would make it seem I knew nothing nor cared nothing for their private business along the barbed wire. But they never even looked at me until I held the cans up to their faces.

Zeke and my dad stared out at the pasture, which was so dry that it had cracks like spiderwebs splitting the earth. The black cows, including the monstrous and bad-tempered bull that a neighbor was lending us, trotted in one mass away from the fence and my dad's voice.

"Thanks, Jackie," he said as I handed him his beer.

"Thanks, Private," said Zeke, but this time he only mumbled the words.

They both opened their beers—which foamed over because I'd been running with them—and my dad began walking along the fence, away from Zeke and me. His own limp was more pronounced than usual. He always said it was made worse by stress. Zeke slowly followed him, and for a moment their limps were in sync, each long, steady step of Zeke's left leg and quick, painful step of his right mirroring my dad's. It only lasted a few seconds, and then they walked at separate jerky paces, shifting their weight from side to side like wind-up toy soldiers.

The problems with my dad's sciatic nerve had started during his last year in the service. It was the first sign that his athleticism was truly slipping. Even after his semi-pro ball days, when he was in the Marines, he remained proud of his abilities. One weekend a year they'd conduct their PFT, and in his forties, competing against teenagers, he'd return home and flex muscles for us in the kitchen. "Sub-twenty three mile. Twenty pull-ups. Eighty sit-ups. I got my full three hundred points. Made all the pups take note." And my mom would kiss him then, running her hand over the crew-cut stubble on the back of his head.

Now the sweat soaked through the back of his shirt. He tipped his head and took long swallows from the can. Zeke barely sipped at all, and my dad noticed. "Now I know you can drink better than that." And guiltily, Zeke took a long sip, forcing it down.

My dad looked at me and used his beer can to point at the backyard. "Get, Jackie. Go play."

It was something a parent would say to a five-year-old whose toys were scattered across the lawn. He should have noticed that the only things I'd played all summer were pitcher, catcher, and outfielder. I set off in the direction of our black-and-blue trampoline that I never used any more. Then I checked over my shoulder. When my dad wasn't looking, I steered toward the granary.

The granary was a small red structure that the previous landowner may have actually used for storing grain, but as long as I could remember, it was my mom's domain. She was a teacher, and she'd redesigned the inside of the granary to make it look like an old country schoolhouse. There were two rows of antique desks, an old blackboard, and Norman Rockwell prints of happy children with books and cowlicks and red apples. When we had people over for hayrides in the fall, we would all sit at the small desks beside the wood-burning stove, drinking hot cider with our knees pressed against the bottoms of the desks.

But in the summer it was best to stay out of the place. All of the windows were sealed shut by layers of old paint, and, without a breeze, the granary was oppressive with heat. The only reason to go in there was to climb up into the loft, which my parents used mainly for storing boxes of baby clothes, Christmas decorations, and artifacts from their youth. Once I climbed up there looking for my dad's old catcher's mitt, and instead found a box of Marine gear. There had been a tightly rolled green sleeping bag, green flack jacket, green socks, green canteens. There'd also been a camouflaged helmet, and when I put it on, the weight of it bent my neck and pulled my head to the side. I dug around looking for knives or grenades, but never found any and never really expected to. I asked my dad about the box of equipment. The next day it was gone.

When I walked inside, the heat was like something I could

poke at with my fingers. I walked to the far wall, next to the wood-burning stove. My dad and Zeke were on the other side of that wall. I crouched down and tried to look through slits in the old red planks. I couldn't see anything, but I could start to make out their voices. I stared down at the cement floor, trying to discern the words, and as I stared, I watched drops of sweat fall, making wet constellations on the cement. I was at the age where I was just beginning to sweat the way a man does, the way my dad did, and I liked it.

"Don't give me that, Zeke."

I pressed my ear to the wood. It was warm, the sun bleeding all the way through from the outside.

"I'm sorry, Sergeant Major, but that's what you said."

"You're not listening." My dad paused. "Why should that surprise me? Why should it?"

"Am I supposed to answer?"

My dad chuckled but didn't sound happy. I wished I could see his face. "No, you can answer to other things."

"Like what?"

"Like what. Like that moneybags on wheels out there."

"My truck?"

"Your new-as-spit F-250."

"I needed a new car."

"Oh, I *know* you did."

The small wet spots on the cement accumulated until there was only one large spot as the sweat rolled out from under my hairline, down my forehead, and off my nose.

"Is that supposed to mean something too?" asked Zeke.

"Yeah, it means maybe if you hadn't been stoned you wouldn't have slipped off the road into an irrigation ditch and into a tree, you'd still be driving your old car, you wouldn't be walking like an old man, and you wouldn't be here at all today because you never would have needed any of my money."

"There we go," said Zeke. "You should've just said that when I got here, Sergeant Major."

"Don't call me that any more, Zeke."

"I don't owe you anything, sir. I don't even need to call you 'sir.'"

"At this point, I'd rather you didn't."

"I don't believe you, Sergeant Major. The second I set foot on your farm you were making our relationship clear. Goddamn, you should've just held me up, like a bank robber."

"Oh, Jesus Christ."

"You could've used that baseball bat you got there to break my kneecaps."

"Your knees are bad enough." I could hear my dad sigh. "My right hand on the Bible, I have never met a person who pisses in the wind the way you do. You're twenty-one years old. Do you know what I was doin' on my twenty-first birthday?"

"Were you in Nam, Sergeant Major?"

"Yes I was, smart-ass. And you wanna know what else happened to me when I was twenty-one?"

"That's probably when you got engaged, sir. And now this can become a lecture about my little girl and how I'm not married to her mom and how I've ruined my little girl's life by not bein' around. Right?"

I turned and looked in the direction of the voices, although I was only staring at knots in the grain of pine planks. I didn't know Zeke had a daughter.

"We'll get to that," said my dad. "In fact, yes, I did ask Sal to marry me when I was twenty-one. I wrote a letter and mailed it from the war and asked her to marry me. But do you know what made me decide, on that day, to ask her and mail that letter?"

"No, sir. I'm completely dumbfounded."

My dad laughed again. "There's no argument to that. I asked her because I needed something to look forward to. I was feelin' like the shit of the earth. Earlier that day there was an ambush."

"Sir?"

I wanted to see Zeke then. I couldn't tell if he sounded sincere or was mocking my dad. I tried to peek through the planks again, but I saw nothing.

"And it became hand-to-hand, and it turns out all that training paid off," said my dad. "Somebody died, and as you can see, it wasn't me."

I pulled my ear away from the wall and sat up, bumping an antique tea kettle that was sitting on the wood-burning stove. I froze, wondering if they'd heard me, but also wondering why my dad had shared his secret, especially with Zeke.

"And at twenty-one, I was flat gone, in every possible way. It didn't matter that the guy was tryin' to kill me. I mean, it mattered at that exact moment. But when it was over, it didn't really matter."

I waited for Zeke to say something, but he didn't.

"God, I cried all the time. I thought the other guys would give me hell for that, but they just kept their distance, which was sort of worse. Twenty-fuckin'-one."

Zeke spoke quietly. "Sir, I'm not sure what to say."

"I know," said my dad. "I'm tellin' you some stuff you probably don't need to know. You've been through shit too. Different shit, but here you are. And I invited you here so I can try to drive into your brain the idea of this gift. At twenty-one, you have a second chance—from God himself—and you're fucking it up. You fucked it up."

"I'm leaving, sir."

"Now's not the time to run, Zeke."

"This is shit, sir. I have *always* been grateful for your help, and I have *always* thanked you and been kind to you and your family. Is this 'cause of the truck? Fine, I'll sell it tomorrow and write you a check."

I folded my legs to sit Indian style and ran my hands through my hair. My hands turned wet, and I wiped them on my shirt.

"Hold up, hotshot," said my dad. "I asked you here to open your eyes, not twist your goddamn arm. I'm not the one who most needs all this money you just won."

"Then who?"

"Christ, you have to ask? Your daughter. How's your child support these days? You told me a month ago that she needs glasses but Shannon can't afford them. And suddenly you get this gift from the skies. You need a car? Fine. Buy a used Taurus and use the rest to buy some glasses for your girl."

They were both silent for a few moments. Then Zeke spoke, almost in a whisper. I pressed my ear all the way against the wood again.

"I've never won anything. So I bought myself a present. So?"

"So everything," said my dad. "So set up a college fund for your daughter. Let her and Jackie go to school and not be plumbers and construction workers."

I shook my head. I had no plans for college. I was going straight from high school to the minors.

"Twenty-fucking-one. You don't got a clue, and I'm sick of pointing out the obvious to you. You could've started over and set stuff straight. Man—if it was me? Man, I'd have given anything."

There was a long stretch of silence, and as much as I wanted to hear the rest, I stood up, thirsty. The air felt too thick to breathe. My shirt was damp and stuck to my back. I began to walk to the door when I heard my dad speak. I paused and listened again.

"What're we gonna do?"

"I don't know, sir."

"What're we gonna do? We gotta settle this. I don't want it to end like it is now, with both of us feelin' like we lost at something."

I could hear footsteps over the brittle grass approaching the granary wall. There was a sound on the wall itself, someone touching the wood.

"The world doesn't wanna watch a fistfight between an old E-9 with a bum leg and a skinny E-2 with one to match," said my dad. His voice was loud, coming from just the other side of the wall. He laughed. "You wanna play a game?"

"What game?" asked Zeke.

"Jackie!"

I jumped.

My dad called again. "Jackie!"

I stepped to the granary door, opened it slowly, and walked quietly to the corner of the structure so that my dad wouldn't know where I'd been.

"What?"

"Sir, what's goin' on?"

My dad was swinging the bat now, warming up. "Jackie, go get—why are you sweatin' so much? Go get a tennis ball, some chalk, and one of Hank's water bowls."

"With water in it?"

"Yeah. And grab your mitt, too. Hurry up."

I turned and ran back toward the house, the tall grasses of the field scratching my legs. There was still no wind, and in the summer stillness there was nothing but the crunching of dryness under my feet and insects, always invisible, speaking from the earth and the sky.

A dark slit in the mini blinds disappeared as I approached the porch. Underneath, Hank hadn't moved. He remained in the shade and raised his head a little when I grabbed his bowl and a ragged tennis ball on which he sometimes gnawed. Then he lowered his head again and exhaled deeply through his nostrils.

I turned and headed back toward the granary, scooping my glove out of the grass on my way. Water splashed out of the bowl and onto my shirt and shorts. Even *it* was warm, and now I had to go back inside the granary—back into the heat—to rummage through the antique desks for a piece of chalk. I checked all the desks, all around the blackboard, all along the floor, but I couldn't find a piece.

"Jackie!"

I ran outside and around the back corner. "I can't find any chalk."

"Hank probably ate it again, the beast." My dad took the water bowl and tennis ball from me. "Grab a piece of sandstone from the cutaway by the tramp."

I rolled my eyes, turned, and ran some more. The sweat came from all regions of my body now. It had already lost its appeal.

When I returned with the sandstone, my dad was swinging the bat again, and Zeke was sitting down in the grass, plucking blades of it out of the ground. My dad took the stone from me and approached the red granary wall. Then he spoke to Zeke, who didn't seem to be listening. "You're taller than me, but it'll do." He drew a sandy vertical line on the wall. Then a horizontal. He drew a rectangle. "This is gonna be our strike zone."

Zeke looked up, his hair obscuring his eyes. "What're we doin', sir? I gotta get goin' soon."

"We're havin' a contest, like a game show. Home Run Derby. If you win, you drive away in a beautiful new Ford F-250." My dad took another swing with the bat, this time in slow motion, his eyes following the arc of an invisible soaring ball. "And if I win, you sell that same truck and find somethin' better to do with the cash."

Zeke shook his head. "I can't swing a friggin' bat."

"I'm gimpin' around as much as you these days."

"Sir, I couldn't swing a bat *before* the accident."

My dad smiled. "Tough. House rules." He picked the water bowl and tennis ball up off the ground and walked to a small pile of dirt that we always used as our pitching mound. He set the bowl down, dipped the ball into the water, and slowly wound up into his delivery. "Jackie will pitch." He fired a fastball that smacked the inside of the sandstone rectangle, leaving a dark splash mark that immediately bled down the red wall. "We get three swings each. Whoever hits a pitch over the barbed wire and into the cow pasture the farthest wins. You don't have to swing if it's out of the strike zone, but if the ball hits the wall and there's a big wet spot there in the square, it's an out. So look sharp."

Zeke stood up, wiping grass off his jean shorts and shaking his head again.

My dad handed him the bat. "Like in any ball game, the visitor's up first."

Zeke limped over to the granary, lazily swinging the bat with one hand at a grasshopper that fluttered in front of his path. "This is bogus."

"You wanna Indian leg wrestle instead?"

I slipped my glove over my left hand. The leather was hot, inside and out. Zeke now stood beside the rectangle in one of the worst stances I'd ever seen. His knees weren't bent, he leaned slightly backward, and the bat hung loosely in his grip.

My dad stepped out of the way. "Nice and easy, Jackie. No heat."

I dipped the ball into the water and went into my motion. I tried to take the whole scenario seriously, but the sight of Zeke made it tough.

His at-bat was an exercise in apathy. He didn't swing at my first pitch, and the ball left a magnificent splatter mark within the rectangle.

"One out," said my dad. He was smiling in a way that was uncomfortable to watch.

Zeke swung wearily at my second pitch, but by the time he reacted the ball had already hit the wall and was rolling in the grass.

"That's two," said my dad. "Come on, Zeke. There's thousands of dollars on the line here."

"I didn't agree to anything." Zeke gripped the bat tightly this time. His eyes focused firmly on me as I delivered the third pitch. And although he took a serious cut at it, he still missed, the momentum of his swing twisting his legs up. He flipped the bat end-over-end and then rubbed his knee. "Bogus."

"And that makes three," said my dad. He sounded disappointed. There was no challenge left. At this point he could have bunted and technically won the contest. But as he picked up the bat and walked to the sandstone rectangle, I knew he wasn't thinking about the truck or the money or the loan any more. He was thinking about AA ball in Birmingham, being a teenager, and hitting four-hundred-foot blasts, like no other pitcher in the league.

As he stepped up to the invisible plate and gripped the bat, he looked again like the Marine after his PFT, flexing muscles for my mom in the kitchen. "Jackie, you better warn those cows way out there. They're in imminent danger." I turned and looked. The herd was a long ways out, resting under a cluster of weeping willows.

I dipped the ball into the bowl and pulled it out. Strings of water trailed behind. I settled into my stance.

"Hold up, Jackie." My dad rested the bat against his leg, unbuttoned his plaid shirt, and pulled it off. Underneath was a white tank-top that clung to his wet flesh. His nipples showed through, huge and dark, and his chest hair sprouted out from the edges. I looked behind me at Zeke. He sat on the ground pulling out fistfuls of grass and tossing them above his head. He refused to watch.

"Serve it up," said my dad. His arms flexed and the bat hopped a little in his energized grip. I'd never seen him swing all-out before, and I tried to work up an excitement fitting for the moment. But Zeke Mockerman was lying on his back now as if looking for shapes in the clouds. My dad's determination felt extravagant.

I fired the first pitch. My dad didn't swing, thinking it was a ball. But it smacked the granary and left a sun-shaped mark of water on the inside corner of the rectangle.

"Just waitin' for a perfect pitch," he said.

I dipped the ball into the water, went through my motion, and sent the second pitch his way. This time he swung but was a moment too anxious, missing by only a sliver of air and time. Neither of us said a word, and he avoided eye contact with me until he was in the batter's box again, ready for the final pitch. I glanced over at Zeke. He still reclined in the grass, but his head had perked up. He was watching now.

I looked at my dad again. "Ready?"

He nodded, and I lifted my left knee, twisted my waist, and hurled the wet, ragged ball at him. He swung, and he connected.

But the cows lived to see another day. My dad hit a soft dribbler right up the middle that rolled past my feet, slowing down in the long grass and stopping about a foot short of the barbed wire fence.

Zeke stared hard at my dad. "Looks like you win, Sergeant Major."

My dad grimaced and walked gingerly past me in fresh pain. "I aggravated it," he said. He limped to the barbed wire and picked up the tennis ball, rolling it around in his grip and examining it like an umpire checking for scratches and scuffs. "See what I mean? Best days behind you." He turned and threw the ball as hard as he could, in the direction of the cows. "Fuck it!" He walked to the gate of the fence, opened it, and entered the pasture. He started walking toward the herd, and then, over his shoulder, called out. "Keep it. Enjoy it. Just let me borrow the damn thing when I clean out those fallen trees by the creek."

Zeke remained silent and sitting, his arms resting on his bent knees as he stared at the dirt. He wasn't going anywhere.

I watched my dad turn smaller as the distance between us increased. He kept walking toward the herd, but all of the cows, even the bull, stood up and trotted farther out into the pasture, away from him.

I dropped my glove and ran toward the fence. I tried to slip right through the bottom two wires as I often did, but they snagged my shirt and shorts. Fabric tore, and I struggled to free myself. Barbs cut into my skin, into my back and shoulders and thighs. I tried to pull free, but I just scraped more skin against the steel. I hung limp in the wires.

"Dad!"

He didn't hear me, or he ignored me. He continued walking, to the willows, until he was among their sagging branches and hidden by their soft, swaying green.

time by the seasons within the season. Tomorrow, bow hunting begins again. My other neighbor, Luke Sheparski, was also honing his aim about an hour ago, and I heard him shout at his little boy, "Stand way back when Daddy's shooting!" It was more fear than anger.

I rise with my book and cup of coffee and climb the wooden steps, up the eroding hill to my small white house. Another arrow pierces the target. Through the slender skeletons of the paper birches I see Jim, at the far edge of his yard, wearing stiff blue jeans that hang low on his hips. His belt doesn't round out over him like most men's, but rests flat and rectangular on his trim frame. His brown flannel sleeves are rolled up to the elbows, and rods of muscle run laterally along his forearms. His sandy hair is trimmed to Marine Reserve regulation, short on top, shaved shorter on the sides, with his mustache not extending past the corners of his mouth. When he prepares another arrow and pulls back through the grim motion, rods rise up along his neck. He's just home from work, his wife, Caroline, still away. His house and yard are quiet except for the sudden thump of the weapon. My footsteps over the crackling branches and crisp leaves don't disturb him. He's focused on the burlap archery target. Mulch is piled up around it in case any arrows miss. None do.

I open the door. Behind me, I hear another arrow strike. I walk inside, wanting to watch Jim and figure out what's going on in his head right now, so I take the binoculars from the top of my refrigerator. I usually use them to watch geese and herons sail and slide onto the water's surface. Today, I use them to spy on Jim. I stand in my small kitchen a few steps from the window, the backs of my legs pressed up against the stove, and I aim the binoculars through the mini blinds. I see him through dark horizontals, and as he pulls back on the bowstring to fire again, the delicate arch of the weapon reveals its taut energy, like a big cat or any other predator of the forest. I can't fit both the target and him in the circle of my view, so

I pan back and forth, unsure of what to focus on: the hunter or the thing taking the blow.

The target has eight black circles arranged in a ring. In the center of the ring of circles is another circle, a red one. Two arrows have already sunk into it. The rest are damn close. I pan back to Jim, and he's looking at me. I pull the binoculars away from my face and step back, clanging an empty pot off the stovetop and onto the floor. I look again, and he's preparing another arrow. He never really saw me. I'm too far away, it's too bright outside, and it's too dark inside my house. He fires a silent shot. It's disorienting being inside and witnessing the sight of the impact but not the sound. I need to hear the heavy strike into that straw-filled body to get a sense of the arrow's real power, and Jim's.

There's a restless intensity to his action, as if he wants the day to end. I'm sure that tomorrow—the beginning of October—will represent some truly new season for him, or at least the end of an old one. Last September at this time we could see our breath, and Jim's yells clouded out from him. We could breathe in his fear or walk right through it.

•

That night I could hear him calling Toby's name loud enough that the sound spilled through my windows along with the twilight. He put his two index fingers into his mouth and let out one of the shrill whistles that he always used to call the boy in from playing. Toby was seven. He looked like all the Dutch kids I knew, blond and fair-skinned. His hair was shaved short like his dad's. I brushed aside Jim's calls at first, because parents up here always yell for their kids as the sun sets and Saturday evening meals are prepared. I was in my kitchen frying up a steak and filling a tumbler with boxed red wine. The Notre Dame/USC game was on in the next room. It was late in the fourth quarter. Time was winding down.

I sat in my rocking chair with the steak just as the game clock hit the two-minute warning. The meat was overcooked and hard to cut, so I picked up pieces of it with my bare hands and dipped it into the A1 sauce. Someone excitedly knocked on my door.

"Shit." I set the plate on the floor and furiously wiped my hands and face with a thin paper towel that turned soggy with grease and tore. The knocking started again when I touched the doorknob. My hands slipped while turning it. Outside stood Luke. His long, dark hair was pulled back into his signature ponytail, making his head look sleek and round on the top. He wore a heavy orange jacket. His beard was fuller than usual. He was ready to hunt.

"Hey buddy," he said. His hands were in his pants pockets and his head was bowed. He looked nervous. "Sorry to bother. Jim's wonderin' if you'd help him out. Toby's been missin' for a little while and the dark's at the doorstep."

"Yeah," I said. "Let me get my shoes."

It all seemed like an overreaction, but I didn't know either of my neighbors well enough to say so. These were men I'd wave at from a distance. Sometimes one would bring a chain saw over to help me cut up a fallen tree or I'd help the other install a basketball hoop. But I'd never been invited into one of their houses, and they'd never been invited into mine. My running shoes were still laced tight from my run the day before, and I sat down in the rocking chair with my index fingers pulling at the heels, trying frantically to force my feet in. Luke stood just inside the door, ready to quickly get back outside. One hand was still in a pocket, and the other held the doorknob. "He was playin' his little war games in the woods with those older kids down the road," he said. "But they've been back for a while and haven't seen him in an hour or two." I was surprised and intimidated by his sense of urgency, but, again, I have no kids of my own.

We stepped out onto my front porch. The sun was behind the tree line, but the sky was still a glossy pale blue. There was a little time until all the light would drain into the horizon, but not much. Even with the leaves thinning out, it was always darker in the woods.

My breath bloomed out in a small fog. Luke stooped down and picked up two heavy black flashlights he'd set on the porch steps. As we jogged over to Jim's place, Luke tossed me one. "Here." I dropped it and bent down to pick it up out of the fallen leaves by the road. Luke impatiently jogged in place. "Luckily it's still harvest moon," he said, "so we may get some extra light."

Jim and Caroline were shouting at each other as we neared their house. They were inside with all of the doors and windows closed, but the noise filtered through. The words were unclear. Jim emerged from his house wearing a camouflage jacket, mud-stained boots, and a floppy Boonie hat. He acknowledged us without making eye contact, nodding once and walking quickly past in the direction of the road. He held a large spotlight shaped like a gun with an enormous halogen bulb that was already turned on. The beam was absorbed by the last light outside and didn't cut anything new into the dusk. We turned and followed him.

"Caroline and I both got cell phones," he said. "She's callin' people in the area and stayin' here in case he shows. Us three will hit the trailhead at the end of the road and follow the Refrigerator Trail loop."

The swiftness of his strides evolved into a march, and in his hunting camouflage I could see the Marine in him, the Gulf War veteran. I couldn't keep up at the walk and had to jog again. About two hundred yards from our houses, the road came to a stop sign and met with the perimeter road that circled the lake. At that junction was the trailhead. The sandy path climbed a short, steep hill. We clumsily scaled up to the top. I was only twenty-eight and in decent shape, Jim and Luke were both in their mid-thirties, but all of us looked older as we struggled with our footing and the sudden rushing of our pulses. I'd often seen Toby and his friends shoot up the hill as though they were helium-filled.

I wasn't sure who owned all of the woods. I'd seen NO TRES-
PASSING signs sprinkled throughout the area, and no doubt devel-
opers were just sitting on parts of it and waiting to see if the new
golf course and resort in Rothbury would take off. But much had
always been seen as public domain. Clean, dark trails crisscrossed
the land and were used mostly by kids. At the top of the hill was a
huge beech tree peppered with two-by-fours and bent nails they'd
stolen from their fathers' toolboxes to make forts and watchtowers
for their elaborate capture-the-flag games. I'd often seen Toby trailing a group of older boys—eleven- and twelve-year-olds—down our
road. They usually wore dark colors, the better to blend into their
surroundings and sneak through their opponents' guarded lines.
But Toby—maybe because he was the slowest runner and needed
every additional advantage, or simply because he idolized his dad—
suited up in miniature hunting gear like Jim's: camouflage jacket,
pants, gloves, and Marine Corps cap. Sometimes he even smeared
brown and black grease paint over his cheeks and forehead so he
could slip into enemy territory or dissolve into the brush. I'd once
been on a walk down the trails with my ex-girlfriend and saw one
of their colored flags—a filthy red dishrag—tied to a pine branch
high in the air. The boys tore down the trails, then cut through the
thick underbrush and wet leaves saying, "Don't tell anyone you seen
us," as they raced past.

Just over the crest of the hill, about as close as you could get
to the road yet still be out of sight from it, were piles of garbage.
The area had been used by many for dumping once the Lake Tahoe
Property Owners Association ended its community trash pick-up.
There must have been twenty or twenty-five plastic bags, many of
them split and bursting, leaves spilling from their bloated bodies. There were newspapers and magazines scattered around, white
plastic diapers, and children's toys, including a couple of broken
Big Wheels and several naked dolls with dirt and broken leaves
in their hair. A couple were missing arms or legs, and one was

headless. All were contorted under other garbage or half-buried in the dirt.

Our trail pushed farther into the trees and then slowly curved out in two directions like a wishbone. Refrigerator Trail was about a two-mile loop with smaller trails branching off from it. Luke turned to Jim. "Which way you wanna go?"

I squinted, already having trouble making out shapes in the distance as each end of the trail wandered into thicker shadow.

"To the right," he said. "They play in the open fields a lot because they can dig trenches for ambushes." I could feel the pull of Jim's leadership. I felt like one of his men. He stepped into the trees, and now the spotlight caught the emerging darkness and lit up yellow circles on tree trunks.

A slight wind shook the dry leaves at our feet and above our heads. A gaggle of geese passed over us, loudly and unexpectedly honking in the quiet. Luke looked up and twisted around, startled, aiming his light into the tree canopies. Then he looked at me with a foolish grin. "Jesus H. that surprised me."

I smiled and nodded, but then buried my smile under the same look of concern I'd had since Jim first marched out of his front door. I felt as though I had no right to speak among these sportsmen and fathers.

The trail was only wide enough for us to go single file. Jim naturally led, Luke was behind him, and I was last.

"You think he's hidin'," asked Luke, "or that he's really lost?"

"Really lost," said Jim. "You've seen him. Always movin' and bouncin' around. He couldn't stay still long enough to hide quietly in one place." He abruptly stopped to shine his light into the trees. Luke stopped, and I stopped too late, bumping into his back.

"Damn. Sorry."

They were both quiet. They must have heard something. "Toby!" yelled Jim. He steered the light into the interior of the trail loop, into its dark core.

"Hey, Tob!" yelled Luke. "Come on out, buddy!"

Jim continued walking, and we followed him farther down Refrigerator Trail. I don't know who gave it that name, but because of its simplicity I'm sure it was a kid. On the far end of the loop, at just about the halfway point, someone had dumped an old refrigerator. It was light blue and left there like a piece of modern art or a tombstone, slowly being engulfed by the ground. Each fall it was buried a little deeper as a new layer of leaves blanketed it with fresh decay. The rest of the trail stretched through a varied landscape of dark pine groves, beech forest, and open fields of rolling hills marked with the occasional swatches of Christmas tree farms—small spruces like the kid soldiers who played there, in matching colors and imperfect formation.

The wind picked up again. There's no sound equal to that symphonic crescendo as the brittle leaves flutter more and more violently, like cicadas in the summer but with a refreshing clarity that always makes me want to lie down where I'm standing and go to sleep. A falling leaf brushed against my cheek, making me flinch and hurl the beam of my flashlight into the trees. Luke and Jim picked up my movement, weaving their own light into the woods, thinking I'd heard or seen something.

"Nothin'," I said.

The trees thinned out as we headed for the fields, and I realized it was still dusk, not true night, because I could again see the landscape in all directions. The open sky was a sudden comfort and gave me the confidence to express what I'd been thinking the whole time. "I bet Toby's at a friend's house," I said, "or playin' on that old jungle gym at the park."

"That'd be good," said Jim.

I wanted to keep lightening the mood, for Jim's sake and mine. "I bet this area would be good for hunting."

"Not allowed," he said distantly, half speaking to me, half listening to the woods.

"Actually," said Luke, "there's a patch a little south of here, just inside the trail, that's privately owned. This skinny guy Dean from the other side of the lake has a tree stand there and permission to use it. I've talked with him at the bar. Says he never gets much."

In the open fields, Refrigerator Trail forked into a minor path that arced to our left, to the interior of the loop. "Let's stay on the main way for now," said Jim. "I'm sure if he's anywhere, he's on the perimeter."

"Toby!" yelled Luke.

I decided I better join in. "Toby!"

Luke had been right about the harvest moon. It was rising out of the field behind us. I turned and saw it low in the sky, bloated near the horizon and greater than it would eventually become. It would climb above us and shrink in size but turn pure and crystalline, its light focused and sharp, as though slicing through a magnifying glass.

The fields were hilly and sandy, and along the edges of the trail were huge rocks that I'd never seen anywhere else in the area— glacial residue glowing under a cool glacial moon. Tumbling over the boulders were shriveled ferns. The woods looked thinner without their normally knee-high sea of green. The ferns had died out before the leaves of the taller trees, yet their frail bodies still stood clustered together in clumps and twisted waves, falling over one another like foaming rust.

"Hey!" shouted Jim in surprise. Two deer bounded through the edge of the field and crossed the trail a little ways in front of us, and Jim miraculously kept the ray of his spotlight on them the whole time, his hunter reflexes always simmering under his skin. My heart pounded heavily in my chest, and later, each rabbit or squirrel that scurried along the forest floor made the pounding recur.

"Toby!"

"Come on, bud. It's us!"

The moonlight cast a grayer grimness onto Jim's face. The

shadow from his mustache covered his mouth and chin so that it looked as though his face simply fell away into a cavernous moan.

"Maybe he wandered back home to Caroline by now," I said.

He didn't respond. He took the cell phone from his pocket and dialed. "Is he there?"

Luke and I stared into his eyes, trying to learn the answer before we heard it.

"Okay." He hung up but didn't look at us. "It's really gettin' dark now. I'm not fuckin' likin' this."

We followed the trail out of the fields and back into the woods. The subtle curve toward the south helped me picture where we were on the trail. Sometimes I went for runs on the loop or just took strolls by myself. I knew we were bending toward the halfway point, toward the refrigerator.

Massive beech trees guarded each side of the trail. Their silver bark reflected any shafts of moonlight that made it through the leaves. One of them split out from the earth into several smaller trunks that rose up and then curved back toward one another to form a sort of birdcage. I'd seen this on past walks. The boys—or boys of some other generation—had wrapped a thick, rusty chain around it several times. And as we came upon it that night with our false light, the strange merger of silver wood and tarnished metal and the darkness it held captive chilled me like the air.

"Hey, Toby!" Jim put his fingers in his mouth and let out a sharp whistle. "Toby!" He looked back at us. "I'm not likin' this."

It was now genuine night. In the thicker parts of the woods, where the leaves hadn't begun to fall, the moonlight wasn't enough, and we still needed flashlights to find some sections of the trail. I figured that if Toby wasn't home and wasn't in the open fields, he was struggling to find his way, wandering far off the trail, in more distant woods or dark orchards. Otherwise, we would have heard him yelling for help. Any kid would have been yelling.

Luke shined his light to the left to unveil a thin minor trail—

a capillary—that trickled off the loop like so many others. "At some point," he said, "we may want to consider splittin' up."

"What's that?" I asked. My light was focused on something in the brush, a brightly colored mound that didn't resemble leaves.

"Carrots and apples," said Luke. "Bait. I think we're close to that Dean guy's huntin' area and his piece-a-shit tree stand."

Jim was peering down the minor trail and breathing heavily through his mouth, the exhalations steaming out into the rays of his light. "Let's fan out in this direction. Luke, go down this new trail." He aimed the spotlight at me, burning my eyes and making me shut them and cover my face. "You keep headin' along the main loop. I'm gonna cut in between them and trailblaze a bit."

Luke shined his light on me. "You okay?" I felt a sudden heat, but not from the light.

"Yeah," I said. "I know the trail."

We split up, and suddenly my flashlight seemed like a thin dagger compared to the huge chunks of darkness Jim's had been slicing away. I heard his footsteps off to my left and felt a comfort in that. I was almost to the refrigerator.

While we'd been approaching it, I'd started running through worst-case scenarios, and the overriding one was related to ridiculous warnings I'd heard as a kid about refrigerators. Parents told us never to play around them because we'd get locked inside and suffocate. A Saturday morning public service announcement had shown a group of boys playing hide-and-seek and one of them closing himself inside a refrigerator. These weren't the modern appliances that closed tight with magnets and could be easily pushed open. These were the older ones whose heavy doors latched tight, and only their outside handles could reopen them. The light-blue model half-buried in the woods we were searching was one of those.

"Toby!" I shouted.

Jim's footsteps through the leaves sounded farther away now, but I could still hear his whistles and his voice calling out his son's name. They started to sound more frantic. "Toby, Daddy's lookin' for you! We're comin', honey!"

The tenderness of it, from a tough guy like Jim, made me want to lie down again where I stood, this time to fall asleep amid the desperate crescendo of love.

Then the refrigerator caught my light, its pale-blue skin emerging from the dark. I started to jog as I approached it, my light bouncing over the surrounding trees. I turned my head to the left. "We're halfway! I'm at the refrigerator!"

It lay on its back. As I came to a stop in front of it, I should have been scanning the entire area as I'd been doing the whole time, but my whole focus was on the fallen appliance. The moon—now higher in the sky—washed a subtle blue over everything, yet my flashlight burned into the door and glimmered off the steel latch. I stood over it, catching my breath. Then I bent down and coiled my fingers around the icy metal. I pulled at the handle so that the door squeaked on its hinges and crashed open onto the ground, sending up a dusty debris of sand and broken leaves. I shined my light into its dark hollow and jumped back. "Fuck!"

My arms and legs shuddered as I turned and jumped away from it. I quickly flashed my light at it again.

I'd been tricked. Someone—probably a kid—had put a mutilated doll inside along with some broken toy trucks and scattered cards from a kid's card game. The doll was a plastic twin of those by the trailhead. Its white skin and bald infant head glowed like the moon. An arm was missing, and one of its eyelids—which was supposed to blink shut when the doll was lying on its back—was stuck open. The iris was blue.

I heard murmuring behind me and turned around. Jim stood with his light aimed at the forest floor and the green glow of the cell phone illuminating his fist. "Oh Christ," he said. His voice was tight in his throat as he swallowed. "Caroline says he's still not home yet."

I wasn't sure if he'd seen the doll. I bent to close the refrigerator door and then walked over to him. I felt as useless as I had all night and patted him gingerly on the shoulder. I noticed Luke's light slicing through the woods, coming our way. "Luke'll be here in a minute," I said. "Rest up. Stay calm. I'm gonna walk a little ways ahead and check out the cathedral."

Maybe I had wanted to feel helpful and pretend I was taking charge, but I left Jim there alone for a few moments, and I regret that.

Walking down the trail, I sensed that I was bending east, and that hope was turning in on itself a little as the trail began to loop back toward its own source. I realized Jim didn't know what the cathedral was—the Silver Cathedral. I'd come to the woods once with a woman named Briana Cole because I'd always found this area of the forest especially beautiful. Briana came up with the name. It's a sloping shoulder of land, not terribly large, where the undergrowth thins out into moss and the trees are spaced farther apart. Its edges are raised up by tall, gothic pines that surround an assembly of beech trees, their silver skin like cool marble and their leaves letting in prismatic sunlight.

But it looked different in the dark. The tallest pine trees were only silhouettes, and the harvest moonlight shined through the branches. Its effect on the skin of the beeches was even greater than the sun's, and the ghost trees shimmered more than usual. I couldn't see the beam of my flashlight in the Silver Cathedral because there was enough ambient light to absorb it. I walked slowly in a circle, scanning the dim landscape and peering into the few dark pockets that the moon didn't touch. "Toby!"

In a world of gray and green and rust, foreign colors catch the eye. I saw bright purple and white, making some sort of zebra pattern. It was hovering over the ground in the interior of the loop, a short ways off the main trail. As I approached it and shined my light into the interior, I noticed a minor trail that was probably the end point of the capillary Luke had started searching when the three of us had split up. I aimed my light at the foreign colors and realized they were feathers. From an arrow.

At first I thought the rest was just a heap of leaves. I was away from the glow of the moonlit beech trees, and the camouflage blended so well with the earth. But as I got right up to it with my flashlight I could see the boy, lying on his back with one arm strung out to the side. The patterned brown-and-green hat lay next to him on the ground. And because of the dark grease paint on his face, it was only when I stood right over him that I could see his white skin, smooth and unreal in whatever silver light could reach us. The arrow was buried in his chest.

I turned and screamed, running zigzag away from the body toward the columns of beeches, desperate for light. A rustling of frantic footsteps came down the trail and into the area. I screamed again, imagining for a second that the footsteps were Toby's, that he'd stood up and was running after me. But then I heard the horrifying wails of Luke and especially of Jim, whose expulsion of sound was like the collapse of the soul. I leaned against a tree, weeping and cringing as I listened to him.

He stopped suddenly. I could still hear Luke mumbling "Toby, Toby, Toby," but Jim's voice had fallen away. I ran back in the direction of the body and realized Luke was stuck in some eddy of shock, fingering the shaft of the arrow and just repeating the boy's name. I'm not sure he realized that Jim was face down. Jim had fainted, and the only sign of his own life was the plume of frosty air seeping from his mouth. I flipped him over—blood streaming down his forehead where he'd hit it on an exposed root. As he came to and began to open his eyes, I backed away. I glanced quickly at Toby. There was an enormous dark blood stain on his jacket, but amid the patterns of the camouflage, it was nearly hidden.

Luke started screaming. There weren't any words. Jim's light was already upside-down in the dirt, the ray stretching out to the sky, so when Luke dropped his own light amid the hysteria, everything turned darker.

"I'll get help!" I howled. "I'll get help! Call 911 and send 'em to the trailhead." I raced forward on the trail, knowing it was a little under a mile. I'd run it before. I was the swiftest of any of them. I ran like a deer, terrified, imagining arrows raining down on me from tree stands, from a man who would confuse me with an animal that night, as he had Toby, thinking his only crime would be a little poaching a few hours before the new season had begun. And even through the darkness and confusion I never slowed down. But I could only think of two things as I ran. The first: that I had to be the one to tell Caroline. The second: a lingering dream image of me scooping Toby out of the dirt and placing him inside that refrigerator with the other doll, to preserve him.

•

This past summer I walked the trail loop's interior by myself, past where the piles of bait had been, to the rusty tree stand that, like the refrigerator, is still there—another piece of trash. Olive-colored fish net was draped over it, and hanging from the ladder was a small black sign with white letters: DEAN HOLYFIELD, 822 TONAWANDA DR., PERMISSION TO HUNT BY OWNER. He lived on the opposite side of the lake from me. Sometimes I aim my binoculars at his place, but I never see anything. In that night of lights and sirens, I heard he was found under his bed, bawling like a child.

But now I focus my binoculars back on Jim. Tomorrow will be his first time hunting since Toby's death—his first time stepping back inside any woods. I'm amazed he even wants to walk trails again, that he can release even a single arrow. I don't think he'll be able to fire one tomorrow. Not even if a deer walks right underneath his stand. He'd probably just keep gripping the bow, the tautness making his arms ache and shake as he waits and verifies, waits and verifies that it's okay for him to shoot at this life. Yet what if he does shoot and his aim is true? What of the blood?

But as I said, I'm not a hunter. I'm not a father, and I offer up no sacrifices. Yet with the bright harvest moon back this week, I have to think Jim draws the blinds tight at night to sleep, to keep out the familiar wash of silver light. He'll probably sleep better during the new moon, which is really no moon at all. And as the colors approach their fall brilliance of yellows and reds—my favorite time of year—I don't doubt that Jim will be relieved when they pass him by and he can sink into the late October rust, the forest like dried blood, bitter and metallic.

DEER RUN

Last Thursday, while idling at a red light, I witnessed a desperate attempt at escape. The rest of the story I got from Channel 8 News, the *Press*, and my neighbor Dave Greeno, who was driving his tow truck down the East Beltline when the final scene unfolded.

Four deer broke free from the narrow confines of Plaster Creek, an urban waterway running through Grand Rapids that's as filthy as it sounds. I was on my lunch break from the architectural firm where I work, headed east down 28th Street and stopped at the Kalamazoo Avenue intersection, when the deer crossed a grocery store parking lot and plunged into traffic. All four were does, and to my human eyes they all looked the same, especially at that speed, at that blur. The deer didn't hesitate. They were bigger than most deer I've seen during my walks in the woods, all obviously mature. They knew what they were doing, even if they were influenced by The Grays, which may make animals crazy from a sky full of clouds, the way some go crazy from a full moon. The four of them must have detected some slender opening through the city that, like their trails through the woods, was invisible to most human eyes.

•

This is the season when invisible streams are visible again, the in-between season. The Grays. This is my name for the narrow crawl space between the last snow melt and the first spring rains, when the skies stretch and smooth out from horizon to horizon. These are the early March days, when low clouds are like flat stones and I'm wishful for a wind gust, for any movement in the atmosphere.

.

The four deer rushed into the congested intersection as one mass. They were headed north up Kalamazoo when the first deer, who seemed to lead them, was clipped in the chest, went down in the middle of the street, and lay still. The second and third wove through traffic. Cars screeched to stops, some swerving to avoid the deer, others swerving to avoid other cars. Then all of the traffic was still, and the fourth deer, falling slightly behind, leapt onto the hood of a Jeep in a metallic clatter, scraping its hooves over the surface until it was continuing on, through the new gridlock, following the other two deer to the golf course across the street.

.

I work in Grand Rapids, where I specialize in the art of enclosed space. But I live in Allendale, by the Grand River, surrounded by shrinking farmland and a growing college town. A nature trail coils through these woods at the university, over the hills and down the ravines, until it runs along the river for about a mile. I come here most weekends for a walk, and have been since moving here five years ago, wanting to somehow distance myself from urban living, and usually failing. Over the five years, I've only seen other people in these woods twice. Both times, the people and I were startled. It's far more common to see deer.

.

Indian Trails Golf Course is eighteen holes of flat fairways with scattered trees, and in March, during The Grays, it is devoid of golfers. I rolled down my window and stuck my head out to see the three remaining deer cross the practice green near the road and continue in a direction that can only be described as due north. When they ran behind the clubhouse, I lost sight of them for good. But I imagine them stretching their legs in perfect ease, feeling a trimmed turf under their hooves softer than any surface they'd ever run on before. I imagine them slipping into long strides under the low skies, catching their breath, and for those few moments when they were free from the chaos of traffic, mourning the one that had led them.

•

Today on the trail, The Grays are at their grimmest. I have to stop halfway and turn back on some of the loops. Mild temperatures have melted the lingering snow and the river has let itself go, gorging on the flat flood plain between the hills. If there were ferns and wildflowers and green saplings, they would drown. But those are things for April, and this is the season of sticks and stones and little else, except for deer sightings, which occur through the gray branches of the end-winter woods. I walk the trails of mud, which chirp and smack with each step and make my cheap hiking boots turn heavy, clogging the tread until they're as smooth on the bottom as old penny loafers. I grab saplings as I skid down the hills, and admire the deer that bound through the mud with the same grace they'll exhibit over the baked, cracked earth of August.

•

When the stoplight turned green, we all drove slowly and arced out of our lanes to avoid the blood-soaked body of the first deer.

•

I saw twelve of them today. Groups of three, then four, then five. The first was a doe with her two fawns. Their fur was different from most I've seen. It lacked a warm chocolate hue, and instead was gray with white flecks trickling down their backs, becoming larger and turning all white near the hindquarters. Maybe in the coming

months, the summer sun will add a richer tone. Maybe in March,
it reflects the sky like the cold, quick waters of the river.

Or it could be The Grays. What if these animals have some
powers of camouflage, blending with the clouds and branches and
the silt left over from the floods? Think of the fawns. They've
known nothing but The Grays in their short lifetimes.

•

Channel 8 picked up the story once the deer had made it to East
Grand Rapids, after the three of them cut through the golf course
and adjacent cemetery, probably leaping gravestones like hurdles.
They must have run the three-mile stretch down Plymouth Avenue,
over sidewalks and through front lawns, until they reached the
mansions and oak-lined streets of the city's wealthiest neighbor-
hoods. The news reported several near-misses with cars at the intersections in East Grand Rapids, but since all were four-way stops,
the traffic was moving slowly and had had time to brake.

The event that made the lead story on the six o'clock program
occurred in front of Blodgett Hospital on Plymouth, where an
ambulance, screaming southward in flashes of red—in a direction
opposite the deer—swerved to miss two of them but hit the third,
*remarkably skidding as it swerved and actually balancing for a precarious
few seconds on two tires. It then turned into the curved drive leading here to
the emergency doors. Hospital officials report that, thankfully, the patient
inside the vehicle was not harmed further by the events of the collision.
Unfortunately, the same cannot be said for the deer.*

The newscast said little else, except for briefly mentioning the
first deer, which was killed in front of me, and having no human
explanation for such a run. It also reported that the two remaining
deer continued north, eventually leading to a final incident on the
East Beltline.

•

I must have seen hundreds of deer by my old house in New Era. When I was a kid, I used to walk through the woods with an old spiral notebook and a dull pencil, searching for animals such as deer, hawks, and raccoons, and making a small vertical mark for each sighting. I was more observant then. I walked quietly. Wearing a pair of leather moccasin slippers, I glided between trees, always holding out hope that I'd spot a bear. And during the brief moments when I predicted and envisioned my future life, I was always living up north, in the Upper Peninsula, in a log cabin where deer would eat out of my hand and bears would rumble past my front window in the middle of the night.

•

What transpired over those two miles between the hospital and the Beltline is sketchy. We know that the last two deer made it to the wooded campus of Aquinas College as they pressed ahead, northward, farther into the urban heart of the area. According to the *Press*, students "sprinted for cover behind trees and parked cars, and one of the deer apparently bounded completely over a parked vehicle. 'It was a small car,' said Ashley Dombrowski, 19, 'but the deer flew right over it without slowing down.'" Several other students reported seeing the deer race through the parking lots of the campus to Fulton, where, in unison, they turned sharply to the east and continued down sidewalks like humans who had determined a route beforehand and were following a mental map. I imagine them slicing through front yards and then once again taking long strides as they cross the expansive green grounds of the Grand Rapids Dominicans. If they're anything like humans, their rising heartbeats would start to drown out the sounds of traffic as they neared the edge of the city.

•

The two deer made it down Fulton, through the low-lying areas of the old wetlands, until they reached the divided highway of the

East Beltline. They crossed the southbound lanes without incident, slipping through another opening in space and time, a window between traffic that a stoplight farther up the road must have caused. After hitting the grassy median they then, according to my friend Dave Greeno, turned left simultaneously, pushing north again, skirting the limits of the city.

·

They must have envisioned the same thing as I did: living up north in deeper woods with wilder animals. Although I see many deer by my house, along the widening and slimming river, I have to remind myself that they're here because—in a growing city—there's nowhere else for them to go. I sometimes feel nature reclaiming itself along the trail. The wooden bridges—which students made just a few years ago to cross the wide gullies—have collapsed. The seasonal flooding lifted them off their foundations and sent them splintering into the water, or carried them farther downstream before dumping them along the banks. The boardwalks through the swamplands have buckled and split. The steps made from old railroad ties are caked in moss, rotting and being swallowed by the soil.

And there are deer everywhere. But it's because this is where the new houses are pushing them. As a kid, I used to approach with silent steps, trying to get as close to the deer as possible. Now I make sudden movements, waving my arms over my head and sometimes shouting out sounds that aren't really words. This sets them running. I'm training them to fear me.

·

Dave Greeno was driving his tow truck down the southbound lanes and saw the deer running up the median in the opposite direction. He quickly steered into the left lane to make a U-turn. Dave's an opportunist, and he sensed business.

The deer came to the interchange of the Beltline and I-96.

The concrete and congestion snared them as they crossed the overpass. When Dave approached, he was forced to come to a stop like everyone else in the new traffic jam. One of the deer had been hit and suffered what he believed was a compound fracture, the femur "sticking out of the fur like a broken arrow." The wounded deer hobbled between cars, crossed the on-ramp, and lay down by a tree just off the road. With three of its legs delicately tucked underneath its body and the fourth splayed to the side, the deer, according to Dave Greeno, laid down its head and died.

Blame The Grays. I do. Among other things. The media made no attempt at blame. Where would they begin? But Channel 8 did mention that the fourth and final deer continued, according to witnesses, to run north, toward the botanical gardens. Dave said a child, sitting in the back seat of one of the stopped cars, stretched his arm out the window and waved to her as she sprinted by.

•

Some of the runs are hidden from view—slender trails weaving through the brush, too narrow for most people to travel down. Some of them are completely invisible, cutting through cities we thought were our own.

I sometimes discover the first type. Today, on my walk, I have to avoid a part of the nature trail that's choking. Old oaks have fallen and died, and no one has come with a chain saw to carve new pathways. Another part of it's blocked by thin, thorny branches that rise from each side and arc over the path, clutching one another in the center like kids playing London Bridge. I left this trail to find another way, and that's where I found a run made by deer, slicing nimbly between obstacles. I only took a few steps down it before feeling guilty, as though I was trespassing, and worrying that my human scent would scare them off their own paths.

•

The botanical gardens. I smile at this, imagining that final deer striding through the green grass under the still, gray skies, along the glass building and surrounding sculpture park. Whether any employees or visitors to the gardens saw her, I don't know. There were no reports. There's no story in a lone deer running through a semi-rural area.

Here I envision her bending east, toward Ada, where there are more woods. She doesn't slow and doesn't scramble, but runs in tune with her own set pace and her own decision, slipping through an opening in the city as though it was a heavy, closing door. She probably makes it to Cannonsburg State Game Area, but I don't think she's foolish enough to stop there. She probably curves north again, into the farmlands, and then into the thickening woods. She knows what she's doing.

And she's probably still heading north, to live where I once saw myself living. I try not to think about what will happen when she comes to the Straits of Mackinac and can't cross. Maybe she'll wait for the winter freeze, running in place or in small, tight circles at the tip of the Lower Peninsula, waiting for the ice to become firm enough for her to race across the water, and then making the final leg into the deep woods, where all the trails are invisible, even to people like me who are looking for them.

THE LAKE EFFECT

New Year's brought a new storm, a drizzle of freezing rain that looked harmless until a person stepped outdoors. The day before, on New Year's Eve, a cold front had dipped down from Canada, and somewhere over the unseasonably mild and unfrozen Lake Michigan, the air brewed the phenomenon known as lake effect snow, dumping well over a foot of it on the lakeshore in less than a day, shutting down roads, church events, and airports. Now the rain covered the fallen snow to make a hard crust, difficult to walk through and impossible to walk over.

Evan Rumishek was trapped, and his use of the word "trapped" didn't help matters with Claire. He was trapped in Michigan. His family's flight home to San Francisco had been canceled like nearly everything else. He was trapped in the home of his in-laws, Larry and June Dykstra, where they'd been staying, at seemingly the only event not canceled due to weather: the Dykstra family Rose Bowl party that his brothers- and sisters-in-law, nieces and nephews had reached on roads driving fifteen miles per hour.

Evan's six-year-old son, Jared, sat at the kitchen table. He'd opened up a massive coloring and activity book that resembled a phone book, which his grandparents had stuffed in his Christmas stocking the previous week. He concentrated on a page with six cowboys. At first glance, all the cowboys looked the same, but really, only two were twins, and the rest had some slight discrepancy—

a missing scarf, a black spur that should have been white—which made them unique but incorrect. Jared had narrowed it down to three. He stared at each one, waiting for a little boy's breakthrough.

Evan stared too, out the kitchen window to the backyard, where the more slender branches of the beech trees dipped like those of a willow, heavy from sheaths of ice. He could hear Claire's family cheering and laughing in the basement and found himself rolling his eyes to his own half-lucent reflection in the window. None of this felt like home to him any more. He and Claire had lived in San Francisco since Jared was an infant, when he'd signed on as a partner for an accounting firm called The Davidson Group. Evan's own parents had moved from Grand Haven to Florida; he'd lost touch with most of his old friends. His only connection to the Midwest was this house, in North Muskegon, across the street from Muskegon Lake, which was still unfrozen despite the storm. The water was gray, but it flowed, through the channel to Lake Michigan. Even this made the place feel somehow alien. The channel water should have been ice by now, and the waves along the shore should have been frozen for hundreds of yards out, past the end of the pier. He wondered what the big lake looked like now. During his week back in Michigan, Evan hadn't bothered to check.

He was too busy working and hiding the work from Claire. She'd made him promise to limit his phone calls and e-mails to an hour a day during the week-long vacation between Christmas and New Year's, but before the storm hit, he went for long drives up and down US 31, talking with West Coast clients the whole time. He'd set up several meetings for January 2, the day he was supposed to return to the office. But now his flight was canceled and he was trapped on a frozen coast, spending his allotted hour on the phone rescheduling meetings and apologizing to people who had money.

Jared gave up on the cowboys and checked the answer in the back of the book, quickly glancing first at Evan to make sure he wasn't seen cheating. He set his pencil down, stood up, and pushed his chair behind Evan, who still stared out the window at the clouds, hoping for breaks of blue.

"Piggy back," said Jared. He climbed up and stood on the chair before climbing onto Evan's back, wrapping his arms around his father's neck and his legs around his waist.

"Off!" Evan unclasped Jared's arms and dropped him onto the chair. "Damn, you know better than that," he said, turning to face the boy. "You know about my back."

"Sorry," said Jared quietly. He lowered his dark eyes, jumped down from the chair, and walked out of the kitchen, shoving the massive activity book off the table on his way out so that it smacked on the linoleum floor.

Evan arched his back, trying to crack it. He tightened both of his hands into fists, settled his knuckles into the grooves of his spine, and pushed. The pain had been getting worse over the past year. He was swallowing a Demerol and a muscle relaxer with dinner each night. He performed stretches twice a day to loosen the knots and relieve the pains. And he ran less. Throughout all of the late nights at the office and cross-country business trips, he used to find time to run at least five miles a day. But now, with the pain, he was down to four or three or sometimes no miles at all. His running clothes were packed in a duffel bag down the hall, in the guest room he and Claire had been sleeping in, but he hadn't worn the clothes the entire trip.

Claire appeared in the arched kitchen doorway, her arms crossed and her black hair pulled back to make her round, white face look rounder and whiter. "He's downstairs telling everyone you yelled at him."

"You could sneeze in that kid's direction and make him cry."

"No, *you* could sneeze in his direction and make him cry. And everyone downstairs sees it."

"Well, more ammunition for your parents." Evan walked to the refrigerator to get a beer. It was opposite from Claire, so he could keep his back to her.

"If you're going to avoid them, make it less obvious," she said.

He waited for her to take the next logical step, to say he was avoiding her.

"Go downstairs. You look ridiculous moping around up here by yourself."

Evan knew the things Claire's parents said about him. They resented the fact that they'd waited ten years for their first grandchild, and once Jared was born, Evan took the job in San Francisco. During his in-laws' first visit to California, he tried to show off their Pacific Heights home, the esteemed private schools, and the water of the bay, which, to him, always seemed a deeper and richer blue than the water in Muskegon. Later during the visit, June had sat Claire down and said how she worried about Evan. She said he was too driven by money. She wanted him to join a men's Bible study.

And now, in June's house, he dwelled on such things. He'd never called her "Mom," and she'd never called him "Son."

"Your parents love when Jared's upset at me," he said. "They love to baby him."

If Evan had been looking at Claire when he spoke he might have seen an eye twitch or a nearly imperceptible wince when he said the word "baby." It was the root of most of their recent fights: about his working too much, about his not being there enough for Jared—at the root of her doubts about Evan as a father.

They'd been talking about having another child. Claire, especially, wanted to try for a girl, and with both of them in their late thirties, she didn't want to put it off any longer. But if necessary, she would put it off indefinitely. He'd said many times that he wanted to have another child, and in glimpses of him—like a person running on the other side of a tall picket fence, the mind seeing the whole picture even though it only saw those moments through the gaps—she believed this. Evan kneeling and tying Jared's shoe, or reading him a bedtime story with both of their heavy eyes nearly tumbling into sleep. But she worried that these moments were too few and, like glimpses of anything, quickly over and their existence quickly doubted. And then there was his promise.

He'd said he would work less. He'd said that when she went back to work, as a freelance corporate trainer, that he'd work more from home and spend more time with Jared. But Evan always had meetings at the office, and she had to juggle her own hours, turning down several training opportunities, until the companies stopped calling her altogether.

She couldn't say anything about this now. Not until they were back home. Evan was right. Her parents didn't need any more ammunition, and she didn't need to sell it to them.

Evan turned and, from across the kitchen, gazed outside again. The rain had started to soften back to snow, large flakes like bits of the clouds drifting down.

"You're just going to stand there all day, aren't you," she said.

"All day," he said.

"If I was like this with your family . . ." she said, letting the words trail off.

"Okay, here I go," he said. He sipped his beer as he walked toward her. "Down to the pit." He tried to pass through the door-way, but Claire spread her arms out like a crossing guard, pressing her hands against each end of the arched wall to trap him.

"Don't be an ass," she said. "And don't take it out on Jared."

He shoved her left arm down and walked past. Then, holding the neck of the beer bottle between two fingers, he clenched his hands into fists again and pushed against the middle of his back. With voices rising from the basement, Evan turned and walked down the hall to the stairs.

The basement smelled like sand. It was from years of living by the lake. Children and grandchildren had brought grains of it in on their feet and clothes. He walked down the creaking stairs to the cold concrete floor and its dirty rugs tossed about, all filled with sand as if woven into the fabric. Cut into the wall next to the stairs was a cubbyhole—a diorama of a beach scene that Larry had made for the grandkids. He'd carved a little wooden dock with a little wooden fisherman sitting on the end. Beneath the dock was soft white sand, taken from the beach, or maybe gathered up in handfuls off the floor. The basement felt as though it was slipping down to the shore and all of the lake's sand was leaking through the walls and seeping into shoes and ears and underneath fingernails.

All but one person looked up from the game as he stepped downstairs. There were ten of them: Larry and June; Claire's younger sisters, Sally and Margo; her sisters' husbands; their toddling children; and Jared, sitting on Larry's lap, making sure to keep his eyes locked on the television. Michigan was playing USC. Half of the family was decked out in maize and blue, even though none of them had gone to the school. Evan nodded and tried to smile at the young children, who seemed the most surprised to see him mingling with the rest of the family.

"Who's winning?" he asked. He sat on an old leather chair.

Larry spoke from his La-Z-Boy. "Your California boys. By ten."

"They're not *my* California boys," said Evan.

The family spoke among themselves about the game, or sometimes swore under their breath, trying to keep it from the kids. Evan ate Spanish peanuts that had been poured into an old ashtray. He watched the game with little interest. His loyalties didn't lie with either team, and he hadn't followed sports in years. His weekends were rarely free, and if a client or vendor invited him to watch a Giants game from a luxury suite, they always spent the innings talking business.

About every twenty minutes, the sounds of the game—the crowd and the announcers—were interrupted by a piercing alarm. The alarm always quickened Evan's pulse and reminded him of all the emergencies he'd ever lived through: floods, tornadoes, earth-quakes. Across the bottom of the screen ran a blue ribbon of words updating the viewers on the blizzard. The roads were still slick, they said. A jackknifed semi had blocked all of westbound I-96 near Coopersville. As the rain turned back to snow, another six inches were expected by midnight. There was no news about the airports. None was necessary.

Between alarms, while pretending to watch the game, Evan listened to Claire rummaging through the kitchen upstairs, loudly cleaning up after people, doing dishes, or preparing food. She slammed cupboard doors and clattered silverware. He knew she did this for him to hear. He tried to concentrate on the game.

Just before halftime, the shrill alarm came through the TV again.

"Let's hear how worse it's gonna get," said Larry.

But instead of a blue ribbon of words, a trail of orange moved across the bottom of the screen.

"Why's it orange?" asked Jared.

AMBER ALERT . . . AT 3:32 P.M. A BLACK CHEVROLET IMPALA WAS STOLEN FROM THE KONVENIENCE KORNER ON RUDDIMAN ROAD IN NORTH MUSKEGON . . .

"That's right down street," said Margo.

. . . THE OWNER OF THE CAR WAS IN THE STORE WHEN IT WAS STOLEN . . . AN INFANT BOY WAS LEFT IN THE BACK SEAT . . . MICHIGAN STATE POLICE HAVE ISSUED AN AMBER ALERT TO HELP LOCATE THE INFANT . . . THE BLACK IMPALA WAS SEEN HEADING WEST DOWN RUDDIMAN ROAD . . . THE SUS-PECT IS DESCRIBED AS A WHITE MALE, AGE 25 TO 30 . . . THE CAR'S LICENSE PLATE IS 672 ABC . . . ANYONE WITH KNOWL-EDGE OF THE WHEREABOUTS OF THE CAR, INFANT, OR SUS-PECT IS URGED TO CONTACT THE MICHIGAN STATE POLICE OR DIAL 911 . . . DO NOT CONTACT THIS STATION . . . STAY TUNED FOR MORE DETAILS . . .

"Holy shit," said Larry.

"Grandpa cursed," said Jared.

"Quiet," said Larry. He turned to the rest of the family. "That's right in our neck of the world."

"It's horrible," said June. "And can you imagine? He stole a car—okay, that's bad. But now he's a kidnapper."

Evan shook his head and spoke, to the surprise of the family. "Where's he gonna go? The roads are hockey rinks. They'll find that Impala. In a ditch."

"Maybe," said Larry, not looking at Evan. "Or maybe the cops are so busy with jackknifed semis and a thousand other accidents and cars in ditches that they can't spare extra men for this."

"What happened?" asked Jared.

"Shh," said June. Then she spoke to the family. "Someone should stand by the front window and see if that car comes down the road. He was heading this way. And I'll call neighbors and tell them to keep a lookout."

"I'll go," said Sally.

"I'll take the car and drive around a bit," said Larry. "See if I pass him."

"No," said June. "I don't want anyone driving. It's too terrible out."

Evan rolled his eyes, but barely, so that no one noticed. He stood up with his beer, stretched his back, and walked up the creaking steps to the kitchen. Claire was wiping off the countertops with her back to him. "There was a kidnapping," he said.

"A what?"

"North Muskegon is plunging into the deep end of crime." He turned and walked down the hallway, toward the guest room, where he and Claire had slept all week in separate twin beds. Her clicking footsteps trailed behind him over the hardwood floors.

"What kidnapping?"

"Your family can update you. They're on active hero duty."

They stepped inside the guest room, and Claire closed the door behind them. Evan began unbuttoning his shirt with one hand and tipped the beer back with the other to finish it off.

"What are you doing?" Claire asked.

"Going for a run."

"No you're not. You can't even walk out there. And it'll be dark soon."

"I've run in worse."

"Who's the hero?" she said, brushing his temples with her fingers. "I like your gray hair. I think it's attractive. But it's definitely not a sign of youth."

He pulled his head away slightly and stared across the room at a full-length mirror, at his reflection with the hair that still had some traces of brown, at the tautness of his face, the sharp edges of his jaw and chin. And then his image disappeared as he pulled off his T-shirt. The motion stoked the flames in his back. This was what Claire meant by a sign.

"The cold's never bothered me," he said. "I know how to run on ice. I used to do it every winter during conditioning between cross-country season and track." He unbuttoned his jeans and pulled them down along with his boxer shorts.

"You were sixteen."

"Yeah, and now it's like day eight of being trapped with your family. Call it a jailbreak."

"Nice," said Claire, turning away. She opened the door wide. Evan stood naked, looking out at the empty hallway. Then she walked out and slammed the door.

He rummaged through his duffel bag for clothes. He slipped on a pair of briefs, black running tights, and nylon running pants over them. He looked up as he changed and saw himself in the mirror again. He was still trim, still possessed the distance runner's lean muscles, which amazed him, considering he'd cut back on his miles. Claire had once said he stayed trim from stress, the acidic burning of calories that leaked to the rest of his body. But what if he did? She didn't see the upside, what he accomplished at the office, the way he never slowed down.

Attached to the guest bedroom was a bathroom. Evan walked across the room and opened up the medicine cabinet—the vanity mirror giving him a close-up of graying stubble on his face—and removed a box of Band-Aids. He sat down on the edge of the bathtub, removed a pair of the small round bandages, unwrapped them, and placed them over his nipples. The sweat and snow that drenched his shirts often rubbed them raw and made them hurt for days. He turned to look out the small bathroom window and saw the heavy snow, and because of the darkness of the clouds was able to see his own reflection in the glass. The Band-Aids made him look effeminate, as if he were wearing pasties. He walked back to the bedroom to put on the rest of his clothes.

He dressed himself in layers he hadn't worn since moving out West: short-sleeve shirt, long-sleeve shirt, sweatshirt, earmuffs, hat over the earmuffs, gloves, two pairs of socks, a scarf wrapped tight around his neck and tucked into his shirts, and a nylon vest with a silver reflective strip across the front and back so drivers would see him as they approached in the dark. The weight of all the clothes made him more aware of his body. He cracked his back again.

Indoors, the heat brought on a quick sweat—down his back, in his crotch, over his face. The hardwood floors in the hallway creaked under his running shoes as he walked to the kitchen, and the rubber soles that would freeze and harden when he stepped outdoors for now, at least, made his footfalls cushioned. Most of the family's voices remained downstairs, but he heard Jared whining to Claire, begging for a can of Sprite.

"No. You can have apple juice."

"I hate apple juice."

"Don't say 'hate,' " said Evan, stealing Claire's line but not really meaning to.

She stared at him standing in the arched doorway of the kitchen. He seemed to take up twice as much space in his new clothes. A soft flash of a smile almost lit up her eyes, but she buried it.

"Where are you going, Dad?" asked Jared.

"For a run."

"No!" Jared ran to him and clasped his waist, then pulled his legs up and wrapped them around Evan's legs, like a monkey. "No go. No go."

"What's with the baby talk?" Evan asked. "Ow." He clutched his back with one hand and pried Jared loose with the other. The boy fell backward. His head bounced off the linoleum.

"Shit, I'm sorry."

Jared's face contorted into a cry.

"Goddamn it, if you're gonna go, go," said Claire, "before anyone else sees you."

Evan tried to make her and Jared smile. He turned around slowly, displaying his layers of protective clothing. "What, afraid they'll think you married an astronaut? Maybe a deep-sea diver?"

She turned and started pouring apple juice into a glass. "I'm afraid they'll be happy when they see you leave."

"I'm only going a couple of miles. I'll be back in about twenty minutes." Evan glanced at the stairs leading to the basement. "I thought they'd be up here on hero duty by now."

"Go," she said again. He turned and headed for the front door. "And it's not funny making light of what happened to that baby. Jared just told me about it."

"I wasn't making light," said Evan. He opened the heavy door and then the thin glass door behind it. The air changed as he stepped outside, turning not just colder but almost more fragile. All sound seemed frozen still or was maybe absorbed by the heavy cushion of snow. It made him less certain as he closed the door behind him, but he thought he heard Claire say from the kitchen, "You never take children seriously."

Memorial Drive ended at Muskegon State Park, a wooded
dunescape with a long stretch of beach down Lake Michigan that
curved along the channel to Muskegon Lake. Just before he came to
the park entrance, Evan ran past a few of the seasonal businesses in
the area, all of them closed now, forming a wintertime ghost town.
There was a market, a ten-room motel, and a bait and tackle shop.
The wind picked up as Evan strode past these, sending snow and
bits of ice into his eyes. His nylon clothes broke most of the wind,
but some of it still leaked through to his flesh. Snow on the ground
lifted up and filled the air with a white fog, obscuring his view of
the buildings. Ice began to form on his eyelids, soldering them shut
with cold.

He entered the park at a hilly, wooded stretch of road. The dark
pine boughs and gray clouds above darkened the place. Evan sensed
the coming nightfall. He rubbed a layer of slush off his watch: four
thirty. It would probably be dark by five.

The roads were worse inside the park. The plows had turned
around at the entrance, probably figuring that no one would be
heading to the lake anyway. Evan found truck tracks and ran within
their slim paths. After some rolling hills, the road dipped steadily
down, and by the distant sound, like thunder, he knew he was
approaching the lake, where the wind and water were shattering
against the land. Then the sky broke off from the trees to reveal a
vast, grim horizon separating two shades of gray. Above the horizon was a lighter gray with swirls of darkness where Evan could see
the churning air, the stew for the lake effect snow. Below was the
lake—gray in parts but in other areas bright green, a shade Evan
had never seen before, especially in a landscape so overwhelmingly
colorless. He descended the road and approached the beach.

Larry had told him it had been a mild winter, but Evan had
figured it was just for effect, that Larry had wanted to make the
storm seem like no big deal and intimidate someone now living in
California. But he must have been right. As a kid, Evan would go

to the lake in Grand Haven and walk far out on the floes, tracing the breakwater. But, like the channel, Lake Michigan was entirely unfrozen. As if to take full advantage of its unexpected freedom, like a dog loose from its leash, the lake was frantic. Waves with sharp edges curled into the shore. Evan stopped and looked at his watch. This was where he had planned on turning around in order to make it back by dark. He stared out at the water. The sound of the wind and the sound of the crashing waves seemed to compete with each other, quickening his heartbeat. He was standing in a storm, smiling. Before him was an expanse of white, untouched beach—no footprints. Instead of turning around, Evan turned left, following the road that paralleled the lake.

He continued to run in a lone pair of tire tracks. To his right, most of the beach was covered in snow, but in some places the wind had created huge drifts and in others had exposed patches of sandy earth. It had sculpted crests and curves into the snow so that, in a way, it mimicked the white waves cutting through the water. To Evan's left were small, rolling dunes. Excited by the thought of the view from the top, he turned toward them and began to climb. As he reached the top of the first hill and began to run down the far side, his right leg disappeared into a drift where there was no sand underneath. Evan's leg sunk up to his groin, he lost his balance, and fell forward. Although he stretched his hands out in front of him to break the fall, both arms simply pierced the snow and sunk up to his shoulders. His face struck the snow.

A quick sense of panic filled his chest. The snow was like quicksand, and as Evan shifted and tried to push himself up, each arm or leg made a new, deeper hole. For a matter of only seconds he again experienced that sensation of danger which said this was a place where he could, in fact, die. He could drown in snow, just like water, and no one was around to save him. But he was able to find the sand underneath with one foot and push himself backward to the top of the dune, again to rest. With his earmuffs still on, he could hear his heartbeat within his own body, one of those sounds no one else could have heard, even if he hadn't been alone.

Evan ran back down to the poorly plowed road, cut across it, and ran to the beach. He realized he was running faster than he had since he left the house, not only from the adrenaline surge of the fall, but from a childlike excitement brought on by his surroundings. The landscape looked otherworldly. He'd had the same experience when he'd first moved to California and gone for a run in a redwood forest: the landscape was foreign, or he was.

He ran farther down the beach. A few times, when he came across exposed patches of sand, he tried to run across them, just for the summer sensation of sand under his feet. But it was coated in ice and hard as rock. Some grains of it came free in the wind, stinging his cheeks and forehead and getting in his eyes. Dune grass stuck up from the snow, white and crusted, reminding Evan of sea creatures, upside-down jellyfish. Some blades of the grass were sheathed in clear, smooth ice. Evan was thirsty. He bent down and slid some ice off in one piece. He put it in his mouth and let it melt. The quick stop brought on a quick sweat that the wind chilled over his body. He kept moving, farther down the shore, toward the pier.

As he ran across the smooth, flat stretch of the snowy beach, Evan lost all depth perception. There were no shadows or edges in the white. The ridges and mounds and dips became invisible, and he felt as if he was flying. The wind added to his sense of dizziness and sense deprivation. He began to feel more numb, and the sound in his ears was loud but droning, moving through him like pulses of the sky. It reminded him of standing alongside the railroad tracks behind his grandparents' house as a child, waiting for the next train to pass, feeling the waves of energy as the cars rushed in front of him just a foot or two away, and losing himself in the steady thunder.

He looked at his watch. "Shit." It was a quarter to five. He looked up at clouds that were now a dusky charcoal. He reached a sidewalk that extended down to the end of a pier where the channel spilled into the lake. He knew it was getting dark, he knew he was already later than he had told Claire he would be, but Evan wanted to run to the end of the pier, to get close up to the waves crashing into it and all that energy colliding with the earth. He ran with one hand hovering over the round blue railings, which were coated in ice as well, useless should he need to hold on. Ahead, the blue railings on both sides continued until they reached a vertex. The wind off the lake blew pieces of ice into his eyes again, so he bowed his head as he slowly moved forward. He was breathing hard, but more from excitement than fatigue or the cold. He didn't have any back pain, but he didn't realize this yet.

He glanced to his left, the shreds of ice stinging his right cheek. No one stirred across the channel, where a few houses sat clustered with golden lamps shining in their windows. There was no traffic. The only life Evan noticed were a few ducks bobbing beside the pier. Nothing else seemed alive, except the lake.

He approached the end of the pier. From there, with the loud drone of the waves crashing to his right, almost everything was out of his field of vision except the elements: lake, horizon, sky, and—encompassing everything—wind and snow. He'd heard of a teenager who'd committed suicide in a storm by doing just this, standing at the end of the pier and waiting until he was swept off. But the waves didn't quite reach Evan today, and he didn't want to die. He stopped to catch his breath, aware of the low drone of wind and waves and how it almost became transparent and inaudible. There had once been a *National Geographic* article where he'd read how people in the desert could hold their breath to experience true silence for the first time in their lives. And with the rustling leaves gone, the people gone, the traffic gone, this would be his chance for that. But he knew nothing could stop the storm at that moment. He probably couldn't even hold his own breath. Excitement quickened his heart and lungs and mind. He was the opposite of the teenager. Standing at the end of the pier, Evan wanted to feel all of the earth.

His sweat had chilled him and he wanted to move again, wake up the blood in his body. He turned and ran back down the pier toward shore. Dusk obscured the distance now; Evan wanted to make sure that he was at least to the main road before it got fully dark. Where the pier met the shore he decided to veer left, across the beach, as a short cut. The ground was icy but rough, and with small steps, and with his arms flared out to the sides, he could gain traction and balance as he headed toward the road.

It must have been something like a freshwater tidal pool, a depression in the beach where old waves had crashed and been collected when the water had been higher. Evan ran across ice that wasn't fully frozen and that had not sand underneath but water. He plunged up to his knees before tripping and falling forward. His entire body crashed through the thin ice and into the sharp shock of water.

In an explosion of adrenaline, he lunged back up to his feet. The water was only knee deep, but now the nylon running pants and vest that had shielded him from the cold clung to him, making it difficult to move. Evan shouted and began trudging forward, but each new step broke through ice to more water until, after several steps, he reached ice that broke through to sand. With the clothes stuck to him, with his body shaking, Evan started to sprint.

It didn't last long. The ground was too frozen, and the faster he ran, the faster his feet simply slipped out from under him. The deep cold settled in, and with it the panic, sharper and louder than when he had earlier fallen into the snowdrift. Nightfall had come and gone and left only night, the bizarre five o'clock night of early winter. There was still no sight or sound of anyone but him: his sharp breaths, his crunching footfalls, and the drips of water falling from his body onto the ice below.

Evan reached Memorial Drive and began running up the hill,

heading through the pine trees where the dark became darker. It was a mile and a half to Larry and June's house. He decided that if a car or snowplow drove by he'd wave it down and ask for a ride home. He'd never done such a thing, but he'd never had this sensation before, of true danger. By the time he reached the edge of the park there was still no trace of life, only the little seasonal ghost town. He wondered if maybe someone lived at the motel year round, but as he ran by, he saw no lights. Farther down the road were houses where he could knock on a door and ask for a ride. But then he caught sight of a blue pay phone sign in front of the bait and tackle shop. He ran toward it. The flesh on his legs and chest burned, and he could no longer feel his fingers or toes or penis.

When he got to the pay phone sign, he saw that the phone had been removed. There were holes drilled into the wall of the shop where it had once been bolted. Evan turned to run back to the road, and then he noticed a car parked in back of the market. He quickly glanced at the building's windows, but all of the lights were off.

His focus returned to the car. There was an orange streetlight in front of the parking lot, giving a dim, Martian glow to the snow and surrounding area. The car was parked askew, one of the front tires lurching on top of the curb. There were tracks leading from the road to where the car now stood, but they were on the verge of disappearing. About a couple of inches of snow had accumulated on the hood and roof of the car. It had been parked for a little while, but not all day. Evan looked around again, wondering where the driver was so that he could beg the man or woman for a ride home.

Then he wondered if the driver was still in the car, maybe taking a break, weary from the condition of the roads and deciding to just wait until the salt truck made another pass. Evan approached it from behind. The car was darkly colored, but under the dark sky with the white ground and the orange light above him, he couldn't be sure if it was blue or black or green. He made a fist, preparing to knock on the trunk of the car. He didn't want to hastily wipe away the snow because someone could be in there, maybe sleeping, and he didn't want to startle them. But as he got to the back of the car, Evan glanced down at the license plate: 672 ABC.

It didn't click right away. He thought, for the second time that night, that it was funny—a license number with the letters "ABC." But as he settled his gloved, numb hands on the snowy trunk, he noticed the silver logo of the Impala.

Then he could tell that the car was black. He jumped backward and—despite the bitter cold clinging to his flesh—a surge of hot pain shot down his spine. Evan stared at the car. All of the windows were covered; he hadn't been seen by anyone inside. He almost began running again, unsure if his legs could even start moving. He figured the person inside was armed. Evan began to jog, wanting to get to a nearby house where he could call the cops and say he'd found the car.

And then he remembered the baby. He jogged in place, moving his legs more and more slowly and then stopping altogether. The car's tracks were almost entirely gone now. There was a moment when the wind died down and he could hear the large snowflakes hitting the ground. He held his breath and walked toward the car again, staring at it through eyelids crusted with ice. His shoes squeaked loudly across the fresh snow, and Evan was thankful when the wind rose up again and masked the sound of his approach. He stood next to the snowy driver's-side window and extended his open hand. A yell poured out from him like an expectation of pain as he brushed the snow aside with his gloved hand.

The front seats were empty. He tried the door, but it was locked. Evan gasped for breath, tired, but not from running. He stepped backward and then, pushing himself to do what he didn't want to do, to check what he didn't want to check, he frantically wiped the snow away from the rear window. He peered inside, wincing from the possibility of a frozen, abandoned child. But silhouetted against the ambient orange light was an empty car seat, its handle tossed up almost playfully, like a child's hands during patty-cake.

Evan turned and ran. It was still useless to attempt speed over the road, so he left it, running in the deep snow that covered the adjacent lawns. He approached a couple of houses, planning on ringing their doorbells for help. But the windows of all the houses were as dark as the night, and instead of possibly wasting his time checking to see if anyone was home, he trudged the last mile through the storm, trying to reach Larry and June's house, trying to reach Claire. While he ran across the frozen lawns, his feet kept breaking through the icy crust and his shins scraped against the sharp edges. He had to lift his knees high to get through the snow, fighting his wet nylon pants in the process. But he was able to gain some speed, and he ran the final stretch down Memorial Drive to Larry and June's house without ever seeing a car pass in either direction.

When he approached, he saw the large bay window first. The drapes were still open and the lamp near the window glowed. As he got to the end of the driveway he saw Jared sitting on the living room sofa, flipping through a book. Evan continued to run through the icy crust, battering through with his feet and shins. He scrambled up the driveway, balancing against parked cars as he tried to get up the slope. Then, finally, he entered the garage and went in through the side door that led to the kitchen. He didn't want to go through the front and disturb Jared, who looked so peaceful reading in the golden light.

But as he smashed into the kitchen, that became impossible.

"Claire!" he yelled.

She came around the corner, her shirt sleeves pulled up to her elbows and her arms dripping wet. "What?" She looked at him with enormous eyes.

"I found the car," he said. He walked toward her, into the

kitchen, to get to the phone. He stumbled forward. In the sudden warmth of the house, his legs shut down.

"Where have you been?" she asked. She bent down and helped him back to his feet. She touched the back of her wet hand to his forehead as if he had a fever, but she was checking for degrees of coldness.

"I found the car. I have to call the cops."

"What car?"

"Dad!" Jared rushed in from the living room and hugged Evan's leg, almost knocking him over again. "Why were you gone so long?"

"Claire, I'm serious. I need the phone. I found that stolen car with the baby. But there wasn't a baby." He tried to walk but, with Jared attached, fell down on the hardwood floor. Snow was melting from him, making a pool on the wood, and the front of Jared's shirt was wet.

"Jared, you have to let go right now," said Claire. "You can see Daddy in a minute." She picked Evan up again and led him to the guest bedroom. Larry came up the stairs from the basement.

"What's goin' on?"

"Nothing, Dad," said Claire.

Evan saw Larry's face and wondered why it looked stunned.

When they got in the bedroom, he sat on the bed, across from the full-length mirror. And then he saw what Larry had seen. His eyebrows were white like an old man's, covered in ice, and the skin surrounding his eyes was green and fishlike. The eyes themselves were only half open, crusted with ice. His face was in full bloom— red and flushed.

Claire shut the door and then walked across the room, into the bathroom, and began filling the tub. She returned to Evan on the bed, who was sitting slouched and leaning against a pillow with his eyes closed in exhaustion.

She unzipped his reflective vest and took it off. "Lift your arms," she said.

His eyes opened. "I'm serious, Claire, I have to call."

"They found him," she said.

"Who?"

"The baby boy." She pulled at Evan's soaked sweatshirt that was clinging to his skin. "They had a news brief. The kidnapper dropped him off at his sister's house down the road. And then he ditched the car someplace and took off on foot." Claire tossed the wet clothes onto the floor. "I don't think he's gonna go far in this weather."

"I did," said Evan.

Claire pulled off the long-sleeve shirt, the short-sleeve shirt. "You must have," she said. "You were gone forever."

Someone knocked on the door. "Mom?"

"Not right now, honey. I'm gonna get Daddy settled and then I'll be right out for you."

"I wanna see Dad."

"Just a few minutes, buddy," said Evan. "I'll read you a story in a bit."

"Okay." The boy's footsteps faded down the hall.

"Stand up," said Claire.

Evan stood, wobbly. In the mirror he saw that his chest, arms, and stomach were as red as his face. He removed the round Band-Aids from his nipples. Claire kneeled and pulled off his nylon pants, tights, and underwear in one motion, tugging hard to peel them from the wet skin. He saw his bright red legs and his shriveled penis. "I can't feel it," he said.

"Have a seat." He sat, and Claire pulled at his ankles until all the layers were off except for his wet, dangling socks. Then she pulled the socks off and winced. "Oh, Evan." He looked down at his shins, bruised purple with red lacerations from the ice. Blood ran down to his ankles and feet. "Come on."

They walked across the white tiled floor to the tub, and the cold of the tile on his feet was the first indication that he was now somewhat warmer. "It's not too hot," said Claire, dipping her hand in the water up to the wrist. She held him underneath the armpits as he got in so that he wouldn't slip.

"I really wanted to help," said Evan.

"I know," she said.

He sat down, wincing from the sudden heat. Then he got used to it and eased into the water—his legs, his torso, his neck. He felt no back pain, but he still didn't realize this. Snakes of blood spiraled to the surface. Only his head floated above the water. "I'm serious," he said.

"I know."

Claire ran her hand through his wet gray hair. The ice from his eyebrows and eyelids was melting and trickling in small, cold streams down his face. He took a breath, held it, and immersed the rest of his body in the silence of underwater warmth.

CURBSIDE

Abby noticed the cross first. We'd driven twelve hours that day—all flatland hours—stretching from our dawn departure of Fargo over five state lines, and my vision was a little hazy in the dusky, nine o'clock light of July. We'd been on our first long road trip together: two weeks in Yellowstone, Glacier Park, Seattle, and a three-day visit with Abby's aunt in Idaho. The last two days had been nothing but highway, thirty hours of burrowing head-down through serrated mountains before gliding through the plains. Abby was ornery and anxious, and the familiar Midwestern lake-scapes of Minnesota and Wisconsin toyed with her, making her think we were closer to home than we really were. She wanted to talk with friends, see the cat, and sleep in our own bed, where we'd try once again to get her pregnant.

She'd been off the pill for two months and took her basal body temperature every morning to pinpoint ovulation. She packed lingerie for the trip and smuggled scented candles and silk sheets in the interior pocket of her suitcase. She must have imagined it as a second honeymoon, forgetting that there was no luxury on the itinerary. From the Teepee Motel to the Rapid City Super 8 to our rustic cabin at Yellowstone, she postponed the seduction during the first leg of our trip, and then realized that there'd be no great opportunity until our three-star hotel in Seattle. I'd returned one afternoon to failure, opening the door to our national park cabin,

drenched in sweat and bug spray with my boots and backpack covered in dust, and found her inside with the curtains closed as tight
as she could get them, surrounded by washed-out candlelight as
the sun broke through the edges of the windows. Flies buzzed and
rattled against the glass. To my right, through the thin wood paneling, a man's voice leaked into our room from another cabin. I
approached Abby, my heavy boots thudding against the uncarpeted
floor. She slipped the straps of her lavender teddy over both shoulders until her breasts were first flattened and then roundly released
from the fabric as she pulled it to her hips. I set one knee on the bed
and leaned into her. We kissed each other's necks.

"God, forget it. I'm sorry," she said, sticking her tongue out a
little and touching the tip of it with her fingers, still tasting my bug
spray. The curtains trembled as the flies buzzed more frantically.
"This is gross. We can fool around in the shower or something, but
I can't do it in this room with flies all over and people hearing every
sound we make."

And it never happened in Seattle. We ruined it the first afternoon there with a huge, wildfire kind of argument that started
small and accidental and consumed the rest of the day. We sat at a
busy restaurant in the Pike Street Market overlooking the sound,
and I read the *Post-Intelligencer* aloud to her while she ate a salad. I
came to an article about a fourteen-year-old boy who'd murdered
his six-year-old neighbor, teasing her and then pushing her into a
swimming pool with the solar cover still on. The cover had folded
in on her like a flower in reverse bloom as she sank to the bottom of
the deep end. The boy was to be tried as an adult.

"Poor kid," I said.

"She was only six," said Abby.

"No, the *kid*," I said. "The boy."

I'd been thinking about a high school freshman named
Deshawn whom I'd mentored through the YMCA. He'd committed some petty crimes—shoplifting and underage drinking—and

after reading the article I imagined him in a courtroom, during a murder trial, trying to look tough but crying in one of his dead father's ties and a used suit that didn't fit.

Abby looked disgusted. "How can you sympathize with him? What about *her*?"

"I sympathize with both of them."

"Oh, bullshit. You're way too forgiving when it comes to violence, and boys."

I tried to explain. At one point I mentioned Deshawn.

"Who?" She shook her head. "Screw it. I don't want to hear it." Her voice swelled in the restaurant. The woman sitting behind Abby turned around and pretended to look for the restrooms but instead stole a glance at our table.

After a few more angry volleys, Abby quickly flashed with embarrassment and turned cold silent. Then she shook her head, stood up, and walked out, her fork still jabbed into a tomato and the salad only half-eaten. I put money on the table before our sandwiches even arrived, the woman at the other table looking at me, no longer trying to be subtle. When I reached the sidewalk, Abby was gone. We spent the day separated from each other in the city. I ascended the Space Needle by myself. And we never made love out West.

It added to the allure of home, for both of us. Before the trip, all I'd wanted was to drive through the mountains and across the enormous expanses of sagebrush on their leeward sides—the *West*. But as we approached Michigan, the pale green fields, even in July drought, looked lovely, and without any mountains the horizon again felt properly distant. Adventure was replaced by the instinctive push toward familiar comforts, including our bed and our bodies in it.

We were both too tired for anything that night. I just wanted to make it home by eight, to drink a beer, watch the All-Star Game, and sprawl out on the basement beanbag chair that smelled like cat piss. But construction through Chicago slowed us, and the game, on the car radio, moved to the fourth inning. We didn't hit Grand Rapids until dusk. During the final hour, Abby reclined her seat and closed her eyes. She talked some more about starting a family. It was the same daydream she'd invented before, of moving to a suburb a little north or east of town, into a bigger house. My home office took up the second bedroom now, and the third was too small for a child. Our school district wasn't great, and we lived on the corner of a busy street, where training-wheeled bikes and stray basketballs were too dangerous.

As we finally neared our street, Abby leaned forward and looked for our home as if it was a lighthouse and we were approaching some shore.

"What's all that by the curb?" she asked.

"Where?"

"By the streetlight." She pointed. "God, what'd Cornelius plant flowers or something?"

"Is it the garbage?" I'd lost track of the days.

"No, today's Tuesday," she said. "It's not garbage."

We pulled into the narrow driveway, and as we passed the streetlight, Abby twisted around in her seat, catching her chin on the seat belt until she slipped her arm through the harness and unbuckled it. The evening was creeping quickly from blue to gray, and I didn't get a good look at the curb as we passed. I put the car into park, and Abby was out before I turned the engine off. I followed her down the driveway to the worthless strip of grass between the street and the sidewalk, the strip good only for streetlights, fire hydrants, and stop signs.

Abby didn't say anything when she got there. Instead, she crouched down and wrapped her arms around her knees, immediately tumbling into grief.

A mound of white tulips and lilies slumped against the streetlight. Three white balloons were tied around the pole, bobbing to a breeze I hadn't noticed before. Rising up through the flowers was a little white cross, made of two thin paint stirring sticks. They were nailed together and planted in our lawn. Down the post of the cross, someone had written the name SAMANTHA in black paint, the H and the final A written small and sloppily because they'd run out of room. On the horizontal stick, the person had painted two black hearts.

I felt as though I was trespassing, that it wasn't our house any more. "Wow," I said. I meant it to sound differently. Like her, I was in awe, shock. *My God. Wow.* But it came out somehow playful sounding, and Abby turned and looked up at me, a hint of that Seattle disgust returning to her eyes. I looked away from her stare and focused on the cross. I wanted her to see me, to see my respect.

Other artifacts were scattered around the foot of the cross: a bag of jelly beans, a pair of mud-stained running spikes with the laces tied in perfectly circular bows, an orange-and-black varsity letter from Ottawa Hills High School, a framed photograph—a senior picture—showing a dark-haired girl smiling in a blue top and white shorts, sitting on the white sand in front of the lighthouse at the Grand Haven pier. There were also little squares of folded paper, strewn like a fallen deck of cards. Ink bled through some of them, as if they'd gotten wet from dew or nearby sprinklers. One of them was drenched, and in huge letters, the shadow of the words leaked through the outside of the paper: U R MISSED!!!

"Does this mean she died right here?" asked Abby, pointing at the curb. "Like, on our property, while we were gone? She *died* here?"

"I guess," I said. I reached out my hand to touch one of the white balloons, but then pulled it back, worrying that it might burst at my touch. "What do we do with all this?"

A screen door clicked shut across the street. Our eighty-year-old neighbor, Cornelius Quist, descended his front stoop and walked in our direction. He'd fed the cat and collected the mail while we were gone, and although we'd told him not to trouble with it, it was obvious by the short, green blades that he'd watered our lawn and trimmed it with his old push mower. He wore a white tank top and blue shorts and cradled his old dachshund, Frank, in his thin, white arms. The moon was now out above our tree-lined street, and it waded above Cornelius in that river of sky, along sycamore banks.

"Hello kids," he said softly. "How was your trip?"

We didn't say anything.

"How was your homecoming?" he asked, looking down at the cross. "Yeah, a girl died. Two days after you left."

Abby sighed and fingered the stem of a tulip. I nodded at him and was aware of my own face. I could visualize it: eyebrows too angled, lips too narrow. My concern probably looked phony. I could never express sincerity, even when it was sincere.

"From what I hear, she was walkin' her dog," said Cornelius. "It was about as dark as now, and she crossed from my side of the street to yours. Truck full of boys turned the corner goin' way too fast and hit her. Never saw her. One was the Maddux boy a few houses down." He stared at the wobbling white balloons and gave Frank a pat. "Dog was fine."

I turned and looked at a yellow two-story a short distance away—the Maddux house. The garage door was shut, and an oscillating sprinkler sent an arc of water over the sidewalk, and then eased back, over the grass, then straight up, falling in on itself, before making another arc that splashed the bay window at the front of the house.

"I don't want this in my yard," said Abby. She stood up and was smiling a little, the way she smiled from her claustrophobia on airplanes as the panic crept in. Then she shook her head. "I don't want it. It's like a cemetery." She took a few steps back toward our house before turning back toward Cornelius and me and kneeling down by the sidewalk again.

"No drugs. No booze. Truck just missed sight of her," said Cornelius. "Shame."

"Yeah," I said.

"You said it was going too fast," said Abby. She looked up at Cornelius. "Right? That's what you said?"

"That's what I said."

"Then maybe that's why it 'just missed sight of her.'"

Cornelius scratched Frank's ears. "Maybe I should've called you when it happened."

"No," I said. "It's fine."

"I didn't want to ruin your trip and have you worryin' about somethin' you couldn't do anything about." He looked over at Abby. "I know you said call in an emergency, but I couldn't tell if this was one or not. For you two."

"It's fine," I said.

"Have a lot of people been over here?" asked Abby.

"Police and ambulance, of course. Probably lawyers behind all of them. And over the days since it happened, lots of family and teenagers. Lots of cryin'. Lots of flowers."

The three of us stared down at the shrine.

"Thanks for everything, Cornelius," I said, letting him know he could leave. "The lawn looks nice."

"Here," he said. He shifted Frank onto his left arm while his right hand dug into his pocket. "Your keys. Mail's on the kitchen counter. Cat only hissed at me a little. And the dehumidifier was workin' fine, so no worries there." He made a ticking sound with his tongue, tapping his fingers onto Frank's back to the same beat. "I think that's it."

"Thanks again." I took the keys.

Cornelius smiled weakly and crossed the street toward his house, holding Frank's paw in his hand and making the dog wave goodbye to Abby. She smiled, but forced it to disappear. "I'll be back out in a few minutes to haul stuff out of the car," she said to me.

"Where are you going?"

"I'm gonna call my mom. And then I'm gonna call some flower shops."

"Why? Wait, they'll be closed."

She unlocked the side door of the house, stepped inside, and shut the door.

I looked at the shrine again. Poking up through the flowers and folded letters were several long grass blades, tangled like strands of uncombed hair. Cornelius hadn't gotten too close with his push mower. The streetlight was now on overhead, and the balloons and the cross glowed orange. A few days earlier I'd seen several of these crosses, little markers of tragedy that always made my foot move toward the brake pedal. Driving through northern Montana, on a steep, curving Highway 89 through the Blackfeet Indian Reservation, small, white crosses on metal poles were planted along many of the curves, where a guardrail might be. Sometimes, just a single cross hovered above the ground. At other sections of the road, five or six were clustered in a triangular bunch, like grapes, bright against the bark of aspens, the same trees the cars may have struck. All of the crosses were identical in shape and size and were mounted on identical poles. They were prefabricated products, and I wondered how many of them were ordered in advance of the actual deaths. Were there a hundred other crosses stored and waiting in some shed or a volunteer's garage, set aside for the next hundred accidents in those hills?

I decided to leave the luggage in the car overnight; I was sick of looking at it. I walked to the garage, opened the door, and got my gas-powered weed trimmer. It was late now, and little kids were probably asleep on our street, but I grabbed it with both hands and walked with it anyway, to the narrow strip of grass that no one but the city really owned, although it was in front of my home.

I wondered if Abby was really inside calling flower shops, trying to make the house hers again with a dozen white roses, the yellow pages open in front of her as the phone rang and rang on the other end and nobody answered.

I approached the flowers that surrounded the cross. I'd bought enough flowers for Abby over the years to know that certain types, like carnations and daisies, could easily last over a week, but tulips and lilies like the ones there in the grass lasted only a couple of days before drying and fading to brown.

All of these were fresh. They were probably left that morning, and those from the day before had been gathered up and thrown out. I imagined sitting in my living room over the coming weeks and seeing people through my window, out by the sidewalk, grieving on my front lawn. I hoped that someone would take the cross down soon, but I knew that when a kid died, the crosses stayed a long time and maybe rotted into the ground over the years. And even then, people still left flowers.

I heard something a few doors down. A silhouette under a porch light walked from the front door of the Maddux house to the bushes. Metal squeaked against metal, and the patter of the sprinkler, which had been so gentle as to be imperceptible, was followed by a silence that now loomed in the new night. Mrs. Maddux, walking gingerly through the stones in her stocking feet, stepped out from behind the bushes and quickly slipped back inside the house, shut the heavy front door, and turned the porch light off.

I leaned the weed trimmer against my leg and pushed the primer bulb several times. I pulled the starter cord, and the engine rumbled but didn't catch. The front door of our house opened behind me, and I turned to see Abby, shadowy from standing on the other side of the screen. She didn't ask what I was doing, but watched as I pulled the cord a few more times and got the trimmer to roar and overwhelm the neighborhood's stillness. A plume of exhaust rose up around my head. I stepped toward the shrine, self-conscious with Abby behind me but glad that she was there, to see me taking care of the cross and all that surrounded it. Then I focused my attention on the long, sad strands of grass and trimmed them, careful not to nick the cross, shred the squares of folded paper, or bruise one petal of that day's flowers.

AFTER THE RECESSIONS

for John Crouse

The beaches were too big. I couldn't tell at the time there was any-thing wrong—Henry had yet to enlighten me—but as I approached on the deck of the *Emerald Isle*, I stared for a time at the island's thick, sandy skin. In other years the deep green of the trees might have easily, from a distance, blended into the blue of the water. But today that wide, white membrane of sand defined the boundaries of land, lake, and sky, while at the same time inching gradually, in all directions, toward the mainland.

The *Emerald Isle* was a slow-moving car ferry that, I'd heard, was the newer and swifter of the company's two-boat fleet. It was painted white and green with a shamrock on the smokestack. Irish and American flags flew from small poles at the stern, and the wind was so brisk that they remained taut and rectangular for most of the two-hour trip from Charlevoix to Beaver Island.

The sky was a clear, flat blue. In no way did it resemble the lake. Whitecaps cracked like rough glass against the side of the ferry, which rose and dropped in great surges. I'd only seen the lake like this a couple of times, and then, only under darkening skies at the onset of storms. It seemed to have taken the guise of something salt-water—huge and dangerous—reminding me of a whale-watching trip I'd taken two years ago with my ex-fiancée, Olivia, on Monterrey Bay. The whales had come remarkably close to the boat, surfacing and then plunging so that they splashed the tourists taking pictures.

But the two of us had barely seen them. We were vomiting over the railing and then rummaging for loose change to buy cans of Sprite from a vending machine in the cabin.

This time I was out of change, so I sat on an outdoor bench on the second deck, breathing the fresh air and staring at a fixed point on the horizon. I thought of Olivia, and the sudden starkness of my house, and how I hadn't realized how much of the furniture had actually been hers until she took it with her. I'd started hanging posters of baseball and football players on my bare walls, as I had in junior high. I'd bought a card table and steel folding chairs. It was not what most expected from one recently promoted from illustrator to art director.

The ferry was crowded with end-of-summer travelers. Few of them spoke. Many held tight to handrails, resting an open hand over their stomachs or swallowing their saliva repeatedly. A few rows in front of me, a group of students from Michigan State with baseball caps and hooded sweatshirts passed around a stainless-steel flask, looking sick, all of them, but drinking anyway.

I hoped Henry and Jo had some Maalox or Pepto-Bismol when I got to the island, but I doubted it. They had no medicine cabinet. They had no house. I hadn't seen them since their wedding, which had come only a month after Henry, along with half of Ivey and Associates, had been laid off. I'd packed a pillow and a sleeping bag because we'd be sleeping in tents.

I'd worked with Henry for five years and we'd become friends. He and Jo would have Olivia and me over for dinner every couple of months. They were like an aunt and uncle. Olivia and Jo shopped for bridal gowns together.

Their invitation had come by postcard. On the front was an aerial view of the island—almost all of it cloaked in trees—and on the back, Henry's heavily slanted scrawl: *Care to visit God's country?—H.* He'd written nothing else except for a P.O. box number. He insisted we communicate through letters. The obvious reason was that he had no phone, but it was more than that. I could already tell he was distancing himself from what he called "the mainland," which was not, to him, simply the land, but its people, technologies, and pace of life. He was probably so distant that he hadn't heard I was the one promoted to his old position at the agency.

An elderly employee of the boat company emerged from the lower deck with an aluminum pole wrapped in blue nylon cradled under his arm. His neatly trimmed white mustache added to the dignity of his walk across the rolling deck, and he moved with perfect cadence, never stumbling or extending his arms out to the side for balance. No one else seemed to notice him, lost as they were in the worlds of their own nausea. He approached the back railing, next to the flag poles, and pulled the American flag from its bracket. Then, without holding on to anything, he unfurled the blue nylon roll, revealing the elk and the moose and the entire state flag of Michigan. The new pole dropped securely into the bracket with a metallic click, and the flag made a few sharp whipping sounds as the wind pressed against it. The man rolled the American flag up and placed it under his arm, while the state flag stretched into a perfect rectangle beside its Irish twin.

I pulled my wallet out of my back pocket, hoping for at least a dollar bill. I wanted a Sprite. One would think the new art director of Ivey and Associates would have some cash on hand. Olivia wouldn't have been fooled. Instead, I had plastic: identifications, a security key card that got me into the office, five credit cards. Each time I received a paycheck, Olivia had described me as a little boy with his First Communion money, eyes huge with the sight of it and, a week later, surrounded by a new batch of toys. She'd paid all our bills. I put the wallet back in my pocket, swallowed my spit, and stared at the horizon.

A half hour later the ferry arced to the west, passing the old white brick of the Harbor Light at Whiskey Point, and entered St. James Bay. I learned all of these names later, from Henry. At first sight, I felt a subtle tug of what he must have felt on some far greater scale, the calm waters of the bay like cupped hands, welcoming and protecting all those in need of rest. He would have said we were just two in a long line, from Indians to Mormons to Irish fishermen. And I would have rolled my eyes at him.

The ferry approached the docks. In 1856, the Mormons were driven off the island here, by a mob that was supported by speculators who had their eyes on the green land and ample fishing. Henry had absorbed all of the island's history, made it his own, and spread this new knowledge like gospel. I stood up and walked to the end of the deck, looking for him and Jo. A small group of islanders watched us come in, alongside another, larger group lined up beside a yellow chain with luggage at their feet, ready to return home.

People around me stood as well, reinvigorated by the decreasing speed, the calmer waters, and the approaching land. The ferry finally drifted up to the docks, and young men in green polo shirts and khaki shorts hustled to secure the boat to the docks and get the steel staircase in place. I lined up in a sudden crush of people and made my way down. As I descended, I looked out at the small crowd of islanders again, and this time spotted them.

"Marcus Furey!" shouted Henry. "The golden child of the mainland returns!"

I walked toward him, smiling, and shook his hand. "What do you mean 'returns'?" I asked. "I've never been here before."

"But it doesn't feel that way, does it? Admit it, it's like you've come home."

He wore an old T-shirt that said PEACOCK TAVERN, one I'd seen on him before, although the words seemed stretched across his belly more than usual. His denim shorts revealed skinny but deeply tanned legs. I stared at his eyes for a moment, looking for some sign that he knew about my promotion and was being—in even the slightest way—falsely pleasant. There was none.

Jo stepped toward me and wrapped her arms around my neck in a maternal hug. Her hair was still cut short, except for the bangs, which blew forward and backward in the swirling wind. "My surrogate nephew," she said loudly, and then, in a whisper to my ear, "How are you?" She meant since Olivia had left.

"I'm fine," I said, nodding and smiling. "A little seasick. It took forever to get here."

"You know that boat can go a hell of a lot faster," said Henry. "But they're only allowed to top out at fifteen miles an hour. Don't wanna make it too easy to get here."

Jo wore sunglasses, and she dabbed a finger underneath one of the lenses, drying a tear. A distorted, embarrassed smile surfaced. "You're seasick? We'll go to the store and get you something. I used to have pills and such in my purse, but I don't carry around my purse any more."

"It's fine," I said.

"Look at her, Marcus," said Henry, "all motherly and such. Been like this since I made an honest woman of her."

I'd been to their wedding that spring. It was Henry's second marriage, and his son, who was my age, served as best man. Jo had never been married before, and her father gave her away at the ceremony. He was frail and gray but jubilant. At the reception, with the rest of us watching silently from the environs of the dance floor, he smiled and cried while he led her in dance to "The Way You Look Tonight." It was a lovely day and evening, and would have been perfect were it not for the guilty look on Jo's face every time we made eye contact. Olivia had broken off our engagement only a month earlier, around the time of Henry's layoff.

The three of us began wandering back toward the boat, looking for the luggage.

"We're glad you could come for a couple of days," said Jo, "especially in the middle of the week."

"I got some extra vacation," I said, and then realized I'd showed my cards. The extra days had come with the promotion. "Hey, I get some rest and I get to see you two. Killing two birds."

"We'll kill more than that this weekend," said Henry. "We'll kill all those mainland demons of work and worry hangin' over a man's head."

"Has it helped you?" I asked.

"Are you kidding? Really, are you kidding? Look at me." He extended his arms and turned in a tight circle, like a model showing off a gown. "I'm the epitome of the resuscitated man. Guys your age are coming up to me and asking how I got my healthy glow."

I set my open palm over his belly. "How far along are you? I think I can feel the little one kicking."

Jo laughed, and Henry playfully pushed my hand away and patted himself. "That's what happens on a diet of milk and honey. Jo finds it sexy."

"Incredibly," she said. She placed her hand on his back and gently rubbed it.

Porters began wheeling carts of luggage down a ramp. As we approached, Henry took a slim silver case out of his pocket. He removed a cigarette and set it in his lips, among his gray beard and the subtle yellow stains around the edges of his mouth. As he smoked, he pointed at the ferry. "That boat," he said, exhaling, "that boat carries a lot of people with just one-way tickets. They sail to Valhalla and want no more part of purgatory." He patted me on the shoulder. "Twenty-four hours from now you'll be like a citizen of this place. You'll be chaining yourself to The Big Rock to keep the mainland from pulling you back."

I found my backpack and sleeping bag among the carts. Beyond them, on the other side of a chain barrier, cars began rolling out of the belly of the ferry.

"Oh fuckhell," said Henry.

I looked at him and then followed his sightline, to the car ramp, where two Michigan State Police cruisers had emerged among the minivans and SUVs. They were a deep, dark blue, almost black. Darker than the color of the flag.

"What?" I asked.

Henry and Jo seemed not to hear me. His head was lowered as he shook it slowly, and she spoke to him with her lips almost touching his ear. "It's okay," she said, and she began rubbing his back again.

"God, why today?" said Henry.

"It'll be fine."

"Why did they have to come today, with Marcus here?" He snuffed out his cigarette on the pavement and then dropped it back into the silver case. "I can't believe I didn't notice the flag."

"Neither can I," said Jo. "But that's because we're distracted by the prospect of good times." She looked at me, smiled, and spoke louder. "Right, Marcus? Good times?"

"The best," I said. "What's going on?"

"Later," said Henry.

"Let's head to the Jeep," said Jo.

"Oh," said Henry to me, visibly brightening, "you gotta see my truck. I've got bumper stickers. I designed them and had my old buddy Wally Whitehead at Elmore Printing make a run of five hundred for almost nothing. He owed me a favor. You can get them at most of the bars or stores on the island."

We approached Henry's green Jeep, which, like most of the cars and trucks in the lot, had a thick coat of brown dust on its lower half. Henry guided me to the back bumper. There were two identical black-and-white stickers reading THE BILL OF RIGHTS: VOID WHERE PROHIBITED BY THE MICHIGAN STATE POLICE.

"It's a little wordy," he said, "but I think it gets the point across. I know the cops have read it."

"We can only hope," said Jo.

The three of us climbed into the Jeep, with me and my gear

in the back seat. Henry started the engine and began to pull out of the lot.

"Better put your seatbelt on," Jo said to him.

"Christ, you're right." He pulled the harness over his belly and clicked it into place. I looked out the window at the little main street. The buildings had rectangular facades like those of Western ghost towns. Trucks with canoes or rowboats tied to their roofs were parked along the shoulders. We passed the office of the Beaver Island Boat Company. A man stood out front at a tall flagpole, pulling at the ropes and raising a blue state flag, which instantly unfurled in a gust of wind.

·

The island's dirt roads were narrow. Trees and ditches came close to the car. Henry drove down the middle because of the deer that had recently bounded in front of him.

"This is The King's Highway," he said, "named for James Strang, head of America's only monarchy. Mormon separatist. Self-proclaimed King of Zion. Killed by a couple of men of his own flock who didn't like all the wives he was keeping."

It mattered little that we drove down the middle of the road because there was hardly any traffic. Whenever he did pass a car going in the opposite direction, Henry lifted two of his fingers off the top of the steering wheel in a little wave, and the driver of the other car almost always did the same.

"Do you know him?" I asked after he passed a red pickup.

"I don't think so. But I know most of the locals. The year-round ones at least."

A short ways later, a blue Geo Tracker passed us, and the driver, a young woman, was reclining with her bare left foot propped up and sticking out of the open window. Henry waved with his fingers, but then said, "Now that was a Yuppie. Anyone driving a Geo Tracker on the island is automatically a Yuppie because those

are the only cars you can rent here. Weekend warriors. Not locals."
He reached into his pocket for his slim silver case. "Plus, she didn't
wave."

I didn't say anything. I wondered if I was a Yuppie.

Jo removed the Jeep's lighter and held it in front of Henry's cigarette. The weekend was full of these simple newlywed acts. "The
cops see that bare foot of hers," she said, "they're bound to give her
a ticket."

"Honey, you're preachin' to the deacon." Henry inhaled from
the cigarette and blew smoke out his nose. "Did you see them flyin'
the state flag at the boat company?"

I leaned forward so that my head was between the two of theirs.
"They put it out on the boat while we were coming over. Do you
know why?"

"Do I know why. Jo, do I know why?"

Jo slowly shook her head. "Oh, he knows. The question is
whether you want to. It's a can of snakes few dare open around
Henry."

He glanced back at me. "Marcus, let me tell you something
about the Michigan State Police."

It was a favorite line of his. "Let me tell you something about
exercise. Let me tell you something about professional wrestling.
Let me tell you something about the Dutch."

"The Michigan State Police," he went on, "have for the last year
been conducting what can only be called an inquisition."

"At least, Henry can only call it that," said Jo.

"Don't give me that. You're on my side. You and Arnie and
most everyone else on the island." He glanced at me again. "The
cops are stickin' in their noses. It's hard to explain. You'll see by the
end of this trip. There's a reason this place was once its own king-
dom. People here feel separate from everyone else."

Jo looked back at me. "The flag is raised as a favor by the boat
company. It lets everyone know the coppers have arrived."

Henry made a turn in a crunch of gravel under tires. "Sloptown Road. Here's our neck of the woods." And it really was woods. The trees were close on both sides, arcing overhead, blocking out parts of the blue sky. Then, to our left, the land opened up to fields with scattered apple trees. Two horses grazed in a field. To the right was a dense mix of evergreens and hardwoods, except for a small clearing with a dirt driveway leading to a large square of cement. We pulled into the driveway.

"Foundation, sweet foundation," said Henry.

We parked and climbed out of the Jeep, and I surveyed their land. A short ways ahead, among the trees, were two small tents and one larger one with side flaps drawn up to reveal a screened-in card table, chairs, and a cooler. Closer to the road were stumps, a fire pit, a fallen log with the numbers 28245 spray-painted on the side. It must have been the address of the house that wasn't built. And near the driveway stood a giant wooden sculpture of a beaver.

"I see you're admiring Bruce," said Jo. "He was a wedding gift from our friend Arnie." Right there—I saw her tense when she said "wedding," as if it would offend me. "Arnie lives a couple of miles from here. You'll have to meet him. He knows a guy who knows a guy who does sculpture with tree trunks and chainsaws. Hence, Bruce."

I approached him and ran my hand over his large, flat tail. "He's a delight."

Henry walked slowly to the center of the cement square. Cinder blocks rose two-high around the edges, except for a wide space in the front and a smaller gap where a door would probably go. He turned to me, smiling and gesturing luxuriously. "If you imagine an invisible house standing here," he said, "and, like a tree, it's been cut down and we're looking now at the growth rings, this, right here," he pointed at the cement, "this is where you can see the exact moment when they laid me off."

"Henry," said Jo, shaking her head. I said nothing.

"What?" he asked. "It's not a bad thing. True, I wish this invisible house were actually visible. That we were sleeping in a king-sized bed instead of tents, bathing in a warm tub instead of knockin' on Arnie's door or hosing ourselves down at the carwash. But, as I've said, early retirement," he patted his belly, "has been very, very good to me."

Henry had never mentioned their financial troubles to me. Earlier in the summer, it had been Jo who phoned—eager to unburden herself through conversation—and told me about their disappearing retirement fund and the temporary halt to home construction. They'd sold their house in Grand Rapids and were camping on their land and sometimes staying at a local motel at a reduced rate; Henry was friends with the manager. When the weather cooled, they'd be renting a small guest house on Arnie's property. I'd been promoted earlier that week, but during the phone call, I never mentioned it to her.

I walked toward Henry and stared at the foundation. "There's no basement?"

"That's the garage," said Jo. "Or will be. The workers never got started on the actual house."

Henry had his back to us. He stooped down, picked up a rock, and hurled it into the trees. He was silent for a stretch.

"Do you mind if I wander around?" I asked.

"Be our guest," said Jo. "We started hacking through the brush a few weeks ago to blaze a trail. In time, it'll wind through all ten acres."

I turned to her. "Do you wanna come?"

"I'll stay here a bit," she said, stepping slowly toward Henry.

I nodded and walked to the trailhead. The shade in the woods was darker than I'd expected, the trees close together and the taller ones rustling furiously, their canopies rocking in the wind. The trail was narrow but clear of all roots and stumps. It went about a hundred yards, coiling between large beeches and aspens, before

coming to an abrupt end at a fallen log. I tried to press ahead, bending and snapping branches where the trail might someday run. But
the brush was too thick—pine needles pricked my skin and thorns
snagged my clothes—so I turned and walked back toward Henry's
naked foundation.

•

He was leaning against the Jeep when I emerged from the woods.
His smile had returned, and his silence had passed. "Wanna see
some sights?"

"Of course," I said. "What do we have time for?"

He opened the driver's side door. "Hell, we're on Island Time
now. There's time for everything."

The three of us rumbled down dirt roads again. "Do you like
big things?" asked Jo.

"Well, I like Bruce," I said.

After a few minutes of driving Henry pulled onto the shoulder
of Fox Lake Road beside a slouching mass of stone. There were no
signs marking the place, no bronze plaques, but Jo insisted this was
one of the island's most famous landmarks. We got out. "This is
The Big Rock," she said. There were no other sizable rocks nearby,
nor cliffs or outcrops. It was a remnant of the last glacial period, but
seemed more like a gray, egg-shaped meteorite, about ten feet high
and longer across, that had fallen to the island. It was worn smooth
in patches from the hands and feet of climbers.

"They say two thirds of it's underground," said Henry, "like a
granite iceberg." He bent down and touched his toes in a motion
that wasn't meant to look comical, but did. "You need a running
start to scale it."

He ran, climbed, and slowed almost to a stop halfway up, but
then pumped his arms, his thin legs a blur of tanned skin, and
reached the top. I followed quickly behind him and was ashamed
at the ease with which I ascended.

"Stay there," said Jo, "let me get my camera." She removed it from the Jeep's glove compartment and sized us up through the viewfinder. We flexed our muscles. "You two look so small on that thing. My little men." She took our picture.

We got back in the Jeep, where Jo offered me some crackers. I shook my head; the dips and bumps from riding in the back seat had unsettled my stomach again. As he pulled back into the road, Henry looked back and winked at me. "Now for the next big thing."

If the rock was a monument to the earth, then our next stop was a testament to the sky. In a sunny clearing, set apart from the brown bark of maples and cedars a little ways off, a white birch caught the light and towered to a staggering height for such a species. Its trunk was really five trunks, like fingers of a white hand, each twice as wide as anyone standing beside it. It seemed to spring from some northwoods mythology.

"That's what I mean," said Henry as we walked toward it. "That's what I mean about this place. You plant yourself on this island, you drink its water, you breathe its air, and look what happens. You rise up and find yourself closer to heaven."

There was a weathered sign that read ISLAND'S OLDEST BIRCH—PLEASE DO NOT DEFACE. I posed by it, and Jo took more pictures. I wanted copies of these. I'd always loved birches and had a daydream of planting one in my yard after the birth of each of my future children. I'd never mentioned this to anyone, including Olivia. I loved the skin of the trees and was tempted to pull it in long strips, leaving tender orange scars like the flesh under a scab. But my grandfather, who'd had a large one growing in his front yard, warned me of their delicacy, so I always refrained.

I wanted to climb this huge tree the way I'd scaled my grandfather's—teeter on its highest branches in this wind—but soon Henry was corralling us back to the Jeep, excited about showing me more of the island's wonders. He started the engine and reached around to a grocery bag in the back seat by my feet. He removed a can of LaBatt, opened it, and began pouring it into an empty travel mug one would normally use for coffee. "In the past, people didn't hide such things," he said. "As long as it was never in excess, people drove around with an open can, or set up lawn chairs and coolers in the back of pick-up trucks and made their own parades. But with the blue flag flyin', we have to be more cautious."

There was a quick succession of sights: the Protar Home, the Old Beaver Head Lighthouse, huge stretches of the Jordan River Forest. One road came to a dead end at the north arm of Lake Genesareth. "I wanna show you something else," said Henry. "I take no pleasure in this sight."

To my eye—my mainland eye—there was nothing extraordinary. Trees and water and sky: a postcard panorama. The lake was quiet except for two distant fishermen in a rowboat sitting with their backs to each other.

Henry stepped toward the shore and stopped a few feet short of the waterline. "Notice anything?" He faced Jo and me and lifted his knees over and over as if marching in place. His shoes made loud suction noises as he pulled them up from the mud underneath. "A couple of years ago I'd have been knee-deep in blue right now. The water levels are sinking like stones." He spit and looked out at the lake again. "It's like this everywhere. The big lake's got it the worst."

I didn't say anything or think much of it. Lake levels rose and fell. More rain one year. Less snow the next. But Henry looked uneasy.

"One more stop," he said, "and we'll call it a day."

He drove us around the south end of the island while the late-summer evening seeped in. My eyes grew heavy in the back seat, and my appetite began to return. Sleep, even in a tent, was an alluring thought. I yawned as we got out at Henry's final destination, which was a flat stretch of brown muck, puddled in a few areas. If Henry had meant to show me water, he'd failed. "This is Miller's Marsh," he said, "named after Harrison 'Tip' Miller, the old lighthouse keeper at Beaver Head. Take a good look."

"Miller's Mud," said Jo.

"Exactly." He stepped closer to where the tall grasses gave way to the gray mud. Driftwood was scattered everywhere on the empty marshbed, like little ships broken and run aground. "Be careful. You could lose a shoe in this stuff."

The mud was supposed to be a lesson of some sort, but its significance was lost on me. Then Henry spoke some more.

"Big ships can't dock in Chicago. There's problems with tankers passing through the Soo Locks. They may even have to dredge here at the island so the ferries can come in." He picked up a long, thin piece of driftwood and stabbed it into the mud so that it stood there like a sword or a cross, marking something sacred. He seemed then to change the subject from water levels, although perhaps it was all one subject. "In the short time since we've sold the house and moved up here, they've started paving roads, building things like gas stations and gaudy convenience stores, and the cops—well, I'll plead the fifth."

Jo hooked her arm under his and began leading him to the Jeep. "If the water keeps dropping and the ferries can't come, then neither can the cops."

"Or the Yuppies," I said, walking behind them.

Henry smiled a little. "Let's go. I'm hungry."

An hour later there was a fire going in their pit that he'd made with a few oak cords, a bed of brittle leaves, and his cigarette lighter. The wood was dry and caught flame effortlessly. I noticed that the wind had finally died down. Jo set a steel grate from an old charcoal grill over the fire pit and then placed three great steaks on top of it. The sun had set, and the new night was dark in the way I remembered childhood nights being.

When the steaks were almost finished, Jo walked off into the woods to pee. Henry and I were silent, staring into the fire, until he said quietly, "I don't know if you've been walkin' on eggshells or what, but I know about your promotion. I keep in contact with some of the guys back at Ivey. And I think it's great. I know they were cutting dead weight—or at least, older weight with higher salaries. I know that youth is cheaper. But you're talented as hell. And I'm glad to be free of such shackles. Let's eat this meat and celebrate."

The meal was not the most relaxing I've had, filled instead with thoughts of whether Henry meant what he said, if he preferred his life on the island, if he was so adaptable to change as he claimed. The mood darkened further as he talked more about the cops. A woman was ticketed for driving a golf cart that wasn't deemed street legal. Two middle-aged twins, Marvel and Johnny Fitzgerald, received DUIs within forty-eight hours of each other, and now both rode around on bright red mopeds. And Henry, about a few weeks earlier, had been pulled over for driving down the middle of the road, although it was nighttime and foggy and he'd worried about deer. He'd escaped a ticket, but that mattered little.

Above, there were stars I hadn't seen since those deep child-hood nightfalls. In that quiet I could understand Henry's love of the place and imagine myself returning to the island some day and staying. A short time later came a silver moon—nearly full—that crested the black tree line. It cast shadows like a sun, and its light drowned out the stars until it had the sky to itself.

•

My eyes opened to the silhouettes of insects on the outside of the tent and the sound of cracking branches and rustling leaves. There was no wind. The blue nylon of the tent was bright with sunlight, already warming the inside where I slept. I was stiff from sleeping on the earth and struggled out of my sleeping bag, unzipped the tent, and stuck my head outside. The sweatsuit I wore had holes and paint stains on it, and I could feel, without touching it, that my hair was sticking up in all places. The island itself made me not care. I walked toward the sounds I heard in the woods.

I followed the trail to the fallen log that, yesterday, marked the trail's end. The log now lay collapsed in its center, resting in a pile of sawdust. A saw lay at Henry's feet. In his hands was an enormous blade—a machete—that caught slivers of sun that had found their way through the trees. Jo heard me approaching and turned around. She held a pair of pruning shears. A circle of sweat darkened her shirt between her breasts.

"Good morning," she said.

I nodded and gave a weak salute with my right hand. "What time is it?"

"About nine. We're ready to take a break here and visit a friend of ours for coffee. You're welcome to come. Or you can borrow the Jeep and explore on your own a little."

"Take the Jeep," said Henry, his back to me. He raised the machete and assaulted the brush. "Connie's a nice woman, but she's a bit crazy. Smokes a lot of weed and likes to hit on young men. Take cover."

Jo smirked and shook her head. "She's a delightful person. Teaches kindergarten in Traverse City and she's heading back tomorrow. The island's just her summer home."

I didn't fear Connie, but the prospect of time alone appealed to me. There were sights that we hadn't gotten to yesterday, including an old Catholic cemetery that Henry had mentioned. Most of the dead were Irish, and I wanted to look for "Furey" among the stones.

I changed my clothes and put on a baseball cap. Henry drew me a primitive map of the island, including directions on how to get to the carwash, should I choose to take a cold shower. ("Beware the underbody spray," he told me.) He then explained the way to the cemetery. I opted not to shower. Again, the island made me not care, and I took this as a good thing.

As I was about to leave, Henry dangled the keys out in front of me. I reached for them, and he snatched them back and grinned. "Be careful of the fuzz. I think they work off commission."

I grabbed the keys. "Enjoy your coffee," I said and walked to the Jeep. Jo handed me a granola bar and said they'd take me out for lunch in a few hours. Then I left them, the Jeep kicking up light brown clouds of dust that made Henry and Jo evaporate in my rearview mirror.

I headed north on The King's Highway, back in the direction of St. James and the harbor that Henry said was getting shallower. I never saw the two police cruisers, and the entire discussion of them began to feel like a rising paranoia, a conspiracy theory that Henry fueled with talk the way he fueled his bonfire with oak. I did, however, pass a white Geo Tracker and, a short distance later, Marvel and Johnny Fitzgerald on their matching red mopeds. I turned when I saw the old rectory and the sign for Holy Cross Cemetery. I entered its open grounds of granite markers and scattered trees. There were no other people.

For a place so old, I expected more overgrowth. But most of the trees had been cut down, and yellow sunlight washed over the entire place. The grass was browning and dry from lack of shade and lack of rain. The older stones were of white marble, and they leaned or had sunk partially into the earth. These held the Irish names: Gallagher, Martin, Boyle. They were straightforward in their grieving, with etchings of birth dates and death dates and little else, except, for some, noting that the deceased had fallen victim to a particular shipwreck. The newer stones were larger and made of gray or pink granite. Pots of red geraniums hung from shepherd's hooks over the graves. I walked down the rows, scanning the names. I found no Fureys. I did, however, find a few newer stones with cryptic messages engraved on them. One said simply, I TOOK THE PICTURES, and another, I TOLD YOU I WAS SICK. They seemed to exhibit a kind of final self-gratification that I could imagine Henry requesting. His might say I LEAVE THIS HEAVEN FOR A LESSER ONE or I HAUNT STATE TROOPERS.

The pity and disgust I felt toward him then were mere sparks that didn't catch on anything—that were extinguished before they grew—and I was glad of that. The same was true of the self-pity and feelings of loss that things like headstones and broken engagements could bring about. But I wanted to leave the cemetery. I walked briskly back to the Jeep and drove off. My mental map of the island was limited, there were no road signs anywhere, and I didn't know how to get to any other new sights. I considered heading back into town, wandering along the docks. Instead, I retraced the route I remembered to the big birch.

Like on the day before, there were no other people there. No tourists, no islanders. The image of that leviathan tree had floated in my head since the day before, and the sight of it again surpassed even my memory of it. I parked the Jeep and approached. As I did, I looked in all directions to be sure I was alone. Then I climbed. I hadn't climbed a tree in maybe fifteen years and couldn't tell if it was my larger feet or greater weight that made this time such a struggle. I tried not to tear the paper bark as I ascended. Soon I was beyond the five large trunks and amid the medium-sized branches. I passed the point where I could fall from the tree without injury. But I climbed higher, until the branches became so thin they'd no longer support me. Then I stopped and peered through the openings between leaves. The view was beautiful but limited, and I imagined that, from the highest branches, Lake Michigan could be seen in all directions. It would look like a moat, separating the island from the mainlands of Michigan and Wisconsin, and it was visibly shrinking, as though an open drain was sucking it from beneath, until the moat would be something any invader—cop or Yuppie or art director—could easily traverse.

•

We were headed to Arnie's for dinner. He'd stopped by Connie's as well, had coffee with Henry and Jo, and invited them over for that evening. During the short drive to his place, Henry described him in a strange series of anecdotes.

"Arnie didn't know he was retired till he got here. Calls himself a pirate, although I'm not sure why. He moved up in the eighties and never looked back. Used to work in office furniture. Now he makes blades. Beautiful blades, like works of art. He made that machete you saw this morning, and I feel guilty using it. His knives are things you mount on walls like trophies or watercolors."

Jo turned to me and smiled. "He's divorced and his kids are grown, but when his daughter was young he took her through one of those haunted barns out in the country for Halloween. A guy in a gorilla suit jumped in front of them, and Arnie about wet himself. Then, boom. Uppercut. Gorilla out cold. Which is shocking, because Arnie's strong but such a sweetheart. The gentlest giant."

His house was a simple A-frame, and the property was wonderfully overgrown with black-eyed Susans, purple thistle, and goldenrod. A stone walkway led to the front door, running past a large, well-tended vegetable garden. Two robins splashed their wings in a birdbath, beside a hummingbird feeder and a small statue of what looked to be St. Francis of Assisi. Toward the back of his land was the little guest house where Henry and Jo would spend their winter.

We didn't knock. Henry simply opened the door and stepped inside. It was dark—all the blinds closed—with a fire in the stone fireplace. A small window air-conditioning unit was running. "Ooh," said Jo. "Ambience."

Two men sat on a leather sofa close to the fire. Their foreheads were damp with sweat. Cigarette smoke hung above them, but I couldn't smell it because of the chopped onions and garlic on the counter and the boiling pots on the stovetop.

One of the men stood up, towering to at least six-foot-three or -four. His beard was gray like Henry's, but the hair on his head was longer, touching his shoulders. "Welcome to the cave," he said, shaking my hand with both of his. He introduced himself and said, "Dinner will be served in about half an hour. Until then, you're all free to raid the wine rack. Nothing's too good for such good people."

The other man then stood up from the couch. He wore a sleeve-less flannel shirt and cut-off jeans. His hair was pulled back into a long black ponytail. "I'm off, Arnie. Call me tomorrow. We'll watch the game." He shook hands with Henry and Jo on his way out. "Good to see you two again. Been too long." He waved at me as he left.

"That was Drywall Frank," Henry whispered to me. "He's an Indian. Fishes waters the rest of us can't. He makes Arnie look like a Yuppie."

Jo selected a Merlot from Arnie's sprawling wine rack. It was built into the wall, as were the bookshelves, which covered half the perimeter of the house. Above me was a loft with a bed and more bookshelves. The rest of the small place seemed dominated by the kitchen, a beautiful showcase of wood and stainless steel with cop-per pots hanging from the ceiling. I expected a woman to emerge from somewhere in Arnie's home, but there was none.

Henry drank a glass of ice water, while Jo and I poured some wine and lounged beside the fire. I could feel the sweat rising to my skin. Henry picked up a paperback copy of *A River Runs Through It*, which, though worn and obviously read, lay diagonally on the coffee table for, I believe, decorative purposes. He flipped casually through its pages.

"So what have all you been up to?" asked Arnie. He stood at a butcher block, slicing tomatoes with a glinting knife.

Jo told him about the sights we'd seen together, lunch at The Shamrock, and our plans to relax on the beach the next morning before I left again on the *Emerald Isle*. The discussion soon turned to Miller's Marsh, the proposed dredging of the harbor, and the third consecutive summer drought.

"It's not just the rain and snow," said Jo. "We need colder winters. The lake doesn't freeze enough and then it evaporates too much."

Henry set the book back down on the coffee table. "I am haunted by recessions," he said.

Arnie cooked the way he crafted blades, so that the aesthetic beauty of the end result made its use—its consumption—seem a sin. We sat around a large oak table, and he began to serve us. There was mozzarella with tomato and fresh basil—from his garden—to start, and then the main course: fillet of beef with wild mushrooms, roasted potatoes with rosemary and whole garlic cloves, mixed greens, and French bread. We drained two bottles of Merlot and one of Burgundy, even without Henry, who drank water through the entire meal, claiming it kept him cool by that summertime fire. The three of them talked mainly of mutual friends I didn't know, but at one point Arnie apologized for excluding me from the conversation and asked what I did for a living.

"He was fooled into taking my old job," said Henry. "Only the young can be so easily jailed."

Jo soon changed the subject as quickly as she could. "There better not be a dessert, Arnie. I'll have to swim to the mainland to burn this off."

"There's two, actually. Your choice. Poached pears with vanilla ice cream and orange liqueur or, for a lighter taste, strawberry mousse."

"I've married the wrong man," she said.

We all smiled and looked at Henry, but he was staring across the room at the fire, not listening.

After dessert we moved to the sofa and lounge chairs and talked until two in the morning about the island's history and some of its colorful characters, past and present. I remember little, due to the wine, but I know there was no talk of anything mainland. We were warm and happy, except for Henry, who was stone sober and began talking about the cops again.

"Let me tell you something about how they operate. One of the cruisers hangs out behind The Shamrock. Then every time someone leaves they radio the other cruiser, who tails the person for a while—rides their ass—until, out of sheer intimidation, if nothing else, the person does something wrong and gets pulled over."

Arnie shook his head and laughed. "You need to lighten up, brother. This shit's eatin' you alive."

"You have no idea."

"You're a tortured soul, Henry."

"I have overcome the world," he said.

We decided to leave once Jo fell asleep by the smoldering fire. We thanked Arnie profusely, and as we walked through the door he said he'd meet us at the beach the next morning.

None of us talked during the drive back to our tents. Henry smoked with the window down while Jo's head drooped and bobbed against the window and then shot up again. I stared silently over Henry's shoulder, out the front window. There were clouds that night, and thus no moon. The night was dark in a way that made me feel completely and comfortably invisible. Then lights emerged from the far side of a hill, ambient at first, and then became two sharp headlights aimed at us. As it neared, Henry raised his fingers in a wave.

In the moment of its passing, in the exchange of illumination, we all saw it was a cruiser.

"Fuckhell," said Henry. I turned, looked through the back window, and saw a bright red burst of brakes.

There was a U-turn, great flashes of red and blue, but no

sounds—not sirens nor words from anyone inside the Jeep. There was not a shoulder to pull on to, so Henry let two tires dip into a ditch on the right side of the road, and we sat and waited with gravity pulling us to the passenger's side. The window was already down, so we could hear the trooper's footsteps over dirt and stones. He shined a light into the Jeep. "Please turn the engine off."

I couldn't see the man very well because of the bright light in our eyes, and his blue hat crept low down his forehead. "I did nothing," said Henry. "I did not speed. I did not swerve. And I have not had a drink since yesterday because I know how you work at night."

"I need to see your license and registration." Jo, with trembling hands, rifled through the glove compartment until she found them. The trooper looked them over and said, "I pulled you over for littering. You tossed a cigarette out your window as I passed, and in this weather, you could set all the forest ablaze."

Henry's head shook as if from convulsions. "What? You're lying." He reached into his shirt pocket.

"Stop!" yelled the cop, reaching back toward his belt. But then he saw Henry's silver cigarette case and relaxed.

"Look," said Henry. "He turned the case upside-down and three cigarette butts fell into his palm. "I put every cigarette I smoke back in this case. You think *I* would do something to cause a fire on this island?"

"I saw you litter, sir."

"Hell you did. You saw a red ember from the inside of this car, knew someone was smoking, and figured he must've been flicking it out the window. Good. You've got your excuse. Now I can do your bidding. Want me to breathe into a straw? Want me to touch my nose?"

"I want to you to stop ranting and step slowly out of the car."

Jo and I sat, leaning to the right, with our seatbelts digging into our skin. A half hour probably passed, and when it did, Henry returned to the Jeep, the trooper returned to his cruiser, and the three of us drove back to Sloptown Road. In the air and space surrounding Henry there was not—as with the yellow tongues of a campfire—wild movement and crackles of spark. He was silent and motionless, like the deep red coals.

•

Arnie removed his left shoe with his right foot, his right shoe with his left foot. His shirt was off, revealing a striking farmer's tan and a good-sized beer belly. He'd been reclining there on the beach for an hour already, waiting for us, while Jo and I had tried to shake off our hangovers.

Henry walked along the waterline alone, about a hundred yards off, swinging a metal detector gently in front of him like a pendulum. He'd spoken little all morning.

The lake was transparent near the shore and remained so for about a quarter mile out. The sandy bottom showed through the shallow water, pressing up close to the surface before falling back and sinking into the deeper shades of aqua and indigo and finally to violet near the horizon. Even a long way out, rocks poked out of the water, exposed from the drought. And on shore, smaller stones, like schools of dead alewives, lay scattered in the strip of wet sand where Henry walked.

Straight ahead, past all the shades of blue, was a dark green ribbon of land: the mainland. My bag was packed and my sleeping bag sat rolled and tied in the back seat. My ferry would depart at two o'clock. I was ready to return. I sat and filtered sand through my fingers. Jo was stretched out on a towel beside me, wearing dark sunglasses. She snored slightly.

Henry walked back toward us with the metal detector slung over his shoulder. It was perhaps his most prized possession because

it helped him find and unearth the real prizes: padlocks, belt buck-
les, and fishing lures, left behind by the Mormons and the Irish. He
sat down by me and Arnie and slowly held out his cupped hand. It
was a shard of pottery.

"I thought it was a penny," he said quietly. "Off by just a couple
thousand years maybe. It could be Hopewell. Or it could not." He
got comfortable and faced the lake.

"We'll have to do some radiocarbon dating on that son of a
bitch," said Arnie. We were quiet for a couple of minutes, until he
asked Henry, "You heard of that sunken lumber schooner out by
Iron Ore Bay?"

"That one that's now sticking out of the water?"

"Yep. John's taking me up in his plane tomorrow to get a good
look."

"That's great," mumbled Henry.

Voices emerged in the distance. To our right, two young men
and two young women descended a dune. One of the girls, who had
red hair and wore a green bathing suit, jogged toward the water.
She also wore white running shoes to protect her feet from the
stones. She splashed a few steps in, and when she walked as deep as
her knees, she turned and looked at her friends. "It's freezing!" The
others weren't dressed for swimming, and they laughed and waved
their hands, motioning her to go out farther. She did, but the water
never rose past her knees.

"Look how far out she's walking," I said.

Farther, then farther. The lake crept only to her thighs. It seemed
as though she could keep walking, twenty-five miles straight out,
to Cross Village on the mainland, passing sunken schooners along
the way with the water never rising above her head. It reminded
me of something I'd learned in a college anthropology course about
the Bering Land Bridge. The oceans were lower during the last ice
age, and an ancient strip of exposed land had surfaced between
Siberia and Alaska. Hunters and whole tribes from Asia followed

the mastodons across this new plain, and they stayed, fanning out and populating the Americas. I'm sure Henry knew that history as well. He was an intelligent man. I was not sure that he was a spiritual one. But when I left that afternoon on the ferry, I could imagine him on the beach, on his knees, praying for rain.

THE FEEL OF MERIDIANS

Abby bought me a globe, one with brown oceans instead of blue. It was for our third anniversary, and she told me it would look nice in my home office. The brown oceans would complement the beige walls.

I set the globe on top of my bookshelves, turning it so that North America faced me. I'd never traveled overseas, like Abby, whose parents were missionaries and had moved the family to Rwanda when she was in high school. I didn't want to glance up while working at my desk and see other continents staring back at me. My work required concentration and was slowed by distraction. Regret was a distraction. I was working on the page layout for an office furniture catalogue, tinkering with typography and second-guessing myself on color schemes. I'd left a large design firm six months earlier to go freelance, enjoying my new hours, often making edits until long past midnight.

I finished the edits at two o'clock. Abby had been asleep since ten. I turned the computer off, walked over to the bookshelves and the globe, and began to palm it with both hands, turning it slowly, reading the small print of cities, the bold print of countries. I remembered a game I played in fifth grade. Every winter day, when the class came in from noon recess with soaked jeans and half-off socks flopping along the carpet, we'd set our hats and gloves and boots along the register at the back of the room. The heater ticked and rattled, blowing warm air, drying the clothes, and filling our class with a sour breeze laced with children's sweat. On a low shelf above the register sat our large classroom globe— a blue-oceaned globe. I'd spin it on its axis, draping my index finger along the surface. I wouldn't let myself sit down at my desk until I'd done it once after recess. All the nations—with their pink and green and yellow political boundaries—would blur with the blue oceans to become a single mass. Tiny days and nights whirred by, and my home and school in Michigan turned invisible. I'd trace my finger over the topography, feeling the ridges of the earth where mountains became plains that tumbled into seas. And wherever my finger lay when the globe stopped spinning, that's the place where I would someday live.

To give all nations an equal shot at my citizenship, I'd move my finger north and south along the meridians as they passed. I usually landed in Canada or the Soviet Union, if I wasn't floating somewhere in the middle of the Pacific. But sometimes I'd come to rest on Belize or India or Rwanda—someplace exotic—and try to imagine living in those places as I returned to my desk, ignoring Mr. Haverkamp's math lesson.

So at two o'clock in the morning, my wife asleep in the next room, I spun the globe, set my finger on its surface, and watched as it came to a stop on Spain. I was dead center on Madrid. It was a nice thought, living in Spain. I thought about it as I brushed my teeth, checked the front door's lock, and settled into bed beside Abby.

This became a routine. Every night before bed, I'd spin the globe to see where I was going to live. I never landed on Chile. Chile was too thin. And my finger never made it down to Antarctica. But there were places, like Spain, that would linger in my head, sometimes until the next morning as I made coffee.

One night, a couple of weeks into the routine, Abby caught me. "What are you doing?"

I stood by the bookshelves with my finger on the globe. She drowsily walked to the bathroom and winced from the light of my office. There was a second or two when I imagined seeing the subtle roundness of her silhouetted belly.

"Are you coming to bed?" she asked.

"Yeah. Two seconds." But it was too early; she was only six weeks pregnant. We hadn't even told friends or family yet because we'd known too many people who'd lost a baby in the first trimester.

The globe kept spinning as I looked at her. When she walked into the bathroom and shut the door, it slowed to a stop. But I didn't turn to look right away. I'd been caught and quickly wondered if I should be ashamed. I was doing something I should have outgrown long before. Three years into our marriage, and I was still playing with a globe, toying with fantasy. I decided it was the last time. Whatever nation was underneath my finger, whatever topography I'd finally come to rest on, that was it. It was the last. Wherever my finger lay, that was the place I would someday, ultimately, end up.

The Federated States of Micronesia.

That was it—gravity, geography, and the Lord agreed—that's where I'd move and make my new home. I imagined being surrounded by salt water, anything other than stuck on this freshwater Michigan peninsula that can't pull itself free from the continent. I decided I'd better go to the library and open up an "M" encyclopedia. I'd learn about my new home's imports, exports, and infant mortality rate. I'd take this more seriously than I did in Mr. Haverkamp's class. I was an adult with money to travel. I could take a class at a community center and learn whatever language they spoke in Micronesia. I was finally mature enough to appreciate the flavor of a different culture and the beauty of a different landscape.

The toilet flushed. Abby staggered out of the bathroom, and we looked at each other. My finger still rested on the tiny chain of islands.

"You coming?" she asked.

"Yeah."

I slipped under the comforter with her, thinking about Micronesia. Abby stretched out on her back, and I slowly moved my open hand over her stomach. I couldn't feel a change yet. Then she turned onto her side, away from me, and my hand followed her slopes, down her ribs, down her side, up her hips.

She'd never leave. I could tell by that serene motion of hers—drawing the comforter up and tucking it tight under her chin. She slept too well here, in our restored house, close to friends and family and church, and only a short drive from Seven's Paint, where she'd already bought a pale shade of blue for the nursery meant to look like the sky. My freelance work might allow me to move, but the baby would anchor us. Abby had said she wouldn't live beyond a sixty-minute radius of her own mother now.

But even her mother didn't know our secret yet. And the darkness of closed eyelids in a dark room encouraged the dark scenarios I sometimes imagined. I played one out in my half-sleeping brain, one where tragedy struck in a month or two. Abby's screams from the bathroom would bring me running from my office. A red string of blood, like a surfaced artery, would leak down her thigh. The grief of the miscarriage would be long and aching for her, something she'd want to run from for a while, something triggered by the smell of fresh paint. I'd persuade her West, to San Francisco or San Diego, the places all Midwesterners see when they dream. A final taste of couplehood, I'd say. Then of course we'll try again.

I turned onto my side, away from Abby, as if the shift of my head on the pillow would dislodge the scenes. I fell back on less wicked thoughts, of Micronesia. It must be small, or why give it such a name? Maybe it was so named because its people were very short, because the skyscrapers were only two stories, because on holidays the marching bands played nothing but piccolos. Or maybe each island, floating in the brown saltwater ocean, was so small that there wasn't room for an airstrip. No planes could land, every islander was stranded, and no vagabonds like me could settle there anyway. Of course it was too small. It was a ridiculous place to land.

There's a reason we can't feel the spin of the earth.

FRESHWATER BOYS

Casey DeHaan swam with his eyes open underwater. He saw through the blue of his backyard pool, the silt-filled brown of Boulder Bluff pond, and the chilled green of Lake Michigan waves. His friends, Jake and Sam, would bring over buckets of golf balls that they'd collected along the netted outer edges of the driving range. They'd toss them into the pool, and the three of them would dive to the bottom of the deep end, frantically gathering the balls in their arms while their lungs caught fire.

They were twelve years old. Their shoulders were still slender, and their legs couldn't push them through the water with great strength. But they'd all been swimmers from birth—Casey and Jake in neighborhood pools, and Sam in the lakes that his father sailed with his forty-foot Chris-Craft. None of them feared water. They wore it over their skin like cool summer bed sheets. Casey liked to float on his back, staring up and squinting so that there was nothing in his peripheral vision. All he would see was blue sky, and when he stared at it long enough it became another lake to him. Then he would close his eyes and smile at the rising, sinking, rising cadence of the waves and the blind thrill in his stomach that came from letting himself be taken where the waves wished.

The sky was calm, and the waves went almost invisible during the first Sunday in August, making Lake Michigan seem more like the lake it really was and not the ocean that those with boats and

beachfront cottages liked to believe. Instead of climbing and curling, the waves moved as tender ridges toward the shore, and when
they met the shore they merely slipped underground. There were no
fireworks, no white, foaming rush.

It was perfect for swimming, even a half mile offshore, where
Gregory Dunn, Sam's father, had anchored his Chris-Craft. Gregory
was a thoracic surgeon in Grand Rapids who kept his boat docked
at the Singapore Yacht Club in Saugatuck. Casey and Jake called
him Dr. D because it sounded tough, and it was funny, because
Gregory Dunn was bald with glasses and was an inch or two shorter
than Mrs. Dunn. Once a month, the Dunns invited Sam's friends
along to trace the coast between Saugatuck and Holland. They did
this especially for Casey, whose parents had been divorced for over
a year.

Parts of the coast were absent of homes and people. Under the
sun, Casey imagined it as an idyllic Pacific island. The trees cast
shadows that looked like oases in the warm sand. But when the
skies were overcast, the shore was a borderland of gray, and the
imagined Pacific island was simply deserted. It was easy for Casey
to play these mind tricks on himself. All it took was clouds, this
detachment from land, and enough water.

Today there was sun. The three boys were sprawled along the
seats of the boat among empty Coke cans, junk food wrappers, and
a stereo playing hard rock that was turned up too loud. Droplets of
sweat marked the boys' hairlines. Their shirts were off and their ribs
showed through their skin. Sam turned his hand palm-upward and
cupped his Coke by the bottom of the can. He gently swished it in a
circular motion, closed his eyes, and inhaled the aroma of the Coke
as if savoring some prized vintage. He spoke with a phony Spanish
accent, trying to sound like the Colombian drug lord in the movie
they'd rented Friday night. "This is the good life, my friends. This
is the good life."

They laughed, and Jake picked up the accent. "Enjoy yourself,

Señor Soriano, for tomorrow you will banquet in hell and be a feast for dogs." He threw a licorice rope at him.

Mrs. Dunn emerged from the cabin. They could smell her before she appeared: coconut tanning lotion that was rubbed into her face, shoulders, and her long legs. She wore a black one-piece bathing suit, but Casey had once seen her in a bikini. "We're getting sandwiches ready. Ham and cheese."

"I want turkey," said Sam.

"You'll get ham and cheese. If you want a quick swim, this is your chance."

She turned and disappeared. The smell of coconuts stayed behind. Sam's Spanish accent returned, and he mumbled, "You will bring me fifty kilos of turkey or you will be a feast for dogs." He stood up. "I'm swimmin'." He turned and climbed over the seats to the edge of the boat, near the motor, where he stood and balanced and looked at the water.

Jake and Casey stood up and walked over to him.

"Dare me?" asked Sam.

"What's to dare?" asked Jake.

"Six-foot sturgeon. This far out, they circle you like sharks."

"Yeah, you've seen sturgeon," said Casey, who was scratching at cuts on his forearms.

"He has," said Jake. "He was flogging his sturgeon in the bathroom a few minutes ago. That's why he was in there so long."

"*Cabrón!*" shouted Sam. He returned to the accent. "I was in there taking a shit, and there was nothing the American swine could do about it."

"Just jump in," said Casey.

"Gringo," mumbled Sam. Then he leapt forward. In mid-air he pulled the back of his bathing suit down and mooned them.

"Gay," said Jake. He jumped next, cannonballing over the splash rings where Sam had just disappeared. Then Casey went, standing on the edge for a few seconds, his blond hair getting tossed up by a brief breeze. He dove headfirst with his arms and legs tight together, his hands angled like an arrowhead, trying to make the smallest splash possible.

All three emerged, their hair plastered to their heads. Casey took in a mouthful of water and spat it at Sam.

"Don't! God, I need cooler friends."

"We're not your friends," said Jake. "We just hang out with you for your boat. And to look at your mom."

"That's sick!" Sam cupped his hand and splashed water at the other two, who closed their eyes and turned their heads. Sam kept splashing. "Come on, open your eyes. Open your eyes. Come on. Come on. Come on."

"Truce," said Jake.

"What? Truth?" asked Sam.

"Truce."

"I'm pretty sure you said 'truth,' Jakey. Wanna play truth or dare?"

Casey didn't. Last month Sam had a birthday sleepover with six or seven other guys. In the middle of the night, in Sam's dark basement, they played the game, and nobody chose to tell the truth. It would be sexual, something about a girl, and there never seemed to be a right answer. You could only incriminate yourself. Have you ever fingered a girl? Has she licked your dick? Say yes and you were a deviant, reeking of semen and musk. Say no and you were a pussy, and quite possibly a fag. So they all chose dares, and again, there was no way to win. Jake had to go through the Dunns' dirty laundry and fondle a pair of Mrs. Dunn's panties. Shawn Steenstra had to page through a Victoria's Secret catalogue and lick the photo of any model in a black bra. Tony Logan had to do twenty naked jumping jacks, but he only did about ten. And Casey had to go outside in the middle of the nighttime road and sketch several large penises, complete with oversized testicles, using a piece of blue sidewalk chalk.

"Sure, I'll play," said Jake. "But first I have to give you a message underwater."

The three of them inhaled, slipped below the waves, and opened their eyes. Casey saw green blurs with bright yellow ripples where the sunlight trickled through. He could see the other two, but only their general form. He couldn't make out their eyes, noses, or mouths. Jake's arm was outstretched. Casey couldn't see his fingers.

They emerged, exhaling and spraying water.

"Did you read it?"

"It's too blurry," said Sam.

"I'll do it again."

Back under. This was something they'd started doing in Casey's pool last year. Their teacher, Mrs. Koop, had taught a lesson on sign language during a week-long diversity unit, and the boys learned enough of the alphabet to spell out an exhaustive catalogue of profanities to one another while underwater.

They came up again. "I still couldn't see it," said Sam.

"It said 'dick.'"

"Wow, that's brilliant," said Sam. "Well worth the time and effort."

"Shut up."

Casey was hoping this would distract them from their plans, but it didn't. He nervously scratched one arm while using the other to stay afloat.

"Just for that, you're first, Jake. Truth or dare?"

The three boys treaded the cold water, barely bobbing up and down in the calm lake. There were no other boats or jet skis in sight. Blue skirted out from them in all directions, and the earth felt flat. Sam's parents could be heard over the metallic riffs on the radio, discussing lunch from inside the cabin, but they couldn't be seen. This would allow for more daring dares.

"Dare," said Jake. He was probably thinking the same thing Casey was, that there weren't any Victoria's Secret catalogues or laundry hampers around. They were treading water in Lake Michigan. There were no props handy, no tools for humiliation.

"Okay, let me think," said Sam. He took a deep breath, puffing his cheeks out as he did, and slipped underwater. Casey looked at Jake, who looked back and smiled nervously. Sam's dares were always the worst.

When he broke through the lake's surface, he shook his head from side to side, spraying water and making his hair spike out in all directions. "I know," he said, grinning. "You gotta swim under the boat."

"What boat?"

Sam looked from side to side. "How many boats do you see out here, *chico?*"

"No way," said Casey, half-laughing.

"Oh, screw that," said Jake.

"Not the long way," said Sam. "Just the width of it."

"*Just* the width of it?"

"You can swim the whole way across Case's pool underwater. That's farther than underneath the boat."

"Yeah, but I could get stuck under there," said Jake.

"That's why it's a dare. You could have said 'truth.'"

"Just make him do naked jumping jacks or something," said Casey.

"No, I don't wanna see that," said Sam. "I wanna see this. Get goin'. Take a deep breath."

Sam started to swim toward the boat, knowing the other two would follow. They did. The three stopped and treaded water halfway down the boat, beside its shiny white abdomen.

"From here?" asked Jake.

"Shh." Sam put his index finger to his lips and then pointed toward the boat, indicating his parents. "Yeah. You stay here for a second, and me and Case will go to the back of the boat so we can see you go under and come back up."

They each swam the backstroke to the stern. Mrs. Dunn emerged from the cabin and was suddenly looking down at their round faces as they slipped through the water. She gathered up the empty Coke cans and tossed them into a plastic bag. Sam waved to her, and she smiled back, flipped the radio to the oldies station, and disappeared again.

"Okay," said Sam. He paused for a few seconds while looking up at the boat, making sure there were no witnesses, only the smell of coconuts. "Now."

Jake rose out of the water as he inhaled. Then, with puffed cheeks, he thrust himself below the surface. Water foamed upward as his trailing feet desperately churned like propellers.

"Go, go," said Sam, and he and Casey splashed their way to the starboard side. They breathed heavily and said nothing as they waited for Jake to reappear.

Buddy Holly was on the radio. *Pretty pretty pretty pretty Peggy Sue.* In his mind, Casey started counting seconds: one Mississippi, two Alabama, three Mississippi, four Alabama.

The water broke like glass, calm and flat one instant and then brightly shattering as Jake arose. His hands came before his head, as though he was pulling himself free from the lake. He coughed several times and ignored the other two boys.

"What was it like?" asked Casey.

Jake kept coughing. "Just a minute."

"You're so out of shape," said Sam.

"What was it *like*?" repeated Casey.

"It was dark, what do you think? Even with your eyes open, you couldn't see anything until you got right to the other edge of the boat."

"Was it scary?"

"*Was it scary?*" said Jake, making a face at Casey. "Stop buggin' me for a second. You want to know? Fine. Truth or dare."

Flickers of truths ran through Casey's mind, like the quick

flipping of pages when a thumb runs along the edge of a book. His dad's confession. His parents' divorce. The pocket knife he used to make the cuts on his arms.

"Dare."

Jake shrugged. "You know what you gotta do."

Casey nodded and began swimming around the corner of the boat.

"About two minutes, boys," called Mrs. Dunn from the cabin. Stevie Wonder was on the radio. *But it's all right if my clothes aren't new. Out of sight because my heart is true.* Casey swam the breaststroke, its long, fluid motion calming him as he approached the invisible spot in the water where Jake had made his descent.

He looked back and saw Jake and Sam treading water next to the ladder, smiling. "Let's do it," said Sam.

Casey nodded again and squinted at the smooth, bright surface of the boat. Around him, the water reflected the sun and shed diamonds. He took a series of deep breaths, trying to find one that felt thoroughly refreshing and satisfying, that made his lungs feel their fullest.

"Come on, Case. Don't puss—"

He disappeared in a slit of water. The breath wasn't full, but as he slipped between waves, his lungs still felt huge in his chest, pressing out against his ribs.

Jake and Sam whooped in excitement as they turned and swam around the stern of the boat. Again, the two boys who were above the water and under the sun quietly waited and watched. Huge smiles lit their faces.

"Okay, come on," called Mrs. Dunn above the music. "The sandwiches are ready. I've got dry towels laid out for you."

Sam and Jake stayed silent. They continued to tread in place, not moving in the soft current, not even feeling the weight of the water. Jake was the first to stop smiling. As Casey had done for him, Jake began to count the passing seconds.

Beneath the boat, those seconds were being stretched by panic. Casey's head and his right hand pressed against the belly of the boat. He had swum with his eyes open, but all he had seen was black water, and his first instinct when the claustrophobia struck was to swim straight up. He thrashed but made only ripples. They were smaller than the waves that day and absorbed right into them, into the larger blue that lay beyond the black.

●

David DeHaan lay asleep in the first pew at Northcentral Reformed Church. His black suit was wrinkled and his gray-blond hair was damp with sweat. He had been sitting, bent over, with his head cupped in his hands, sending silent prayers into the silence. The church was dim and empty, and only a trace of a sweet floral scent remained in the air.

He had fallen asleep in the middle of his prayer and had begun to slowly lean to his left, until his shoulder rested on the wooden pew. Unconsciously, he pulled his legs onto the pew, tucked his left arm under his head, and slept for the first time in forty-eight hours.

The funeral had been opulent and devastating. The flowers, all of them white, nearly hid the altar, and the rows of mourners in black extended to the back of the sanctuary and spilled into the narthex. David's family and friends sat on one side of the aisle, Shelly's on the other. At first glance, it was so horribly like their wedding day.

Shelly wore a black dress. She sat in the first row, across the aisle from David. Her mother was next to her, and for most of the service they sat with their heads tilted toward and resting on each other, their bodies shaking from sobs but neither making a sound.

David's tie was crooked and the knot was loose. The shadows from sleeplessness were so dark that, from a distance, it looked as if he wore grease paint under his eyes, like a ball player. The whites of his eyes were not white, but pink. He didn't get drunk often, but today he brushed his teeth twice before the service. The mourners who embraced him could still smell whiskey.

The small casket had been closed. The mortician had made Casey's skin white again, changed it back from the blue it had been when Gregory Dunn found him and performed CPR, blowing air past his blue lips. But David and Shelly managed to agree, at least, on this one thing. A framed Little League photograph sat on the casket's lid. Casey, in an oversized green batting helmet, smiled and stared back at those who managed to hold their heads up.

Now, as David slept, the Reverend Randall Wierenga came quietly down the aisle from the back of the church, trained from years of walking in sacred places. He no longer wore his black vestment and tie, but had changed into shorts, a T-shirt, and a Boston Red Sox hat after the luncheon, which had been held in the fellowship hall downstairs. He had worn his vestment the entire time because the mourners seemed to want that extra touch of ceremony and solemnity today, and because the summer heat and his personal grief had made him sweat through all the clothes he was wearing underneath.

Shadows in the church were now stretched along the floor as the sun angled toward dusk. Randall sat in the row behind David, never making a sound. He listened to David's heavy breath and slight snores. He reached into his pocket and pulled out a key. Then he leaned over the pew, opened David's hand up slightly, and placed the key in his slackened grip.

David woke. "What?" he said, a little too loudly, sitting quickly upright with huge, pink eyes. "Oh. Hey, R."

He'd been calling him that for years. It stood not only for the name of his friend of twenty years, but also for the title of Reverend, sharing the two worlds that his friend shared with him.

"It's okay," Randall whispered. "Keep sleeping."

David looked at the key in his hand, squinted, and reclined, settling onto the pew again. "What time is it?"

"Almost eight." Randall stood up. "Stay as long as you need." He stepped into the aisle. "I'll call you tomorrow."

"All right."

"Will you answer tomorrow?" Randall walked backward up the aisle, his eyes looking sad and the rest of his plump face looking pink and soft and damp.

David turned onto his side, slipping his left arm between his head and the pew. "Just make sure you leave a message. I'm screening my calls."

Randall nodded.

"R?" said David.

"Yeah?"

"Thanks for your words. The sermon and the eulogy."

Randall's mouth creased into a false smile. "It was like writing a nightmare."

He continued to walk backward, walking slower and slower as he approached the doorway that led to the narthex. He wanted to give David another chance to speak, to ask a favor, to join him in prayer. But there had been enough of these things today, and Randall also wanted to give him this: space. So he passed through the doorway, into the dark narthex, stretching the arc of space between them. Then he leaned his back against the church's main door, the sun slicing gaudily into the dimness, before he disappeared and let the door slam shut.

David jumped at the sound. He took a deep breath and kicked his shiny black loafers off his feet. There was no air-conditioning in the church, and the heat now seemed like a tangible film between his skin and his clothes. The metal key felt cold in his hand. He placed it against his forehead and ran it along his temples, cheeks, and the back of his neck.

He began to cry again. It took nothing today, and the sight of him caused everyone around him to cry as well. He cried mainly today from the kind gestures: the appearance of old friends, the homemade cards from Casey's classmates, and the ever-present goodness of Randall. Randall, who had married them, whom he had confessed his infidelity to before he confessed it to Shelly, who counseled them as they tried to clot the bleeding, and who smoked cigarettes and drank beer with him all night after the signing of the divorce papers.

David spoke little to Shelly today. The sight of her reminded him of all their lost unions, including the lost physical union that had created their only child. Now, there was no trace of them ever having been anything but two divided people.

Before he died, Casey had also been divided, spending most of his time with Shelly, but every other weekend with David.

"You should feel lucky you get to see him at all," she had once told David, and he hadn't argued with her.

When David met with Shelton Thompson, his divorce lawyer, for the first time, Shelton had leaned across his imposing wooden desk, his hands clasped and fingers laced in front of him, and without a trace of humor, irony, or malice, said to him, "Welcome to adultery."

In David's case, the woman was a twenty-eight-year-old colleague, also married, named Jennifer Montgomery, and it was a long-term, habitual deceit, so there was no mercy from Shelly, from the court, or from administrators and faculty at Georgetown High School, where he and Jennifer Montgomery had both taught social studies. Rumors began to circulate among the students. On the last day of school, as those students cleaned out their lockers, David turned in his resignation, ended the relationship with Jennifer, and cleaned out his desk.

That was over a year ago, before this: a man wearing black, sprawled over a wooden pew, shifting from his side to his back to his side, unable to sleep any more. He sat up and scratched his head, and his fingers came away wet. He was no longer crying and felt as if he would never be able to cry again. When he stood up to leave, he lost his balance for a moment and clutched the edge of the pew. He bent down, picked up his black loafers, and then stood staring at the altar: the baptismal font, the ciborium, a few fallen white rose pedals and daisy heads on the red carpet. The sanctuary was so void of sound that David could only hear a ringing in his ears, which he wasn't sure was actually real or phantom. During his Saturday floral deliveries, with the keys of ten churches in his pockets, he would set up the new week's vase arrangements at the altars, and he found all empty churches to be this silent, even the downtown ones, like Northcentral, with the Heritage Hill traffic outside. The sanctuaries were like cocoons.

With shoes in one hand and the key in the other, David walked up the aisle to the back of the church. In his stocking feet he could be as silent as Randall. He went through the doorway into the narthex and past a wooden cross located near the front doors. With the key held between two fingers, he reached out the other fingers on his left hand, gently touching the cross, and dragging them over it as he walked by. Then he opened the main doors to leave.

He had always thought that funerals in the rain were the saddest of all. But when he opened the doors, the low sun blinded him, the great heat returned to his body. And he knew that this was worse: a ball of fire that he couldn't hide from until nightfall, which itself would be more terrible than the day.

·

He still got lost. David had been working at Jenison Floral for a year, after leaving the high school and wanting any sort of shit job where he wouldn't have to interact with a lot of people, where he wouldn't be stuck in one place all day, and where he could get— at the very least—health insurance. But after that year of driving

the delivery van all around Grand Rapids and the suburbs, there
were still roads he'd never heard of, places he couldn't find in the
street atlas that he always kept on the passenger's seat. Some were
new subdivisions that wouldn't appear in the street atlas for another
year. Other times, David simply got confused, especially by the
streets that ran straight through the city for miles and then, like
an aquatic bird or mammal, disappeared, only to resurface several
blocks or even miles later, at the same latitude or longitude, running just as straight after their return.

   He liked working alone, listening to sports talk radio for hours
and then singing along to the classic rock station once all the issues
of the day's sport had been exhausted. He made occasional small
talk with people, mainly the designers at the shop, all of whom
were women. While he picked up and loaded another batch of
arrangements, he would learn little things about their lives, like the
hobbies and talents of their children, the sicknesses or recoveries of
their parents, and who was in love, who was getting married, who
was pregnant. He liked Diana, the owner of the shop, who was tall
and kind with long gray hair that she kept straight and in a pony
tail so that she looked, all at once, like an old woman and a young
girl. She never asked why a man in his late thirties had left such a
stable job as teaching, although, through polite conversation, she
knew that he was divorced and had a son, and she seemed fine not
knowing the rest.

   In a business composed nearly entirely of women, it's the men
who drive, who take all of the colorful goods to people as signs
of celebration or of mourning. He sometimes crossed paths with
drivers from other shops. They were usually old men who had
been delivering flowers for thirty or forty years and who didn't use
maps. They didn't get lost. They gave directions using landmarks
like "Byron Road" or "the Reynolds Metals building," which had
changed names or didn't exist any more, except in their own mental

maps, which never let them down. And they didn't drive like old men. David had seen them relying only on the side mirrors of their vans and easing backward perfectly into parallel parking spaces at Butterworth Hospital, on a hill, in the snow. David was more likely to clip the curb.

He usually saw these men at the funeral homes. Each home had a white door on the outside with black letters reading FLOWER ROOM, where he and the other men would carry in casket sprays, sympathy arrangements, easel arrangements, planters, and satin pillow hearts. On the walls of the rooms were chalkboards with the names of those who had just died scribbled in white. The drivers checked the boards to make sure they were at the right place. The men who died were often named Fred, Stan, Ralph, or George. The women were Betty, Constance, Florence, and Ethel. The names themselves gave away their age and made David think of World War II.

Every flower room was a little different. One in Grandville had a door with an orange biohazard sign. David didn't know what was on the other side, but he suspected it was the bodies, and the fluids and tools and makeup of the trade. In Byron Center, he had to walk through a garage to get to the flower room. It was dimly lit, and the hearses were parked there. Two gurneys sat in the corner, and wooden caskets lined the walls. He knew they were empty, but he always kept from looking directly at them.

David took one week off after the funeral. Diana urged him to take more. The shop was slow in the summer, and her nephew, Jason, was filling in part-time before heading back to college. But David had spent that one week at his small duplex, in bed, with the blinds closed, and with bottles of Jack Daniels and warm Pepsi on the nightstand that he sipped from a Georgetown High School travel mug to help him sleep. Athena, his yellow Lab, slept next to him in bed for most of the day. Every few hours, she coaxed him awake by lifting his arms up with her muzzle. Then he'd stumble through the duplex to let her outside. When he bothered to dress, he had to cinch his belt more than usual.

He returned to the shop on a hot and humid Wednesday, and Jason was in the garage, loading a casket spray into the newer and nicer of the two vans that the shop owned. David walked inside and found Diana in her office doing paperwork. "Why's Jason here?" he asked.

She set her pen down. "I already had him scheduled for the rest of this week. He could use the money, and you could probably use a bit of a transition."

"I'm fine. I want to work as much as possible."

"Good. Good." She handed him a delivery checklist. "I've already done the routing for you. They're scattered all over, some out in the boonies."

He took the checklist. There were only about ten stops, all of them residential, but they ranged from Allendale north to Rockford, east to Ada, south to Dorr. It would take him all day.

David went to the walk-in cooler at the back of the shop. It was lined with shelves where all the finished arrangements were stored before delivery. The door slammed shut behind him, and he breathed in the cold. He exhaled and saw his breath. He grabbed a vase of iris and stargazers in one hand and a planter in the other. He backed into the cooler door to open it, and as he did, noticed a sympathy arrangement on the shelf that was going to Arsulowicz, the funeral home on Remembrance Road.

He passed Jason on his way to the van. "I'll take the Arsulowicz in the cooler," said David. "I'm gonna be cutting through the north side of town when I go to Rockford. It's right on the way."

Jason was tall and athletic. He was a hurdler at Michigan State. But he was a towhead with a little boy's face. "No, it's cool. I got it."

David shook his head. "It doesn't make sense for you to go. It's out of the way. And it's not a problem." He leaned through the open door of the van and set the flowers into wooden racks so that they wouldn't shift or tip over. Jason walked quickly away.

The van's engine ran while David loaded the rest of his deliveries, the air-conditioning turned full blast to keep the flowers and the driver from wilting. He had finished loading everything and was about to leave when Diana strode into the garage, Jason a few steps behind her.

"Do you have the Arsulowicz?" she asked.

"Yeah, it's on my way."

"No. Leave it for Jason. I already made up your route."

He stared at her. The day's heat was making his shirt stick to his back, and the exhaust from the van made the air a sick thing to breathe. He spoke slowly. "It's on my way."

Diana stepped to the side door of the van, opened it, and pulled out the Arsulowicz arrangement.

"What are you doing?" asked David.

She turned and handed the arrangement to Jason. "For today, just stick to your route."

"You're not letting me go to any funeral homes, are you?"

"I'm having Jason do all the hospitals, nursing homes, and funeral homes today. It's just easier."

"For whom?" he asked. "This is why you're sending me to every sisterfucking delivery on the outskirts of town, isn't it? You think I can't handle the sight of a casket spray?"

"David, don't swear at me."

"I'm not swearing at you. I'm swearing at the absolute absurdity."

Diana spoke deliberately and nodded slightly with each short sentence. "Just do it. Don't question. Don't complain."

Jason disappeared then. David just stared at her for a moment and then shook his head and smirked. "This is cock." He turned, climbed into the driver's seat, slammed the door, and backed out too fast, scraping the side mirror against the garage door rails.

The ten-stop run did take him all day. He kept the radio off as he drove, stewing in Diana's words. The anger and the silence made him think more about the things that whiskey and sleep helped him forget. Not just Casey's death—Casey's life. The loss of custody. That was the real fuck-up, that was the sin he couldn't recover from. Shelly had lost a child she had spent twenty-six days a month with during his final year. He had lost a child he barely saw, who barely saw him. He'd lost Casey before the lake took him, and he was the reason for that loss of time. David thought about the funeral homes he wasn't stopping at that day. He wondered if Jason had delivered Casey's flowers when he died and if he had seen "Casey DeHaan" scribbled on the flower room's chalkboard. Fred. Betty. Stan. Casey. It didn't fit with the rest.

David hated driving the old van. It had over a quarter of a million miles on it. The brakes didn't work. A crack snaked across the entire windshield. And the air-conditioning never did quite perform that day. The roses in the van opened up too much, and he knew the people who received them would call and complain the next day as those roses started to lose their petals too quickly. David was a mess, the sweat not only dripping down his brow but also soaking his back and ass as he sat on the hot vinyl seats. He tried not to hate Jason for taking the good van.

In the end, the run actually took him more than a full day. It was six thirty when he arrived back at the shop. Jason's van was parked in the garage, and all the designers, including Diana, had left for the night. David punched his time card, dropped his delivery checklist on Diana's desk, and walked through the darkened design area. Green stems and ferns covered the floor. It felt like a hot, jungle place. He went into the bathroom, ran cold water, and scooped handfuls of it onto his face. But it wasn't enough.

He went to the large, walk-in cooler at the back of the shop. The shelves were full of flowers, deliveries for the next day. The door closed behind him, and David sat down on the cold cement floor, exhaling a warm cloud of himself. He reclined and rested his

face on the cement. He knew that Randall would have wanted him
to pray then, in that cool sanctuary. But instead he just cried, surrounded by blooms.

•

Randall had bought him a cross a few years before. He and his wife,
Mary, had been on vacation in Bohemia, and he bought it from a
blacksmith who worked out on the sidewalk. The cross was about
two inches long, with a thin strip of black leather looping through
the top. It was to be worn around the neck.

"Oh, wow. Thanks," said David. "You didn't have to buy me a
gift while you were over there."

"Are you kidding?" said Randall. "I'm ashamed to say how little I paid for it. But he was making them right in front of us. I don't
know. I just thought it was cool."

"No, it is."

The metal was a dull gray, so there was nothing gaudy about
it. But it seemed to David a little too large. When he slipped it
over his head and tucked the cross underneath his shirt, he could
actually feel the weight of it pulling slightly on his neck. When
he moved, the cross swung and thudded against his sternum. He'd
always had a problem with men who wore any jewelry more than a
wedding band and a wristwatch. Not to mention any showiness of
a person's faith. So he thanked Randall, wore it for a few days, and
then put it in a shoebox full of photographs and keepsakes, where
it stayed for years.

David found it by accident. He was looking for an old photograph that Shelly had taken of him holding Casey on the beach.
Casey was two, and Athena was a puppy, running madly down the
shore in the background. He wanted to frame the photograph and
put it on his nightstand so that he would go to sleep and wake up
with Casey, so he wouldn't forget what he had looked like.

The photograph wasn't in the box, and David remembered that

Shelly had used it to make a scrapbook of images taken over the years at the lake. Now the scrapbook was hers. When he found the cross, it still felt heavy in his cupped hand, and heavy when he slipped it over his head. But now he liked the weight. At any point during the day, usually in the delivery van, when he thought of Casey—when loss and guilt and fear poured in, like a boat taking in water—he would clutch the cross through the fabric of his shirt.

The last days of August approached. He continued to screen his calls and often returned home from work to ten or fifteen voicemail messages. He hadn't spoken to Shelly since the funeral, and figured she was probably screening her calls too. Catherine Ferenz and Andrew Steenstra, the other pastors at Northcentral, left a couple of messages. Thomas White, an old friend who was also a doctor, left a message saying he'd ordered a prescription for Paxil in David's name that he could pick up at a local pharmacy.

David hadn't seen Randall over the past few weeks, not since Randall had placed the key into his hand the evening of the funeral. But Randall called often, and a few times, David returned the calls.

"What can I do?" asked Randall.

"Nothing. You're doing it. Checking in on me."

Randall rented a beach house in Saugatuck for two weeks at the end of every summer. "Mary and I want you to come up to the beach house for one of the weekends," he said. "We can drink beer and grill meat and build another of those huge bonfires, like we had last year. Remember we couldn't get within ten feet of the thing?"

"Yeah, I'll think about it."

"Or you can come up and just read on the beach, take walks, be by yourself. I don't want you to feel any pressure."

"I know. I don't."

"Okay, good." Randall paused. "You know, we're all praying for you. Me and Mary. Me and the other pastors. The whole consistory."

"I appreciate it, R."

"Don't be afraid to pray for yourself."

"What's to fear?"

"Nothing. That's not what I meant."

"I know."

David had been a regular attendee of Northcentral Reformed before Casey's death, but he hadn't gone since the funeral. It was more a matter of dealing with other people, answering all the same questions, absorbing all the same sympathies. During their phone calls, he could tell there were a few times when Randall was about to ask the big question, the one involving loss and despair and the truly great sin. But he never asked, which was good, because David hadn't lost his faith. He'd never felt angry at God. He was angry at himself, and when he thought about God, he knew God had every right to be pissed at him too.

He prayed. He prayed for strength and he prayed for Shelly and he prayed for Casey's soul. But he didn't pray for forgiveness. Not yet.

Jason returned to Michigan State the last week of August. David was the only driver again, and beginning that Monday he made all deliveries to the funeral homes. Diana had taken an order for an old man named Herman "Corny" McCormick who had died over the weekend. The family made a special request: they wanted a sympathy arrangement done in red and white carnations with a baseball placed in the center.

The designers kept the obituary section from the newspaper spread out over their work area so they had all the information on the memorial services. David scanned the brief write-up on Corny, hoping for a clue about the baseball. It said that he'd had a long minor league career and played briefly for the Cleveland Indians in the early forties before being drafted into the army.

Diana was trimming tree fern. "David."

He looked up from the obituary. "Yeah?"

"I need a baseball. Can you pick one up during your next run?" She reached into her pocket and pulled out the company credit card.

An hour later, David walked through the doors of MC Sports.
He passed the football equipment, the basketball shoes, the golf
clubs. The baseball equipment was in the back corner, hidden
behind all the sports that had overtaken it in popularity. There
were Little League supplies like aluminum bats, stiff leather gloves,
cleats, and batting helmets. David picked up an official Rawlings
ball and walked quickly away. On his way to the checkout, he
passed through a boxing display with speed bags and heavy bags
suspended from the ceiling.

Back at the shop, Diana hot-glued the baseball to a green plastic pick and eased it into the floral foam among the red and white
carnations. David loaded the arrangement and accompanying casket spray into the van and drove to Zaagman Memorial Chapel
on Burton. He parked in the back, beside the white door with the
black letters, and carried the arrangements into the flower room. A
white-haired woman who worked at the home was inside. He said
hello to her and set the arrangement with the baseball down on the
counter.

"Oh, how cute," the woman said. She smiled and reached out
her hand, touching the baseball briefly and delicately. And David
agreed, without saying so, that it did look cute. "Cute" was the
word for it. It looked like something a mother would use to deco-
rate a little boy's room.

Before he left, David scanned the names on the chalkboard to
make sure he was at the right place. Gertrude Bailey. Hank Zylstra.
Herman "Corny" McCormick. Then he said goodbye to the woman,
turned, and walked back outside.

He still drove with the radio off. The sports talk felt annoying
and trite, and the classic rock brought back too many memories
of his teenage years. In relative silence, David made runs to three
other funeral homes that day. He felt little emotion in the flower
rooms of the first two, but at his last stop, at Gillespie on Eastern,

made up entirely of men's and boys' clothes. He had thrown two flannel blankets over the laundry so he wouldn't have to look at the inside-out Pistons jersey and dirty tube socks that Casey had worn the last time he'd stayed over.

David ate a cheeseburger, wiping the grease and ketchup onto his pants, while he grabbed his drill and compared the different bit sizes to the hook he'd bought at the hardware store. He found the right size, tightened the bit into the drill, and then walked slowly around the room while staring at the ceiling, searching for a solid wooden beam that would support the weight. He found one, raised his arms above his head, and pulled the trigger of the drill. Athena began to bark full force and ran in a frantic circle around his legs.

"Shut up!" Sawdust fell onto his face and into his gray-blond hair.

Athena kept barking.

"Shut up!"

The entire bit buried itself into the wood, and he pulled it free and turned off the drill. Athena went quiet and sniffed at the sawdust on the concrete floor. David set the drill down on the washing machine next to all of his purchases, picked up the steel hook, and inserted it into the new hole in the ceiling. He twisted it with his bare hands as far as he could, until it stopped moving and embedded its shape in his palm.

"Fuck!"

His toolbox sat on a shelf along the wall. David opened it and removed a pair of pliers. He clamped them onto the hook and began twisting. When the hook was finally screwed all the way into the beam, he grabbed a razorblade, using it to slice open the cardboard box. He turned it upside down and dumped the heavy bag onto the floor. When the four smaller chains were attached to the bag, he squatted low and wrapped his arms around the bag's girth, lifting it, guiding it upward until, with one hand, he managed to loop the center chain onto the hook. Then David stood back, sweating completely through his shirt now, and stared at the bag as it swung back and forth like a pendulum. He pulled his shirt off over his head and tossed it in a corner by the dog food. His slight paunch spilled over his belt, but he didn't care. Randall's two-inch cross rested on his chest.

David opened the bottle of whiskey. Shirtless, in blue jeans and work boots, he took three long sips from the bottle and set it down on the washing machine. Then he went for the boxing gloves. Athena was suspicious of them and gave a subtle growl. David's right hand slipped easily into the black glove, and he pulled the Velcro strap with his left hand to tighten it at the wrist. The left glove was harder to tighten, and he had to use his teeth to bite and pull the strap into place.

The heavy bag still rocked back and forth, though only slightly now. Its white Everlast logo was about six feet off the ground, where a man's head would be. David approached, guarding his face, as if the bag might strike first. The initial jab made his left wrist crumple, sending pain up his arm. But then he began with combinations. Left, right. Left, left, right. Athena barked frantically and occasionally jumped and snapped at the bag.

David ignored her and connected with high jabs to an invisible jaw, low hooks to an invisible kidney. Sweat ran down his chest and back and gathered at his waist, soaking into his underwear. The cross swung over his shoulders and around his neck until it was turned around and hanging down his back. David began to shout with each punch thrown.

"Take!"

Jab.

"That!"

Jab.

"You!"

Hook.

"Filthy!"

Hook.

"Fucking!"

Jab.

"Fuck!"

Uppercut.

He stopped a few times to cradle the whiskey bottle in his gloved hands and tilt it to his mouth. It spilled down his chest a few times, and Athena licked the floor around his feet. His knuckles turned sore, then numb, and then burned when the skin began to tear. David fought the bag for thirty minutes and stopped only when the hook fell out of the beam and the bag smashed to the floor in a metallic clatter of chains. Athena scrambled to the other side of the room.

David removed the gloves. His knuckles were bloody, and his hands were so cramped that they remained in tight fists. The bag of ice that he'd bought at the convenience store was melting on the washing machine. He'd bought it for the whiskey, but now he tore open the plastic and set his hands inside among the cubes. After a minute, when a different sort of burning filled his hands, David slowly stretched his fingers out so that he could grab the whiskey bottle and the cigarettes, and then he walked upstairs.

Athena followed him through the kitchen and through the back slider to the patio. Outside, he took a few more sips from the bottle and struggled to pick up a tennis ball. He tossed it a few times across the lawn, and each time Athena returned with it and dropped it at his feet.

David's arms were too sore to continue playing. He lit a cigarette and sat down on a lawn chair. When he leaned back he realized the cross was turned around. He reached behind him and pulled the cross to the front of his body, so that it pressed against his wet chest and pounding heart, and with his bleeding, cramped hand he held it there.

·

The fields were filled with goldenrod and Queen Anne's lace, and the corn was as tall as a man. Barns and grain elevators rose out of the wildflowers, but only sporadically and with large stretches of space and sky between them. It was another bright August day— Labor Day weekend—but the humidity was low, and balmy air blew in from the west. David had finally decided to take Randall up on his offer. He drove toward the lake.

He held the steering wheel gingerly, switching between his left and right hands to rest them. This was something he'd had to do all week while driving the delivery van. Most of his knuckles had bright red scabs that split open again every day, and the tops of his hands were swollen and faintly purple. By the end of the week, Athena had stopped barking at the heavy bag. Incessant pounding, grunts, the rattling of chains—she slept through the sounds of the new evening ritual.

The land rolled gently through Hudsonville and Zeeland, and as he approached Saugatuck, sand and dune grass appeared on the roadside. Green trees covered hills ahead of him, like bristles on an animal's back. These were the backs of dunes.

Randall had promised him two days of relaxation, fellowship, and free beer, but the woods and sandy trails were the selling point. Randall had reminded him that the property bordered the state park.

The daily driving of city streets—the traffic and concrete— was finally getting to David. He planned on spending most of the weekend by himself, walking the trails and even leaving them for unmarked paths. He wanted to surround himself with birdsongs and tree bark, but he didn't know exactly what he'd do once that was accomplished.

When he exited the highway and drove a few more miles, David found himself crossing through evergreen nurseries and blueberry fields. Soon the pavement ended, and the car kicked up dust and loose stones. Then the fields fell away, and beeches and white pines clustered and thickened to become woods. He drove slowly, looking for the address, and found it on a wooden sign in the shape of a seagull just off the road. At about five o'clock that evening, he turned into a narrow dirt lane that curved through more trees until opening up to a wide cement driveway. Randall's Toyota was parked there, but so were a white mini van and a red Cavalier that David didn't recognize.

The A-framed beach house wasn't luxurious, except in the sense that any place on the water lent itself to a certain luxury of leisure. The clapboard needed fresh paint, and moss had gathered on the roof in patches. But there were window boxes overflowing with red geraniums, and slender lavender flowers had emerged from the hostas planted in front of the porch.

David heard music coming from the back of the house. He walked around the garage, stepping over twigs and pine cones, until he came to a steep wooden staircase leading up to the back deck. Upon ascending, he saw Randall and Mary sitting at a picnic table wearing tank-tops, shorts, and sunglasses. Mary looked happy and very tan. Randall obviously hadn't shaved during his vacation. The stubble looked grayer than the hair on his head.

They weren't the only ones on the deck. Reclining on a chaise longue was Catherine Ferenz, the church's thirty-something pastor of discipleship, who looked surprisingly athletic and attractive in a red one-piece bathing suit. And sitting up on the railing of the deck was Andrew Steenstra, Northcentral's twenty-four-year-old youth pastor, who up until a few months ago everyone had called Andy. He'd taught Casey's Sunday school class last year.

"This bright day just got brighter," said Randall.

David shook hands with the men and hugged the women.

Andrew pulled a beer out of a cooler and handed it to him. There were already scores of empty bottles spread across the table among baskets of pretzels and potato chips. David opened his beer and took several long swallows. He felt thirsty all the time.

He squinted up at the sky and then nodded at Randall. "Quite a day you made for us."

"I just made the phone call," said Randall. "Someone else made the day."

Mary patted him on the knee. "That's a very old and lame joke, dear."

"Much like the teller of the joke," he said and turned up the radio. "Old and lame and still listening to the Rolling Stones."

David sat next to him at the picnic table. "Is this *Beggars Banquet*?" he asked.

"It is."

"With 'Sympathy for the Devil'? Oh, the scandal, R. What would consistory say?"

"We all have our contradictions," Randall said and smiled as he raised his beer to his lips.

Mary stood up and began collecting the empty bottles. "Now that everyone's here, we should probably start thinking about dinner."

"I'll start the grill," said Andrew eagerly. His face, as it was at the pulpit or in the Sunday school classroom, was happy and sincere. His short sandy hair was uncombed, sticking out in all directions. It looked as though he'd been swimming.

Mary opened the sliding glass door that led to the kitchen, and Catherine and Andrew followed her inside. David and Randall sat quietly for a moment at the table. The deck was high on a dune and the lake a ways below, but the crashing waves created a single drone that the leaves above mimicked as the wind tossed them about.

Randall took off his sunglasses and gazed out at the lake. "Look at how blue it is."

"Yeah," said David. He was staring at his feet.

They sat in silence for a few more moments before David spoke again. "Quite a fast one you pulled on me."

"What do you mean?"

"I mean the pastoral staff at this beach house suddenly out-numbers me three to one."

"It's not like that," said Randall. "I know it looks like that, but really it isn't."

"It certainly does look like that."

Randall smiled. "I thought we'd play euchre tonight. We needed four people."

"I could leave and you'd still have enough."

"Don't you dare." They both looked down at the table and smiled sheepishly. "It was more their idea than mine. They swore no deep discussions. They just wanted to hang out with you and let you know they're there. Call it fellowship and all that."

David stood up and walked to the cooler for another beer. Then he came back to the table, grimacing and struggling to twist off the cap.

"What happened to your hands?" asked Randall.

The cap came off and David sat. "I had to rough up the last pastor who played a trick on me."

Andrew emerged from the kitchen with a plate full of raw hamburger patties. He opened the lid of the grill, turned on the propane, and lit a flame.

"I better see how Mary's doing," said Randall. He left, and David sat by himself, drinking the beer quickly.

Andrew spoke behind him. "I hope it's okay that Catherine and I are here."

"Just don't overcook my burger and everything will be fine."

David finished his beer and slowly turned his head to look out at the lake for the first time that day. The water was blue with silver froth. The wind stoked up whitecaps. He lowered his head and again gazed at his feet.

They ate dinner and then played cards until the sky went orange. They joked and laughed as Randall told stories about when he and David were at Hope College together. The stereo played more Rolling Stones.

The sun slipped beneath the horizon, half of it hiding behind another corner of the earth. The rest was red and huge, its light bleeding into the sky and diffusing at the ends.

Catherine shook her head slowly as she looked out at all of it. "How much do we owe you for this, Randall?"

"Not as much as you owe me for the card game."

David could actually see the sun moving. All of them watched it without speaking until Randall said, "I once baptized someone in the lake. It was this time of night, the sun looked just like it does now. The woman was crying. It was really quite beautiful."

They nodded their heads but didn't say anything. Randall spoke again to keep the night from getting too heavy. "We should really start the fire before it's completely dark out."

"Let me get it going," said Andrew. He stood up quickly, his eyes big and bright.

"Go for it, my man. There's a pyromaniac in every crowd."

"I'll join you," said Catherine. "I want a better view of that sunset."

Mary stood up also. She went to the corner of the deck by the grill and came back to the table with a citronella candle and matches. She lit the candle, and soft light glowed at the table like a miniature setting sun. Then she stepped behind Randall and hugged him. "I'm going down too." She kissed him on the cheek and followed the others.

"Alone again," said David, winking. "I think they're trying to set us up."

Randall sipped his beer. "You're really not my type. I like mustaches."

They watched the other three descend the deck stairs and make their way down the soft, steep dune trail that led to the shore. Catherine and Mary leaned back against gravity. They stiffened their backs and straightened their knees. Andrew bounded downward, his feet in the air more than on the earth. He whooped and laughed when he made it down to the beach, and then caught his breath with his hands on his hips and waited for the women.

"I wish I still had that energy," said Randall.

David picked up the deck of cards on the table and began to shuffle them. "So how did it come about that you baptized a woman in the lake?"

Randall leaned back, stretched, and yawned. He rubbed his gray stubble. "It was years ago, at Camp Geneva. She wasn't a member of the church. She'd never been a member of any church. I think she was someone's guest."

David continued shuffling the cards.

"Toward the end of the retreat she came up to me and asked if she could be baptized. The lake was the most obvious—and loveliest—place to do it."

David began dealing cards between himself and Randall.

"Know any two-person games?" Randall asked.

"War," said David. He dealt the entire deck into two piles. Then he and Randall began to flip their cards, one by one. Jack. Ten. David took the hand.

"Anything on your mind?" asked Randall. Eight. Three.

"That depends," said David. "Am I talking to my friend or to my pastor?" Five. Ace.

"Both." Each of them flipped kings.

"I don't wanna play any more," said David. He stood up and ran both hands through his hair. Randall watched him and didn't speak. The sun was gone. Light the color of rust still floated over the sky's lower boundary.

"Nothing's changing in my head," said David. "I can't think about any fucking thing except me screwing up as a father and Casey dying out there." He pointed at the lake without looking at it.

"It's only been a month," said Randall.

David paced on the deck. "We can have this same talk a year from now, R. I don't see it changing much."

"It will. You'll change between now and then."

"Yeah, I'll be in a rubber room at Pine Rest."

"No, you'll be surrounded by friends and in the hands of God."

David shook his head. The candle cast enough light to reflect off his wet eyes.

"You realize that, right?" asked Randall. "You realize you're forgiven? We talked about this after the affair."

"Casey was alive then."

Randall let him have the statement. He didn't trample it right away with more words. After a few moments, he said, "Have a seat."

"I wanna stand." David paced some more. "I'm not sweating what's going on at God's end of the deal. I'm the one fighting the forgiveness. I don't want it yet. I wanted it when Casey was alive, but I don't want it any more. Everything's changed."

"Maybe at your end. Not at God's."

David walked to the railing of the deck. "I'm sorry about this. We should just talk about baseball or something." He looked out in the direction of the lake, but he could no longer see it. All was black, but the lake still revealed itself through its absence, the large black form darker than the black trees and sky surrounding it. He could hear the waves. Flames began to flicker on the beach.

"What if I asked you to baptize me out there?" he asked.

Randall turned and looked out at the dark. "I'd say that you're my best friend and I love you, but I'm afraid there's no way I could do it."

David propped himself up on the railing to sit facing Randall. He smiled a little and cocked his head. "Why?"

Randall stood up to get a beer. His back was to David as he rummaged through the ice in the cooler. "Because the Reformed Church believes in one baptism, the one bond for the one covenant between us and the one God." He turned around. "That woman I did it for had never been baptized, but you were as an infant, right?"

"Yeah. So? I wasn't aware what was happening. It doesn't mean anything when you're three months old."

Randall sat down and spoke slowly and softly. "When it comes to the infinite love and forgiveness of God, do you really think an infant knows much less than the rest of us?"

David's jaw clenched. He turned his head.

"It meant something to God," said Randall. "It meant that he came into your life first."

"But shit, R, we don't need cleansing as an infant," said David. "Okay, original sin. Fine. But now I've come up with enough sin on my own—years of shit and grime. Now's the time for some fucking cleansing."

Randall sighed and rubbed his eyes with the palms of both hands. He made sure to speak gently. "It's a beautiful thought. A beautiful image. And this lake, with all its beauty, is still a constant reminder of Casey."

"Which begs the question, why did you invite me out here?"

"Which begs the question, why did you come?" Randall paused. "I'm sorry. I don't wanna get preachy. But obviously it was important for you to come back to the lake at some point, and all of us here today wanted to be there to support you when it happened because we knew it wouldn't be easy." He sipped his beer. "As far as what you just asked, I know there's something so alluring about accepting a second baptism, or a third, or a fourth. But when's it end? That's the problem. If we express the need for even a second, then what we're saying is that God's covenant wasn't good enough the first time. That somewhere between that first time the water touched your skin and now, God has let you down and let you out of his embrace. There's something very culturally appealing about a second baptism. It's very American. It appeals to our love of fresh starts and renewed identities. But it ignores our deep, deep conviction—as a church—in the *one* baptism."

"No, now you're getting too preachy," said David.

"I'm sorry."

"Could you be defrocked?"

"Sure," said Randall. "If classis found out. But that's not the point. There are other ministers out there doing it. Wink, wink. You know. But I'm not saying this because I fear classis. It's because I fear God."

Voices rose from the dark beach below. The bonfire lit up a patch of night.

Randall stood and walked over to David. He placed his hand on his shoulder. "Let's head down."

David moved away slightly. "I'll meet you down there. I wanna bring my bags in from the car and change my clothes."

Randall nodded and began walking to the stairs of the deck. "Take your time," he said. "And I really am sorry. I'd do just about anything for you, but there are certain favors—even for best friends and blood—that get trumped by oaths I've already made." He smiled weakly. "Let's talk about it more down on the beach. This is big stuff. I don't wanna end it like this."

David nodded, followed him down the stairs, and then parted from him, heading to the car. He went in the house and changed into jeans and a sweatshirt. He sprayed his hands and neck with bug repellant. He turned on the television, adjusted the rabbit ears, and watched twenty minutes of a grainy news magazine show before glancing at his watch and deciding to finally head down.

A flashlight would have come in handy on the dune trail. Amid the night sounds of crickets and bullfrogs, David had to rely on the soft and shifting feel of the sand under his feet. The night sounds were replaced by the rising hum of the waves. The firelight came through the tree branches, and then he could see the four figures around the fire—two of them as silhouettes, and the other two, facing the fire, glowing.

"There he is," said Andrew.

"We almost started launching flares," said Catherine.

David approached the fire. "I could have used some coming down that path."

He could see their faces now. All of them were smiling, caring. Mary's face was gentle, but her eyes were sad. It was pity. He'd seen it all month. Everyone was quiet for a few moments, including David. He sensed that they'd been talking about him, specifically his request for baptism. Finally, there was banal talk of weather and the end of summer, but then even that was replaced by the real issue at hand—David—and his suspicions were proven correct.

"I was probably out of line in doing so," said Randall, his arms extended and his hands open to warm them by the fire, "but I mentioned to everyone what you'd asked me."

David avoided eye contact with all of them. He sat down in the sand and stared at the fire. The unseen waves rolled in loudly from the lake.

"And Catherine suggested something that, I'll admit, isn't a perfect substitute, but which may help bring about that same sense of peace that you're searching for. What if the three of us each blessed you?"

David continued staring into the fire, too embarrassed to look up. "I'm not sure I get what you mean."

"It'd be simple," said Catherine, "but powerful. You'd bow your head and we'd lay our hands on you and say a brief prayer over you."

They waited for his response. Firewood shifted amid the flames, sending up sparks.

"And this is certainly a beautiful place for it," said Randall, looking around, "surrounded by God's most basic elements. The water. The fire. We could even stand in the lake while we do it."

David smiled slightly and shook his head. "I don't know," he said. "I mean, I appreciate it, but it's okay. I didn't wanna make a big thing out of this."

"It's not a big deal," said Catherine. She smiled. "You know what I'm saying. It's no trouble."

He never took his eyes off the fire. "I think I'm gonna pass. But thanks. I appreciate the gesture."

Over the next hour, the men and women around the fire sifted sand through their fingers and toes and inched closer to the flames. They pointed out constellations and looked for satellites. David spoke little.

Mary stood up and stretched. "I'm sorry to abandon all of you, but I'm absolutely beat. I think I'll go upstairs and read and then go to bed. Some of us are going for a hike bright and early."

"You better pump me full of caffeine first," said Randall.

Catherine looked over at David, wincing almost from her desire to help. "David, are you sure there's nothing we can do for you tonight?"

"Totally," he said. He looked up at her and smiled as best he could.

She nodded. "Then I'll probably go up. Goodnight, everyone. It's been delightful."

Randall moved down by David. He placed his hand on his shoulder and whispered. "You're sure you're all right?"

"Good as ever."

"Good as ever."

"I kind of just wanna hang out alone and think for a while."

"No problem. That's what this weekend was all about." Randall stood up. "Then I guess I'll give you some space and head up too. I'm gonna sit on the deck a while longer if you want some company. "

"I'll be up in a minute," said Andrew. He was sitting cross-legged in the sand. He pulled the hood from his sweatshirt over his head so that his face was hidden, and then he poked at the fire with a long stick.

David felt the need to say something. "I could stare at a fire all night," he said.

"Me too." Andrew turned around to look at the trail. Randall was disappearing into the trees.

"Don't feel like you have to leave," said David.

"I don't." Andrew turned around to check on the dune trail again and then looked at David. The orange light lit up his face, except his eyes, which were hidden by shadows from the hood. He spoke in a low voice. "I'll do it for you."

"What?" David looked up.

"Shh. I'll baptize you."

"When?"

"Tomorrow morning. But it'll have to be early, because Randall gets up around seven."

David checked the trail himself before speaking again. "You're sure?"

"Yeah. Meet me under the deck at, like, six. It'll probably still be dark out, but that way nobody will see us." He stood up and brushed sand off his legs. "Are you still interested?"

David nodded. "But why are you?"

Andrew shrugged. "I'm not exactly sure right now. I am and I'm not. Just meet me at six o'clock. Don't make any noise when you're getting up."

Andrew then turned and walked away. The dark trees absorbed him the way they'd absorbed everyone else. David stayed by the fire, staring into the flames. The fire shrank over the next hour, and he grew tired. He never fell asleep on the beach, but the time passed quickly, as if he had.

·

It was almost six thirty. David stood among weeds and stones under the deck, smoking the last cigarette from the pack he'd bought a week ago. He wore the same jeans and sweatshirt from the night before. He shivered. The late-summer daybreak was unusually cold. It made his battered hands stiffer than usual. He looked at his watch again.

Leaves rustled and twigs snapped as footsteps approached from the side of the house. David dropped his cigarette in the stones and stepped on it.

"Sorry," whispered Andrew. His hair stuck up even more than it had yesterday. All he had on was a bathing suit and an orange Hope College T-shirt. "I slept through my alarm. I'm really sorry."

"It's okay," said David. "Are you still up for this?"

"Yeah, if you are."

"You could get in trouble for this."

Andrew shook his head. "Don't worry about me. You've got your own worries. Come on."

They walked down the dune. David could tell that Andrew, even though he'd just wakened, had to hold himself back from running full stride.

There was light in the sky, but it hadn't come to the land yet, and the shore was a dark strip of remaining night. Behind them, the sky had layers of color: green, blue, violet, meeting with the black above. The brighter colors, and the rising sun, were still below the tree line.

The sand was hard and damp. It was cold on their bare feet and made loud squeaking sounds as they walked, betraying their secrecy. David stared at the lake the way he'd stared at the heavy bag the first time.

They crossed a line of dead alewives that had washed ashore and then crossed a darker shade of wet, cold sand that nighttime waves had reached. David expected Andrew to stop, to say one last thing before they committed themselves to the water. But he only stepped into the waves, up to the knees of his bare legs. He hunched his shoulders and extended his stiff arms. "It's freezing," he said.

David followed him in, trying not to hesitate because of the cold or anything else. The jeans turned heavy at the ankles and clung to his skin. "How deep do we need to go?" he asked.

"At least to our hips, I guess. I don't know. I've never done it this way before."

David walked in up to his knees. The water nearly paralyzed him at first, but then the cold began to burn and he felt almost warm. It felt good on his hands. He pulled his sweatshirt off over his head and tossed it into the water. The cross hung over his bare chest. A cool dawn breeze blew in over the lake; his teeth chattered.

There were sandbars, and the two of them had to walk farther than they had planned to get deep enough, but eventually the water was at David's hips and just over Andrew's waist. The waves were small, but their gentle roll lifted a chill up David's back and chest and up his ribcage. It was worse when the waves receded and left him exposed to the gray morning air.

"This is good," said Andrew. He winced from early light, like a kid woken from a nap. His back was to the shore. David turned to face him and looked at the red light cresting over the treetops.

"Okay," said David. "What should I do?"

"Turn around. No, wait. Stay where you are. I'll go behind you." Andrew moved slowly and awkwardly in the water, fighting the waves and the sand under his feet. He got behind David so that the two of them could face the sunrise.

"Baptism," said Andrew, his voice deeper than usual, "is the sign and seal of God's promises to this covenant people. In baptism God promises by grace alone to forgive our sins; to adopt us into the Body of Christ, the Church; to send the Holy Spirit daily to renew and cleanse us; and to resurrect us to eternal life. This promise is made visible in the water of baptism."

He cupped water into his hand and poured it back into the lake.

"Water cleanses, purifies, refreshes, sustains. Jesus Christ is living water."

Andrew continued to speak, and David's body shook as he listened to the words. The breeze picked up and his skin felt as if it was hardening from the cold. But he was pleased with the pain. He watched as color came to the trees.

"David?"

He was startled. "Yeah?"

"Do you renounce sin and the power of evil in your life and in the world?"

"I do."

"Who is your lord and savior?"

"Jesus Christ."

The questions continued to be asked and answered, and at one point Andrew asked David to recite the Apostle's Creed, which had always come easily to him, but which he now stumbled over. He couldn't annunciate in the cold.

"We give you thanks, oh holy and gracious God, for the gift of water," said Andrew. "In the beginning of creation your spirit moved over the waters. In the waters of the flood you destroyed evil. You led the children of Israel through the sea into the freedom of the promised land."

He continued, and David found himself not listening, only staring at the sun as it climbed over the tree line. He hoped that the rays would give him some warmth. He'd had enough of the cold pain.

"Pour out on us your Holy Spirit so that those here baptized may be washed clean and receive new life."

The sun rose higher, and David watched its yellow light move slowly across the beach and the trees, revealing the shore. It fell over the dune trail, then over a part of the house, and then upon the deck, on a figure standing on the deck, on Randall. He stood leaning against the railing with a coffee mug in his hand. He was watching them.

Andrew saw him then too. He paused in mid-sentence but managed to move forward with the sacrament. He put his right hand on David's shoulder and spoke more quickly.

"David, for you Jesus came into the world, for you he died and conquered death. All this he did for you. We love because God first loved us."

David stared at Randall during the final words and watched as the yellow light washed over the entire property. He raised his right hand out of the water, a string of it like crystal beads pouring from his hand, and he waved. Randall was in mid-sip, and very casually, with the coffee mug to his mouth, gave a quick wave with his free hand. Then he lowered the mug and continued to watch.

"David, I baptize you in the name of the Father, and of the Son, and of the Holy Spirit."

David wasn't paying attention to Andrew, who, with one hand cupping the back of his head and the other under his arm, dipped David backward into the lake. Despite reflex, despite his desire to be fully conscious of the moment when he was submerged and active in that moment of symbolism, he was taken by surprise. He didn't have time for a full breath or to close his eyes. David plunged backward through the skin of the lake, the cold, gray water pouring over his head. He closed his stinging eyes and saw darkness.

But in an instant he was being pulled up, now through the skin of air.

When he opened his eyes, he didn't at first see the yellow sunlight or the remaining pink and orange light of dawn. It was still a dull blue in the spot of sky he focused on—almost gray—but it was, compared to only seconds before, light.